DAZZLE PAINT

*A Romantic Mystery of
the Hudson River Valley*

ERICA OBEY

Walrus Publishing
Saint Louis, MO 63116

APR 0 1 2021

Copyright © 2021 Erica Obey
All rights reserved.

For information, contact:
Walrus Publishing
4168 Hartford Street, Saint Louis, MO 63116
www.amphoraepublishing.com
www.ericaobey.com

Walrus Publishing is an imprint of Amphorae Publishing Group, LLC
www.amphoraepublishing.com

Manufactured in the United States of America
Cover Design by Kristina Blank Makansi
Cover art: Kristina Makansi
Set in Adobe Caslon Pro, OptimusPrinceps, and Exmouth

ISBN: 9781940442365

To the 40 million casualties of one of the most brutal and senseless wars in history. May we one day learn from our mistakes.

And to the memory of my father, the Rev. Robert F. Obey, who taught me to sing *The Halls of Montezuma* before I could read. Semper Fi.

DAZZLEPAINT

Walrus Publishing| St. Louis, MO

Prologue

MEN SEE WHAT THEY NEED TO SEE—especially
in times of war. But what men claimed to have seen during
the Great War defied imagination. Henry V's angel archers
descending to save the British at Mons. Lord Kitchener
lost on a mission to reclaim Ultima Thule. The defeated
Kaiser's rambling claims of a Masonic conspiracy. The
Zimmerman Telegram. The U.S. Marines, *Teufelshunden*
to their enemies, coursing through the mud of Belleau
Wood to snatch the Allies from the jaws of death. Most
of the stories were so absurd that one could be justified in
believing the rumors that the real battles were being fought
on the magical plane by the hidden masters of the secret
orders on both sides of the conflict: The Thule Society. The
Golden Dawn. The Theosophists. The *Germanenordern
Walvater* of the Holy Grail.

    The armies in that shadow war were the shining troops
of the Seelie Court. The Gentry of the Sidhe, they were
true to their nature as Unfallen—the angels who would
not take sides in the great war between Heaven and Hell.
They danced through the trenches with light-hearted

indifference, playing tricks on their allies as easily as they did their enemies. Yet their very fickleness was what drove them to heroism, for when they conceived a passion for a mortal, they would sacrifice all for love.

But what of the other Fae, the Unseelie Court? Exiled to the Middle Kingdom just as their brothers were, they would not consort with humans. Instead, they roamed the woods and the mountaintops, the desert and the other places in-between. But it was said that valor drew these creatures as hungrily as love and beauty drew their Seelie brethren. And mired in the senseless chaos of the trenches, it was only too easy for a soldier to believe that the Wild Ride was mustering to restore the honor of the Sidhe.

This is the tale of one such ride. This is the Tale of the Lost Company of Ker-Ys.

The girls stepped into the moonlight much as they had stepped off of the special train that had whisked them from the tenements of the Lower East Side to a month's stay in the Catskills, where they would enjoy life as it had been lived before there were factories, when simple crafts like spinning and weaving made life itself an art. Kitty was as thin and wary as when she had first been lured into the Settlement School, not by the promise of free food, but by the books the kindly librarian doled out from her cart if she were offering bits of fish to a stray cat. Mellie was her opposite, having learned the power of her blue eyes and red-gold curls early. She took the lead as her right, tugging a reluctant Kitty toward the pool that lay still and silent at the far end of the clearing,

"Don't be a silly spoil-sport," she scolded. "This was all your idea. If you didn't want to come, why did you tell me the story?"

It had been a mistake. Kitty knew that much long before Mr. Adams had surprised her in the library, his breath heavy against her neck, as he pronounced her drawing a Rare Talent. Kitty had been copying the pictures from a book called *Cian of the Chariots*, whose vivid blue cover with its red-cloaked hero and his intricately worked armor reminded her of the pictures in her head she could not yet get down on paper, although the art teacher at the Settlement School assured her she had enough talent that she might aspire to illustrating the ladies' magazines one day. But it was not the noble charioteer who whose story had held her attention. It was Dynan's elfin horn that she longed to draw: transparent as the summer heaven, yet threaded with wild scrollwork of fire.

Mellie hadn't cared about elfin horns. Mellie only had ears for the story that lay behind it, a tale that lay in the distant past when …

There were dwarfs and elves and powers of enchantment in the land, as all men know; and some have lingered on in hidden places, now and then showing themselves, for good or ill, to one of our race. In deep glens and forest shadows you meet them, it is said, and chiefly by the fountains that come bubbling up with the life of the under-world.

In such a country as this dwelt Dynan's mother's mother's mother, I know not how remote in ancestry. One day, passing through the meadows to bathe, as was her custom, in a secret pool fed by undying springs under curtaining boughs, she heard a faint cavern-muffled call from before her, and was minded to return. But coming a little nearer, she found the place quite vacant, save for dipping ouzels and water-rats that went gliding away. Having waited a while, she laid aside her garments, and stepped in through the shallows. Then again out swelled the cry, but now deep-throated, vehement, exultant, and very near, seeming to heave up the water before some bodily presence. It thrilled and wrapped and all but overcame her; yet she sprang away, snatching her clothing, and wrapping it around her as she ran. And, running thus, she heard yet a third time that voice of the under-world, but now sent after her in accents of more than human despair. Yet she had seen no form at all; and the Three Shouts was the only name she could ever give, or which might be given.

"He calls for you in the moonlight," Mellie pressed Kitty. "We all hear the shouts. Why don't you answer?"

Because much as the pain in that midnight cry wrenched Kitty's heart, she dared not help him. She had been warned about what had happened to her mother by a succession of nuns, nursing sisters, and teachers. "I should never have told you," Kitty said, her eyes on the moonlight glinting off the water, as she thought about the poor creature beneath. Trapped. Just as she had been by Mr. Adams' appreciation of her Rare Talent.

"Books are for reading, not telling," Kitty told Mellie.

"Well, you did tell me. And now I'm telling you that the lady was a fool to run away. But I won't be such a fool. No, when he shouts to me, I'll make him fall in love with me and he'll sweep me off to fairy land, where he will shower me with gold and rubies and dresses as gold as the sun and as silver as the moon."

That was a fairy tale. That wasn't how the story went at all. In the real story, the lady hadn't run away:

She must have sought that pool again – overcoming her fear, or because of it, for there are strange things in enchantment. It is thought, also, she made tryst with him otherwhere. A dimness, not human nor heavenly, was seen beside her in lonely rambles; and one starlit eve she had vanished quite away. Long afterward she returned, and bore a son among her own people, with a tale of wedlock in wild, lonely places, by rites unknown; and this magical token, wrought by no earthly hand, she showed as her voucher. When the right lips blow it, the voice of the Three Shouts will be sent abroad, and hosts of terrible power will come to the rescue.

"It's not right," Kitty repeated. "*They exact their price and claim their own.*"

"Well, what do you care—other than you're a jealous little cat?" Mellie asked, pulling her shift over her head to reveal her high breasts and slender waist, displaying them proudly in the glistening moonlight. "He'll not be coming for you when he can have me."

Kitty turned away, her lips moving with lines of poetry culled from her only memory of the sad-eyed woman who once upon a time used to sing her to sleep. "We must not look at goblin men," Kitty repeated the only words she could remember her mother ever having spoken to her. "We must not buy their fruits. Who knows upon what soil they fed their hungry thirsty roots?"

Did anyone know the answer to that question? The god-fearing farmers of Woodstock who gathered nightly around the pot-bellied stove in the general store had opinions. Their families had a long history in the Catskills, rooted in the wisdom of trusting only in themselves and the Dutch Reformed Church as bulwarks against the dangers that prowled these mountains still. But the artists who had descended on their quiet village in search of something called the Light, not only sought those dangers, but tried to tame them and claim them for themselves.

They would learn soon enough that such dangers could never be tamed or claimed. The good Lord had created the Bible and Church Elders for a reason, and woe unto those who ignored such gifts. So, when new girls started to go missing ten years after that first time, the council around the pot-bellied stove dismissed the question as the result of foreign ways and foreign wars. And when one of the missing girls was found floating in the spring that was said to be haunted, they locked their doors and reassured their wives and daughters that such threats would never trouble decent women such as themselves.

Chapter 1

ONCE UPON A TIME, Gavin Fellowes not only believed in magic; he believed he was gifted to command it. At least, he believed he was gifted to command the webs of illusion that passed for magic. Now he was a man who believed in nothing. Indeed, he had built up quite the reputation for believing in nothing: ectoplasm, table rapping, spirit photography, slate writing, and mediumistic trances all fell beneath the rapier of his cynicism as surely as they had before that arch-skeptic, Harry Houdini.

Unfortunately, and to his utter distaste, Gavin now found himself surrounded by belief, in the midst of a hamlet that not only thrived on it, but sought to make a tidy profit from it—at least judging by the volume entitled *The Land of Rip van Winkle*, penned by one Mrs. A.E.P. Searing, an enterprising hotelier's wife, who sought to bolster her husband's business by painting the Catskills as a wonderland where White Ladies, Indian captives, Henry Hudson's crew, and Captain Kidd all roamed—the last in search of the buried treasure he had lost for the love of a dark-eyed slave he had stolen on the high seas. Belief asserted loudly in Woodstock, New York—especially among the Bohemian men and women that sketched *en plein* air on the Village Green and argued passionately about art in the newly opened sidewalk cafe.

A different sort of belief had motivated Morris Newgold, the hotelier who had invested both his money and his pride in building a grand hotel on Overlook Mountain, where so many other attempts had burned to the ground—including that of Mrs. Searing's husband. Newgold's attempt had ended in abject failure, however, largely because of the rising determination of Woodstock not to succumb to the tide of Jews who had already taken over the Catskill boarding house industry in Tannersville, Pine Hill, and Hunter. So, this year Newgold had been forced to lease his grand hotel to a gathering of trade unionists and garment workers, who strode the streets in solidarity, ignoring the contemptuous nickname the locals had bestowed on them: the Bloomer Girls.

The woman Gavin was travelling to meet had a reputation for unconventional beliefs, prime among them women's suffrage, and had just returned from the nation's capital where she had been privileged to witness the passing of the 19th Amendment. Unconventional was one thing, but it would have been too much to think she would have joined the garment workers and other radicals convened in a hotel owned by a Jew—even if that hotel's precursor had once hosted tea for President Ulysses S. Grant. No, despite her liberal leanings, Mrs. Jean Storrs Adams had not strayed far from the Philadelphia Main Line to which she had been bred. So it was natural that when propriety dictated she withdraw from the artist colony she had founded with her husband, she retreated to the staunchly protestant Mead's Mountain House, which, according to the informative booklet that accompanied the letter accepting his reservation, "while not exclusive ... has preserved successfully the character of a private estate, the proprietor endeavoring to guard against uncongenial introductions."

Tea on what the booklet insisted on referring to as the *piazza* of Mead's Mountain House was a tribute to what underlay such solid, unpretentious American values. Instead of scones, fresh-faced farm girls brought platters of early strawberries and local cheeses. Quoits and croquet sets had been set up on the lawn. A telescope lay out on a wicker table for those who might wish to venture out at night to gaze at the stars. Several guidebooks to the fauna, flora, and natural wonders of the Catskills were invitingly display nearby. A discreet notice alerted residents that carriages and well-trained horses were available from the Mountain House's stable for scenic drives.

Mrs. Adams herself had the appearance of a far less socially acceptable true believer: Dark-eyed and hollow-cheeked, she had the burning gaze and gaunt beauty of a Renaissance pieta. A saint, by all accounts, a visionary even. But not, it would be conceded, a peaceful person to live with. Gavin had heard similar things muttered about himself ever since he'd returned from the War which had, he knew all too well, transformed him into a man not given to anything beyond the most rudimentary of social niceties.

He took a seat across from Mrs. Adams noticing that she had, without comment, positioned the tea table so he could stretch out his leg, sore from the ride on the cob he'd rented from the village stable. He must have been limping again. He leaned back in his chair—thankful for the pillow positioned at the small of his back—and got right to the point. "You requested the Society for Psychical Research to send a representative to investigate whether some magical creature haunts the bathing pool in a local artists' colony and is snatching young girls away to their doom. Is that correct?"

"Yes. A poor girl was found drowned in the bathing pool just over a week ago, but already the rumors have begun to swirl," Jean said. "I can only hope that a full investigation is the simplest way to dispel them once and for all."

Gavin nodded slowly. "And what is this creature purported to be? An ancient monster arisen to defend the Algonkian people?"

"Not the Algonkian people, but rather the drowned city of Ker-Ys." She offered a small smile. "A fanciful name for a fanciful endeavor, and, yes, I know many who would say my husband and I are simply paying the price of our own folly."

"You refer, then, to the colony you founded together."

"Ker-Ys," she agreed, as she poured out their tea. "It is the name of yet another legendary city lost beneath the waves—like Atlantis, Lyonesse, or Heracleion. Some of them real, some imagined, and most somewhere in between. But all of them paradises of peace and prosperity. And all of them lost."

Her gaze grew far away, as if she were voyaging to just such a far-off place. "My husband and I chose to name our colony after such a lost city, although the paradise we sought to rebuild was not drowned beneath waves of water, but rather under the waves of time. For we founded Ker-Ys as nothing less than a great social experiment in returning to life as it was once lived—before the factories arrived to leach the souls of villages into the soot of the cities. A time when women spun tales as they spun yarn, men sang as they strode garlanded to harvest the fields, and children danced happily around the Maypole."

And harvests failed. And plagues killed. And armies pillaged and burned whatever remained. "A golden age indeed," Gavin said.

Mrs. Adams stiffened, as if she sensed his skepticism, and her voice warmed with passion. "In those days, Mr. Fellowes, there was no notion of art or artists, no notion of leisure or work. Life *was* art—and every man an artist. And that was the paradise we sought to restore in Ker-Ys. We sought to establish a brotherhood of artists united in the pursuit of beauty while also taking pleasure in supporting themselves by their own hands."

"Useful work," Fellowes offered the aphorism of William Morris, the godfather of such utopias, "as opposed to useless toil."

"My husband and I share a belief that what we have gained in industrial progress has been paid for by the loss of our souls," Mrs. Adams agreed.

And yet a cynic might point out that industrial progress was the very thing that had made this great social experiment possible, for Edward Ratcliffe Adams commanded a fortune merged from two powerful Yorkshire families, which now included railways, mining, and steel. And from what Gavin had read of Ned Adams' forays into the Renaissance harpsichord, pottery, weaving, and now photographing frolicking fairies, the pinnacle of his artistic accomplishment was to have been born into the right family.

"Of course, there can be no question it was nothing but a tragic accident, which the poor girl brought down on herself," Mrs. Adams said, refreshing his tea as she turned back to the matter at hand. "And the Sheriff quite agrees. One of these new Bloomer Girls snuck down from the Overlook hotel to explore the pool and slipped on the moss of one of the rocks—on a dare from one of her fellows, most likely. Not that I don't admire their adventurous spirit. But these girls venture out, completely unaware of the cruelty that awaits them in the wider world."

Just as five million British boys had ventured across the Channel to Flanders Field and beyond, with no idea of the cruelty waiting.

"As I said, nothing but a tragic accident," Mrs. Adams went on. "But we are in the Catskills, where people dearly love their tall tales. As soon as the poor girl was found, wild stories began to arise of other Bloomer Girls being snatched away, when heaven alone knows that these days such girls come and go of their own accord."

"And yet they point the finger at Ker-Ys, and not the cursed hotel?" Gavin probed, when she seemed disposed to say no more.

Her face darkened. "There was … a previous misfortune at the spring. It was a long time ago, but it took years for the rumors to die down so that we could walk through Woodstock without people whispering. As if those artists down at the Maverick had any right to point fingers. Still, I would not care to experience that again."

At last, they approached the heart of the matter. "I read a little of the earlier case," Gavin said. "Two girls visiting from the settlement school you sponsor down in Manhattan crept out of their dormitory at night in order to summon forth some kind of fairy creature from a bathing pool? Instead, they were attacked by … a wild beast?"

What explanation could be simpler? Fishers, bobcats, bears and wolves prowled the woods at night, along with the catamounts for which the Catskills were named. Yet the rumors that still swirled around the story insisted that the true culprit was something far darker and more dangerous than a hungry beast.

"My husband and I resigned ourselves early on to the fact that we were not destined to be blessed with children," Mrs. Adams explained. "And so we sought to bring children to Ker-Ys—children of the less fortunate classes, who might be offered the gifts of imagination and beauty of which they are so often deprived in their narrow lives in the tenements—and steer them to another destiny than work in the factories where their parents—if indeed they were fortunate enough to have parents—labored. But this was the first summer of our experiment, and we quickly learned the perils of overstimulating such young minds. Shouts shook everyone awake in the middle of the night, and two of them were discovered half-drowned in the water—and quite improperly clad."

Mrs. Adams shivered in distaste. "A singularly unpleasant episode that forced us to reconsider the wisdom of wrenching the children from the only homes they knew, and instead focus on bringing art and beauty to them in their natural habitat. And yet there are those in the village who still insist those girls really did call forth an actual fairy. Can you imagine such superstition?"

"Like all that fuss about the so-called photographic evidence of girls playing with fairies over in Cottingley, England? They say Conan Doyle has been thoroughly taken in—and by a clumsy ploy that would not have fooled the most naïve child," Gavin said. "Which is why I must ask whether it might not be wiser simply to weather the current storm, rather than digging up a painful episode from the past, which an investigation will surely do?"

A moment's awkward pause, before Mrs. Adams allowed with a sigh, "There is a further complication. One of the girls from that first unfortunate episode has returned to Ker-Ys a woman, determined to besot my husband as surely as any man has been pixie-led..."

The pain that shadowed her face was impossible to ignore, and Gavin turned away, focusing his gaze on the mountain that towered above them. "According to the legend, it was a woman who caused the first Ker-Ys to sink beneath the waves," he politely changed the subject. "Dahut, King Gradlon's rebellious daughter, a powerful sorceress who embellished the city with the aid of the korrigans and tamed the sea dragons. And then took a demon as a lover who stole her keys and opened the city's floodgates."

Mrs. Adams' jaw set. "There can be no question of this woman having any ability to summon demons, either as a child or now. She is a fraud, Mr. Fellowes, and I need you to prove it." Mrs. Adams shook her head and her expression softened. "Now, if it had been the other one, I might have been given to at least wonder..."

"The other one?" Gavin prompted.

"Such a strange little creature," Mrs. Adams mused. "Furtive. Shy. Maybe even sly. Now, she could have been a changeling. Crept into the alley behind the settlement school at night to open the rubbish bins. But not for herself. For the cats. And she always left a token. A beautiful little drawing of a flower—on whatever scrap of paper she could find. Heaven alone knows where she got the crayons—stole them, most likely, but she put them to good use. Bluebells on fish wrappers, foxglove on the cook's list, hollyhocks on a blotted page from a copybook. A regular little garden, sprung by magic in that alley full of cats. I still have them in one of my commonplace books. It took the workers months just to coax her inside to take some food for herself."

"Irish?" Gavin suggested.

"Irish? Hungarian? Hebrew? Creole?" Mrs. Adams asked with a helpless shrug. "What are any of them really—other than just another orphan from the lost tribes?"

Her gaze moved to the man smoking a cigar at the far end of the piazza—evidence that even Mead's Mountain House was not immune to the influx of foreigners in the wake of the recent upheaval in Europe. Not just the Russians and Hungarians escaping starvation and pogroms, but creatures like this, in a linen suit and a broad-brimmed panama hat, his pinkie ring flashing as he leaned on the Malacca walking stick that he, unlike Mr. Fellowes, had no need of using. One of the myriad counts and barons and princes that had alighted on America's shores, often with no more money and thicker accents than the peasants who rode in steerage—their only calling card the cut of the clothes on their backs. Even Mrs. Adams' impeccable manners were not enough to allow her to hide her look of naked dislike. "First drinking, and now smoking." She cast Gavin an apologetic glance. "Not that I am an intolerant woman. Judge not, that ye be not judged. But a gentleman understands how to take his needs to a place that can accommodate them, such as the Irvington hotel down in the village. Whereas this man left a flask right out on the washstand for one of the maids to find—even though it is stated perfectly clearly in the brochure that this house has no bar and is run strictly on the temperance plan, thereby offering no objectionable features."

At least not objectionable in some people's opinions. Gavin had reacted with far less enthusiasm when he had read that particular sentence in their informative booklet and had made certain to tuck deep within his baggage the flask of brandy he needed if he wished to sleep at night.

"Of course, Meads' has always required references before they book any guest. But several of my nephew's business acquaintances vouched for the man, and so we are forced to accept his presence and say nothing about his rudeness."

Once more, Mrs. Adams' gaze darkened. "I blame that wretched war. We fought to save Europe for the Europeans, and instead find ourselves flooded with those who bring their troubles here and expect us to solve them, willfully shutting their eyes to the fact that the key to their suffering lies in their own national character."

She shook off her aggrievement after a moment's angry rumination. "Not that I would ever blame the children. Indeed, Kitty was enchanting, even if she was a regular little Gypsy—and with the most extraordinary green eyes. It's why we called her Kitty right from the start. How could she not have robbed the rubbish bins to feed the strays? She was a regular little cat herself."

Gavin nodded. A green-eyed changeling who could bring a garden to life on paper as if by magic. He was more intrigued by this Kitty than he would care to admit. "And how did she describe what happened at the pool?"

"She didn't. She wouldn't say a word for the rest of her stay at Ker-Ys. She simply drew. Extraordinary, fantastic pictures of creatures from another realm…"

"Do you have those pictures as well?" Gavin asked, feeling his belly kindle with a fire of curiosity he thought long since extinguished.

"Oh, goodness no! We burned them all." Mrs. Adams looked shocked. "They were … well, it wasn't the poor thing's *fault*, of course. She was merely drawing the stories she'd been told of fairy knights sweeping off mortal brides to Elfland. But they were … suggestive in ways that … well, I don't know where the poor thing might have gotten the ideas from. Then again, it all comes down to the mother, doesn't it? Who knows what the children have been exposed to before they come to us?"

Or when they did come to them, Gavin thought, for he had seen several examples of Ned Adams' fairy photography and hoped not to be forced to view more. But he only nodded understandingly. "And so what happened to her?"

Another expressive shrug. "I wish I knew. I did try to keep track of her. The girl had an extraordinary talent for drawing. I had hoped to apprentice her to someone in the publishing trade. But she simply vanished, with as little explanation as she had appeared. Just as changelings do. As I said, Mr. Fellowes, if it had been her, I might have …" A soft smile and then a crisp shake of the head. "But it is not Kitty who has returned. It is the other one. Melisandre, she calls herself now. And she calls herself an artist's model. As for what kind of pictures she poses for … No, I am being unkind," she corrected herself immediately. "She is an extraordinarily beautiful woman, and who am I to judge to what uses she puts her beauty? Her kind have few enough choices in this world."

"Then why pursue the matter?" Gavin asked. "Men are given to make fools of themselves, yes, but usually they come to their senses and come around."

Once more, she favored him with a smile. "My husband making a fool of himself is nothing new. In fact, he is rather given to doing just that, and it could be argued that is why I wed him. For why should a man not make a fool out of himself over art and beauty? I suppose there would be many who would say the same of me for enduring weeks of incarceration and torture for the abstract right to have a voice in the running of this country." Her face hardened. "No, my husband has every right to make a fool of himself— over art or beauty or any other cause he might choose. But what I will not tolerate is seeing this woman purposefully make a fool out of him."

And Gavin saw the other side of sainthood: the unflinching faith of the righteousness of one's cause and the steely determination to do God's work, no matter the cost. The resolve that seemed to pass from her like an electric shock as she laid a hand on his arm. "Will you help me, Mr. Fellowes?"

Gavin had been inclined to say no, for all he saw here was an oft-told tale of a wandering husband and a scheming adventuress. But the tale of the green-eyed changeling leaving her sketched thank-you posies had stirred in him emotions he had thought himself no longer capable of feeling, the tattered remnants of a time when he not only believed in magic, but prided himself on being able to weave spells himself. He inclined his head. "I will visit Ker-Ys with your permission, and I will ferret out the truth to the best of my abilities."

He fought down the twinge of dishonesty, for it was not the truth that fueled the eagerness in his voice, but rather a little cat with green eyes. "The sun's still high. There should be time for me to take a ride down there before dinner is served. I believe it is but a mile from here?"

"Not even that." Mrs. Adams' face twisted with uncertainty as she cast a sidelong glance at his stiff leg. "But the road is not a smooth one…"

"My doctors advise me that healthful exercise is the best way to rehabilitate any war wound," he assured her. "And it is said that the mountain air of the Catskills is a panacea in itself."

"Yes, yes!" she agreed eagerly. "Of course. One of the finest curatives in the world. And as for the water—well, you are aware that the late Mr. Mead arranged for a series of galvanized iron pipe coils for a system by which guests may have pure ice cooled spring water, with no contact with ice. You must enjoy it, Mr. Fellowes! I'm certain you will find yourself quite restored."

Although Gavin knew full well it was the kind of magical thinking he had schooled himself against long ago, he also knew that if there was anything that might restore him to the man he once had been, it was the promise of encountering a lovely, green-eyed artist who could conjure gardens with her pen. So it was that with a courteous promise of rejoining her for dinner, he called for his mount to be re-saddled, escorted Mrs. Adams back into the hotel common area, and began the slow ride downhill toward Ker-Ys.

At first he was glad of the open space after the morning's long confinement, first on the railway and then on the piazza of the Mountain House, but the balmy calm of the late afternoon was shattered by an automobile rattling up the steep road and startling the cob. A man in a city suit climbed out of the car to confront Gavin before he had even finished steadying the animal. But this one was no foreigner. Rather, he was one of those bluff Americans bred to letter in sports at Yale before turning to the business of Wall Street.

"Forgive my bluntness," he said, "but I'm a direct man." The alcohol on his breath was discernable even from where Gavin sat in the saddle. "Hollis Stanton," the man declared. "Ned Adams' nephew and the man who actually earns the money those two fritter away on lost causes. Am I to understand you're my aunt's ghost-hunter?"

"Gavin Fellowes. FSPR—or Fellow of the Society for Psychical Research," Gavin said, not bothering to disguise his immediate dislike of the man. "And I'm afraid you have been misinformed. By all accounts, it is a matter of fairies, not ghosts. But yes, I have been called in to ascertain the truth of what is happening at the Ker-Ys Colony. And seeing as you are apparently acquainted with my reputation, you must be aware I very rarely discover either fairies or ghosts or anything else from the supernatural realm. Instead, I usually find some human agency at work."

"Usually?"

Gavin smiled. "A true skeptic must leave both possibilities open for consideration."

"And yet surely, you have your suspicions."

Gavin froze him with a glare. "If you are acquainted with my reputation, you are well aware that I never report suspicions, only findings. Until then, I prefer to keep my theories to myself."

He made to nudge his horse back into a walk, but Stanton stepped into his path. "I will be frank with you,

Mr. Fellowes. My uncle is a gullible fool. And my aunt is a wronged woman who refuses to admit how badly she has been treated."

"I would not argue with you upon such short acquaintance, but I can assure you that my meeting with her left me quite firmly convinced she is a woman who knows her own mind."

"This is not the first time he has fallen prey to a charlatan."

Gavin raised an eyebrow. "I beg your pardon. Is it me that you are accusing of being a charlatan or the lady who purports to commune with fairies?"

"The woman, of course. I draw the line at calling her a lady. But, here. I mean no insult. I speak only out of concern for my uncle. And I don't propose that you should cheat my aunt. I am merely asking that you make your findings available to me before you convey them to her—so that I might advise you as to any … unexpected ramifications ahead of time." Stanton reached into an inner pocket and pulled out a thick, leather wallet. "And I am sure that my aunt is so unworldly as not to speak of expenses, so I would handle that as well. She tends to pay her salaries in hand-woven nightgowns and pottery goblets filled mead. I am of a more practical vein myself."

Mrs. Adams' Mainline graces may have been bred into her, but Gavin froze Hollis Stanton with a stare that had been bred into his line since the Norman conquest. "It is a matter of principal that the SPR never accepts fees. And I can assure you that the monies from my estates are sufficient to support me in whatever style I choose—without recourse to sullying my family name by taking up any profession beyond my Captaincy in the War." He favored Stanton with a tight smile. "Business may be the business of America, but in England, my class clings to its old ways. Now if you will excuse me, I have a fairy drowning to investigate."

Chapter 2

KATE AMES DID NOT BELIEVE in automatic writing or waking visions. But how else was she meant to explain the sight that awaited her on her worktable as she prepared to pack up her drawings and deliver them to her publisher with her customary punctuality? The book she was illustrating was entitled *Fairies in our Garden.* And yet the fairies that she—that *someone*—had scrawled across the top sheet were far from friendly.

Not that Kate believed in fairies—friendly or otherwise—any more than she believed in automatic writing. It was a point she took pains to make clear to anyone who might assume the enchanting pixies she drew could only be drawn by someone who was pixilated herself. Kate did not *see* fairies; she *drew* fairies that other people wanted to see. Cheerful little woodland fairies for the youngest ones: The buttercup fairy with a round, yellow smile, a moss elf peeking shyly from behind a boulder, or the thistle fairy with ragamuffin hair and tunic. For the older ones, she drew the fairies from fairytales: Cinderella's godmother, Sleeping Beauty's twelve fairy godmothers, Tinker Bell, the

Blue Fairy—all of them woven with elegant cunning into the decorations of the pages, peeking mischievously from borders and decorated capital letters and sometimes even forming the words of the stories themselves.

This time she had drawn garden fairies rather than wildflower fairies. The rose, iris, and hollyhocks were set in the rows of a cutting bed every bit as tidy as the rows of text through which they were interleaved—the gnomes toiling industriously with tiny spades and forks as they urged the reader to turn the page. Kate's work always had something of the clever optical illusion about it. Yet optical illusion was scarcely a strong enough word for the wildly colored tapestry of goblins that filled the top sheet from edge to edge: Rat-faced, cat-faced, and parrot-faced; snail, wombat, and badger, they danced amidst a frantic paisley of ornamentation out of medieval prayer psalter with the same mania as the unseen voices that had called to her to "Come buy, come buy" as she had tossed and turned the previous night.

It was not an unfamiliar dream. Nor was it a welcome one—no matter how sternly Kate steeled herself to recall that she did not believe in dream-omens any more than she did automatic writing or fairies. For if she had, she would have been forced to admit that this particular dream only troubled her when the rat-faced men knew something about which they were trying to warn her.

If you had watched Kate Ames striding briskly to her publisher's offices to deliver her drawings, you would never suspect she was troubled by such matters—any more than you would suspect the magical worlds contained in the neat portfolio she carried beneath one arm truly existed. In her shirtwaist and skirt, cut sensibly high above her sturdy boots in order to protect her hem from the gritty sidewalks, she appeared to be just another one of the working girls who had flocked to the city in the aftermath of the war, preferring to earn their bread as typists, teachers, and telephone operators than as governesses or lady's companions. But then again, Kate Ames was a master of camouflage, schooled in its arts by its father, Abbott Handerson Thayer, who had immediately recognized her talent and rewarded her with a place in his singular household of exotic pets, apprentices, and worshipful companions.

Kate had been the only girl among the young artists apprenticed to Thayer. Not that Thayer's intimate circle suffered from any shortage of female companionship. But the other women who surrounded him served as ministering angels, both actual and imaginary. After Thayer's wife had tragically lost her reason, he had surrounded himself with lady acolytes he called "companions," who saw to his every need. Then Thayer had cemented his artistic reputation as, in the words of no less a luminary than John Singer Sargent, "the best of them" by capturing their souls in ethereal portraits of his daughters and other young models, robed in Grecian simplicity and graced by giant angel's wings.

But, although Thayer was an eccentric who began the winter in a pair of woolen underwear which he progressively shortened with scissors as the weather warmed, until by summer he was wearing shorts, he was also enough of a realist to admit he had ruined several works of art by redoing them "better and better"—often going so far as to uncrate them in the railroad station and rework them by candlelight. And so, he had recruited a stable of young artists to make copies of his works in every stage of their progress so that he could retrieve the work he himself had ruined. Kate was the first female to join their ranks—although it rapidly became clear that her gift had not been for angels, but rather for Thayer's other great obsession: the protective coloration of animals, the genius of which, he claimed, only a master technician in color could comprehend. Kate had rapidly exceeded her master in this subtle art, her skill at obliterating contrast by the antithetical techniques of blending and disruption arguably as great as that of Mother Nature herself. When war had broken out in Europe, she found herself in demand for turning that skill to practical use, creating disruptive patterns for everything from battleships to horses. In peacetime, she had rapidly developed an equal reputation for hiding her flower fairies so elegantly that it would take months before even a mother reading to her child could be certain she had found every face that peeked out from behind the pages she turned.

The offices of Charles Scribner's Sons were as far from camouflage and nature as they were from her teacher's wild eccentricities. "Publishers and Booksellers," according to the proud legend on the side of the building that dwarfed its neighbors, the business occupied a stately Beaux-Arts building on Fifth Avenue, as befitted the city's largest publisher of both books and periodicals. The bookstore on the first floor was a temple to writing, from the arched windows where elegant scrollwork framed the stacks of books offered for sale, to the marble staircase with wrought iron balustrades that led up to a balcony decorated with potted trees. A lofty clerestory above the balcony saved the room from stuffiness, giving it instead the air of a pleasant arcade, while keeping the sunlight from damaging the books that were shelved not just along the walls, but also in custom oak tables with shelves beneath and books stacked on their tops.

But the bindery and packing rooms, where the real business of publishing took place, were a completely different story—a bustle of humming presses and shirt-sleeved men shouting orders at scrambling printer's devils. The engraver, an old German who had learned his craft with the finest, shook his head at the intricacy of her drawings and the extravagant number of color plates, before gruffly promising to see what he could do—as was their established ritual. Taking her leave of him, Kate returned to the quiet of the editorial offices, where the book-lined hush was only slightly less reverential than that of the store. Mr. Bridges, who had recently replaced Mr. Burlingame as editor, had an entire floor to himself—not quite as lofty as the office in the dome of the *New York World* building from which Joseph Pulitzer once looked down on other publishers—and it was said, on God himself—but still an august setting that Kate would no more think of breaching than the altar of nearby St. Patrick's Cathedral. Even the clerk, who had Kate's cheque prepared and waiting, worked in the august calm of a room adorned with soft carpets and cases upon cases of books.

Alas for Kate's peace of mind, the envelope with her cheque was not the only one that had been left for her. The clerk also passed her a heavily scented lavender envelope with an apology. "This one came just this morning, and I thought it simpler to hold it for you then send a messenger."

One glance at the bold, slashing letters scrawled in green ink, the words URGENT and CONFIDENTIAL underlined repeatedly, and Kate knew last night's rats and wombats had not lied. She broke the seal mechanically and scanned the lines scrawled in handwriting she'd not seen for years, but still recognized as surely as if they were sitting side by side, forming their letters at their desks in the settlement school. "Kitty! You must come! I'm in dreadful danger, and so are you! A girl is dead, and more will die unless you come back to Ker-Ys, for it is you he seeks, not them."

Melisandre hadn't even bothered to sign the letter, assuming, as was typical of her, that everyone simply knew who she was. Pocketing the missive, Kate forced a smile for the clerk. "No harm done," she said. "Just another child writing to her favorite flower fairy. I'll answer it personally. No need to trouble anyone."

Relieved, the clerk pulled something else out of her cubby. "A gentleman called for you earlier this week as well. He left his card, as well as a forwarding address at both the Kingston Telegraph Office and Mead's Mountain House in Woodstock, N.Y."

"Josep Havel, Impresario." The script on the calling card was almost as florid as Melisandre's handwriting. On the back was scrawled, "I beg the favor of an appointment at your earliest possible convenience, in order to discuss a matter to our mutual advantage."

"You certainly are gaining a reputation," the clerk said with a knowing smile that suggested that breaking the seal of a letter was beneath her, but that reading a message left in plain sight on a calling card was another thing altogether. "Trust me, Mr. Bridges has taken notice."

Chapter 3

GAVIN CAUGHT HIS FIRST GLIMPSE of Ker-Ys as he turned off the precipitous road that led down from Mead's Mountain House to the Village and onto a rutted lane between cornfields hewn out of the hard, clay earth by two centuries of sheer determination. The antithesis of Mead's clean clapboard, the Ker-Ys Great House was a fantasia of balconies, porches, and gables, hand hewn from rough, dark lumber, it nestled deep into the trees that clustered near the mountain spring. A few other houses, built by the Adamses' intimate friends, peeped from neighboring groves, but they had been largely shuttered this summer in response to the scandal. The far more modest dormitories further down the hill were still populated by students from the Settlement Schools who acted as unpaid servants in exchange for room and board and a few art lessons.

"Poor girl," Ned Adams mused, as he and Gavin gazed down into the bathing pool whose centerpiece was the stone relief of a moss-ravaged face whose mouth stretched open in a wordless cry. "So young and so innocent. Of course, who can blame her for risking all to win the pleasures of dancing in the fairy ring? But there are dangers. Oh, yes, there are dangers. Treating with the Fair Folk is not for the inexperienced." He shook his head sorrowfully. "If only she had come to me first, instead of venturing to seize them for herself."

Clad in a homespun tunic and gaiters, Ned was a stout man with the pleasant aspect of a child, although his curls were more white than brown. His pride in his handiwork was infectious as he stumped around the art colony to show Gavin its hand-built ateliers and picturesque grottos, follies, and shrines, the rough-hewn Great House built on the lines of an ancient feasting hall—and at last the bathing pool where a girl had been found drowned.

"All of them salvaged from the Ker-Ys for which the colony was named," Ned had informed him repeatedly while gazing fondly on this or that structure or fanciful detail. "You have heard the tale?"

"A lovely old Breton legend," Gavin agreed.

"Not the Breton Ker-Ys, but the Hudson's own Ker-Ys," Ned corrected him. "Fated to vanish beneath the waves when New York City dammed the Esopus Creek to create the Ashokan Reservoir in its greed for drinking water. Scores of villages were drowned. Some, like Brown's Station, simply disappeared. Others—Boiceville, Brodhead's Bridge, Shokan, Glenford, Olivebridge, and West Hurley—were forced into exile from the land they had owned for generations. Not just families, but houses, stores, entire Main Streets were relocated. Even the dead were forced to leave, for the villagers refused to leave their fathers behind and dug up the cemeteries."

Probably a reasonable sanitary precaution, Gavin thought, the stench of the dead rotting in the trenches still sour in his nostrils.

"But there was no one to salvage this Ker-Ys," Ned went on. "For no one knew where it had come from or who its inhabitants might once have been. All that anyone had ever known of it was its ruins: Walls, a ringfort, the remains of a chapel ornamented with strange carvings. And a spring with a curiously carved wellhead that some said was a sacred portal to the Underworld. And so when none of its inhabitants arose to salvage Ker-Ys, I did. Before another Ker-Ys could vanish beneath the waves, I dug up its ruins, and transported them here, stone by stone. The pavilion by the tennis court? Built entirely from the walls of Ker-Ys. The Shakespeare Folly? Reared from the stones of the ringfort. The grotto shelters the remains of the chapel."

He gestured proudly at the moss-covered face that was the centerpiece of the dam. "And as for the sacred guardian of the wellhead, I built him his own watery shrine, so that he might be pleased to serve as a *genius loci* to our new shining city."

Dropping his voice, Ned leaned forward confiding. "Never did I expect to succeed on our very first Midsummer here. I had resigned myself to years of study and careful preparation. But now I know such bookish methods were destined only to failure. For it was not I who succeeded. Rather it was Melisandre that called him forth, armed not with books and knowledge but only the innocence of her soul." His face grew grave. "Alas, I fear these other girls carelessly sought to emulate her childish success, blind to the perils of such an undertaking to any but the purest of souls."

Gavin nodded gravely, although neither innocence nor purity would have been the words that would have sprung to his mind when it came to describing Melisandre. He'd discovered that her career as an artist's model had been followed in short order by a stage tour as part of the scantily clad Living Tableaux that reproduced famous works of art for the cultural enrichment of those who could not attend museums. And the brief conversation he'd had with her before Ned began showing him around had done nothing to change his opinion that Mrs. Adams had no reason to reproach herself for unkindness in her evaluation.

She had laid a hand on his arm with a theatrical shiver, as she explained why she dared not accompany them on their tour of the colony. "Please do not think me an ungrateful hostess, Mr. Fellowes, for we are in dreadful need of your assistance. But the risk of my nearing that place is too great. I am certain it would place us all in mortal danger."

Never one to be comfortable with uninvited physical contact, Gavin disengaged himself as politely as he could. "You have been the subject of threats yourself?"

"A girl is dead, Mr. Fellowes! What more threat do you need?" Melisandre breathed. "Only a fool or an innocent would be blind to the signs. Someone ... or something is stalking Ker-Ys. Someone is stealing away dear Ned's models—stealing away the girls who dared to dance with the fairies. At first, they vanished for only a few days, only to return with wild tales of the lost cities beneath the water. But the last one returned to the surface drowned. And being that I was the first to probe the secrets that lay beneath the surface of the water, how could I not fear the same fate?"

"That first, glorious success was alas, not to be repeated," Ned returned to the burden of his tale with the unerringness of a man who has repeated it many times. "And so, I returned to my years of weary study. I consulted spiritualists, I consulted Theosophists, I consulted the wise men and women of every religion. And now, only now, has a sign been vouchsafed to me that I am near the truth." He cast an awestruck gaze at the woman next to him. "My dear Melisandre is returned."

And if Mrs. Adams' information was correct, three other girls had disappeared—two of them never to return, and the last one returning dead. Gavin reached for his notebook and began to ask, "And what exactly is this truth you are near to discovering?"

It was no more than a routine question, but Ned's next words deprived Gavin of breath, hearing, and sanity all at one blow. "I found a Book of Shadows. An Ariosophic ritual, this time. *The Most Sacred Protocols of the Germanenorden Walvater of the Holy Grail.*"

A hound bayed in the distance, Gavin's vision blurred, and he was back in another time and place altogether.

"Am I to understand that the hospital's alienists want an opinion as to whether this man is not mad, but in fact possessed?" Gavin asked.

The nurse's face twisted anxiously. "It was the patient himself who requested you. He asked for you by name. Indeed, he was quite insistent. There was no other way to quiet him, short of sedating him."

Gavin shook his head, unsure why he continued to protest. They might call this place a convalescent home rather than a lunatic asylum, but the fact remained that this was no place to look for logic or rationality. "I can only repeat that I am hardly qualified to help him. I am no exorcist, nor alienist either. I'm not even a medical doctor. I am simply an enlightened skeptic, a member of the Society of Psychical Research—whose mission is to explore any and all rational and scientific explanations for mystical phenomena before accepting them as real. I am not in the business of banishing demons—mainly because I do not believe they exist."

"The patient," the nurse repeated stolidly, "requested you by name. Captain Gavin Fellowes, formerly of the British Army Intelligence Division."

Her face grew briefly uncertain as she glanced down at his walking stick. "The doctors assumed that you were a personal acquaintance, despite the fact you are English. Perhaps you served together at some point?"

"It's not impossible," Gavin allowed, for the Americans and British had been brothers in arms—even if it had taken three long years of bloody and pointless fighting before the Yanks had at last been persuaded to abandon their lofty neutrality and involve themselves. But there was no point in bitterness. If the Americans had not ridden to the rescue, Gavin would still be shivering in a muddy trench today. Or, perhaps more mercifully, dead.

In any case, as long as he had made the journey here, there was little else to do other than make his way down the corridors of the hospital, reminding himself that, although he leaned more heavily on his walking stick than he would have liked, he was one of the lucky ones compared to these burned, lamed, and crippled men. Not to mention those like the man who awaited him in the locked ward, his eyes vacant and childlike, suffering from an injury of what—the brain? The soul?—that was only now being recognized as equally terrible to the carnage in the other beds.

Soldier's Heart. Shell Shock. They were beginning to find words for it, and yet it remained the wound that dared not speak his name. The man that awaited him displayed the classic symptoms. His once athletic frame lethargic, his gaze not vacant, but simply… disinterested in the amenities that were meant to serve his comfort: The meal waiting untouched on a tray. The songs of the birds in the garden outside that wafted in through the discreetly barred windows. And the easel and paints that awaited him, inviting him to put his well-known talents to use capturing either. According to the urgent summons Gavin had received, once upon a time, Andrew Piper had been the most promising apprentice of the well-known painter Abbott Thayer—so skilled that he had been nicknamed Pied Piper by the Master himself. Now, both of his hands were bandaged so tightly that it was impossible to use them, even to feed himself. "Has he made an attempt to do violence to himself?" Gavin asked.

The nurse's voice lowered. "Slashed himself with one of those things an artist uses to scrape away paint…"

"A palette knife."

"Over and over again," the nurse agreed. "That's why we keep him wrapped up like that. Doctor's orders, you see. Doctor's afraid he's going to do it again."

And with good reason, Gavin surmised, to judge from the madman's vacant eyes. He cast a quick look at the nursing sister. "Would you please leave us alone?"

The obvious suggestion was that he wished to perform a physical exam that would be unfit for the female gaze, and the nurse withdrew with discreet alacrity. But as soon as she was gone, he asked the patient, "I understand you summoned me by name. Why?"

The madman's eyes flared suddenly to life, and he dropped his voice to a whisper, beckoning Gavin closer. "Because I know you. I know who you are."

Gavin took a step backwards. "I regret to say I do not recollect…"

The patient's eyes glittered with fey humor. "Oh, it matters not *what* you *recollect. What matters is that* they *do.*"

"They?"

"The Hounds of Annwn." The madman laughed. "The Gabriel Hounds. The Cwn Annwn. The hunting pack of the Wild Ride whose howls presage your death. They know who you are. They know where you are. And they never give up the chase. Once they have scented your spoor, they will not cease until they bring you to ground. And you know this as well as I do. That is why I can trust you. Because you hear them, too."

It was all Gavin could do not to turn and run—to leave this madhouse before the madman could divulge his secret: that this was where Gavin truly belonged as well. That some nameless lunatic had somehow penetrated the secret that had driven Gavin from England to America, away from his mother's bewildered pity and his father's angry despair. Away from the stolid loyalty of his pretty second cousin, who was unable to hide her relief when he finally released her from their long-shared understanding that they would marry upon his return from the War. Away from his valet who pretended not to notice that Gavin's cultivating a beard had more to do with the uncontrollable tremors in his hands that kept him from using a straight razor than any taste for fashion.

But most of all, away from the hounds—baying for their revenge when he least expected it. Pale, red-eared, red-eyed shadows glimpsed from the corner of his eye at dinner, the opera, a walk in the park—at any moment when Gavin might have allowed himself to believe that the war was behind him, and he was permitted to be happy and whole once more. The shadows that had forced him into a hopeless flight across an ocean—only to follow him even here.

"They will never cease, not until we pay for what we've done," the madman hissed. "Once unleashed, the Gabriel Hounds are relentless, and they will chase down their quarry until they have their satisfaction."

"Satisfaction for what?" Gavin asked, fighting down a surge of panic more overwhelming than even when he had first heard the Gabriel Hounds and had stared death in the face. "Of what dread crime would you have us stand accused?"

"We were desperate! We used them cruelly, yes. But we were in cruel straits ourselves. The wretched war showed no sign of ending. Men were dying—and worse—in the trenches and the Americans showed no signs of being willing to help. They have powers we can only dream of, master of illusions, able to weave castles out of hillocks and feasts out of acorns. Was it so wrong for us to trick and trap them when they have done the same to so many of ours?"

"I am afraid you are mistaken," Gavin said, fighting to hide the tremor in his voice. "I fear I have no real idea of what you might be referring to."

"Don't you?" The madman's face grew sly. "Oh, I do not believe that—any more than I would venture you do. But it makes no difference. What matters now is that new ones seek to capture them and enslave them once more. And we cannot let them have them. Do you understand? They cannot complete the ritual, or all is lost."

The madman grabbed for Gavin's arm only to find himself thwarted by the bandages, "They failed at Midsummer. They will not fail again. For Lammas comes.

And when it does, they will try again. And you cannot allow them to succeed. You cannot allow them to complete the Rite."

When it came to cases of shell shock, scholarly opinion was divided as to whether one should enter into a madman's reality or refuse to engage. But Gavin had no choice. The madman's reality had already intruded into his, in the form of the shadow that would not cease to haunt him. "What Rite?" he asked, although he already feared the answer.

The madman's face grew cunning. "Twenty-four books for the twenty-four Protocols. We thought it was a joke. We thought it was a game. A serious game, yes, but a game nonetheless. But it is no game to the men who sought me—and who seek you." He brandished his bandaged hands. "I have done what I could. I have made certain I will never create any more copies of that cursed book. Now, it is up to you. You must act! You must find the twenty-four books! You must find the twenty-four men!"

"But why?" Gavin demanded. "Who are these men? What powers do they propose to seize?"

Already, the madman's eyes were far away and vacant, and he only uttered one last word—a soft sigh.

"Dazzlepaint."

In the distance, the baying of the hounds redoubled, and shouts drew closer.

"Dear me!" Ned Adams cried, tearing himself from his rapt contemplation of the water. "I'd better see what that is. Most likely a deer in the cornfields. But it could be a fox in the henhouse."

His prosaic practicality brought Gavin back to himself—just as an excited boy burst through the woods with a telephone message from the Mountain House. "Come quick! Come quick!" the lad cried. "It's another girl gone missing from up at the Overlook Hotel. They're sending out the search parties now, and they need every able-bodied man to help in the search!"

Chapter 4

THE STRANGER WAS GOOD at blending in. Then again, it was hard to say what such a term even meant in a place like the Maverick, populated as it was by artists in flowing Bedouin robes, families masquerading as Romany peasants, Highlanders in kilts and bonnets, Pierrots, and a balding man wearing a monocle and a tutu who flitted though the bonfires shooting darts from a gilded Cupid's bow. And this was not even when one of the Festivals was in full swing. The cottages that nestled in the flat farmlands on the far side of Woodstock were hand-built by necessity rather than philosophy—for Hervey White, who had once been one of the Adams' disciples at Ker-Ys, had come to the conclusion that even the most passionately shared visions could not make rich men and poor men friends. Ker-Ys was for visionaries who sought to seek spiritual and artistic enlightenment by sharing the gifts with which they had been showered at birth. The Maverick was a place for poor men: Poets and artists churned out broadsheets with titles like *The Plowshare, The Wild Hawk,* and *The Hue and Cry* on hand-cranked printing presses. Russian dancers performed recitals in the rough timbered concert hall that had been hewn from the surrounding trees, accompanied by musicians playing in their shirt sleeves—or an impromptu rataplan from a tin can band made of buckets and dishpans that echoed off the stone walls of the nearby quarries. Louche New Yorkers who had heard wild tales of the Festivals through which the perennially-impoverished Mr. White sought to raise money for a well and other necessities came up from the city to see the scandalous goings-on for themselves. In short, it was a place where a one-eyed busker who could juggle flaming clubs as skillfully as she could pick your pocket scarcely drew a second glance.

If the stranger had attracted any notice at all, it would have been for his very ordinariness. No one might be able to explain exactly who he was or what had drawn him here. And, true to the spirit of the Maverick, no one asked. He could have equally been a rich lover of one of the Russian dancers or a field hand who was paid in kind for odd jobs building everything from outdoor privies to stage sets. Whatever his story, in the Maverick, everyone simply accepted that he was there—yet another lost soul that had washed up on the shores of Bohemia.

Everyone, that is, but Gipsy Sarah. For Gipsy Sarah, that clever busker whose one eye saw more than most could ever see with two, had seen him for exactly what he was. And her one eye saw better than the stranger's two, for he never even noticed she was watching as he slid silently from the woods surrounding the Overlook Hotel to watch the Bloomer Girls as they danced. Gipsy Sarah hadn't seen how he came or went, but he was always there, just as the sun set and the Bloomer Girls tumbled out onto the lawn, hand in hand with their chosen partners, whirling and laughing beneath the sun that slowly sank beneath the jagged silhouette of the Devil's Path.

He made no attempt to touch them, or even speak to them. Nonetheless, he summoned them. Summoned where and to what purpose no one knew. But summoned *somewhere* to some revel that left them crouched, disoriented and bewildered, by the remains of the Maverick bonfires on the morning after the full moon.

First had been Miriam, shy and pure—at least until the dancing began. Then came Rachel, as shining and beautiful as if she had been carved from the precious stones in which her family traded. Last came Judith—so different from the rest. Judith, so stern and scholarly, before she had unexpectedly whooped with childish joy during the perilous descent of the Overlook Road by bicycle. Judith who had taken unfeigned delight in hand-churning strawberry ice cream. Judith, who had neither vanished during the full moon nor turned up safely the next morning. Instead, her bloated body had been fished from the bathing pool at the fancy art colony on the other side of town—and dismissed by the coroner as yet another artist's model no better than she ought to have been.

No, Gipsy Sarah knew exactly who—or more accurately, *what*—he was. Indeed, he was the one she had been searching for all these many years. And the answer to the question of what had befallen these three girls. But despite her natural boldness, she found herself hesitating when she at last found herself on the stranger's doorstep. His dwelling crouched at the edge of the woods like a wary animal poised to raid the farmyard coops and barns. Half-cabin, half-tent, constructed out of wood, hide, and bent trees, the ramshackle cottage seemed to belong as much to the forest as to man. But Gipsy Sarah had ventured into far more forbidden places than this, even if it had cost her an eye. Tossing off her moment's trepidation, she pushed open the log-framed door from which she had just watched the stranger emerge with a fishing pole and creel and stepped inside with a defiant jangle of the spurs on her high-heeled riding boots.

The interior was dank, dark, and dirty, little better than an animal's lair. But the workbench that lay on the far side of room seemed to pulse with a hidden light that promised the answers she sought. And after her eye had finally adjusted to the cabin's gloom, she saw the beautifully crafted machines that lay there—the very antithesis of the hovel in which she now stood. She ignored the stereopticon—fat lot of good that would do for a one-eyed girl. But the magic lantern that lay next to it was a different thing altogether. She fitted in a painted glass slide and lit the paraffin lamp that illuminated the projector.

Worlds flared to life on the wall opposite. The first slide revealed a castle that lay in the distant mist, guarded by a wall of briar roses whose brambled hedge was crowned with roses that the slide's alchemy made bloom everywhere like drops of blood. Next yawned the stony vastness of the hall of Mountain King, strange eyes glinting in the depths of its reaches with every ratchet of the magic lantern. With the last slide thundered the Faery Rade itself, pounding through the clouds on their pale horses, the jewels that sprang from their hooves sparkled in the air. At the rear of the charge, Tam Lin thrashed from asp to adder and back again, as valiant Janet strove to take him from his horse.

But there, in a separate tray where they awaited the process of being hand-colored, lay a different set of photographs—and the answers to Gipsy Sarah's questions. In each picture, one of the vanished girls danced alone on the edge of a sea strand, oblivious to the menace of the encroaching tide, completely ensorcelled by the invisible music that transformed her. Rachel was a vision of beauty, a rain of precious things brought up from the lost mines that were said to thread beneath these mountains: Onyx hair, golden skin, ruby lips, emerald eyes. And Miriam leapt and dove like the sleek selkies that danced in the very element for which she was named. Only Judith was different. Judith did not dance, nor was she not oblivious to the danger that surrounded her. Judith prowled the shore like the fierce protectress of her tribe that she was, her lips drawn back with a catamount's natural hatred of the water, as she did her best to hide the fear in her unblinking yellow eyes.

Gipsy Sarah didn't hear the door creak back open, nor the soft footfall behind her—until a heavy hand landed on her shoulder, jerking her rudely back to this world—and to the stranger whose fishing tackled had vanished as completely as if Gipsy Sarah had made a coin disappear. "Well, well, well, look what little fish just came nibbling at my hook."

"You laid a trap," she said calmly. "You knew I was watching."

"You're about as subtle as last night's dishpan concerts. My God, if you hope to earn your daily crust like this, I'd suggest you'd be more likely to try the easier methods favored by most of the artists' models in this place."

She tossed her head, setting the mirrors and sequins that decorated her headscarf jingling. "I am not here to steal from you," she said. "Or to model for you either. I am here because I know who you are. And I know *what* you are."

He stilled. "And what do you propose that is?"

"You're the reason Judith is dead."

Whatever he might have expected her to say, it hadn't been that, and it cost him a moment's startled silence, before he gathered himself to say, "A man is likely to take offense when you accuse him of murder. And an offended man can be a dangerous man."

"I didn't say you killed her," she countered. "I said you were the reason she died."

He allowed the point with a raised eyebrow. "A somewhat Jesuitical distinction."

"I don't care about distinctions. Or priests. I said I know what you are."

"And I know what you are," he said. "Nothing but a common thief."

"I stole nothing from you. Nor did I intend to."

"A spy, then? Simply for spying's sake?"

"I needed to speak to you. But first I needed to be sure you were what I thought you were."

He nodded, considering that. "And have you satisfied yourself?"

"How could I not? I have found your pictures, there beside your magic lantern. You cannot deny it."

"Why should I?" he asked with a shrug. "I'm a photographer. Yes, of course, I took your friends' picture. But I have yet to hear why taking a photograph warrants an accusation of murder."

"It's how she died, you know. Drowning. Just like in your picture," Gipsy Sarah said, forcing her voice to a steadiness she did not feel. "Which means you are exactly what I thought you were all along. And that's why you're here."

"I am here to discover for myself the creature who has been slinking after me for days. And now that I see you, I see you were scarcely worth the trouble. Bah! Go on! Get out of here before I change my mind. And don't try to follow me again—I am rarely in the habit of giving second chances, and not at all likely to offer you a third."

"You don't understand," she protested, trying to wrench herself from his grip in a fresh jangle of beads. "I can help you. But in return I need you to help me."

Briefly, his face seemed to soften with something like... hope? But then he shook his head. "I am not accustomed to bargaining with cat burglars."

"I am no thief!" she said hotly. "As is true of any of my people. The Roma do not steal. We bargain. But we are accused of stealing often enough, for we are canny traders."

"And what did you trade your eye for?" he snorted.

She made a show of feeling for the eyepatch, setting her bracelets jangling, then pulled a face that would have made Puck himself blush. "Why I do declare I don't know! I do seem to have misplaced it!"

The hard mouth quirked briefly in unwilling amusement, but he made no answer, simply waiting for her explanation. Deliberately, she conceded it to him. For gypsies were no thieves; they were traders. And a canny trader knew when she had to bargain.

"I traded it for a pinch of fairy dust, so I might see the wonders of fairy land for myself," she said. "'Twas a fair bargain, fairly struck. One pinch, and one glimpse, before they sprinkled more fairy dust in my eye to blind me. But I was cannier than they. When they sprinkled the fairy dust in one eye, I pretended it stung me—as so saved out a few grains for my other eye when I wiped it. And so they plucked out the eye that dared to gaze on fairy land—as our compact stipulated, but I can still see wonders with my other eye."

His face hardened with fury, as his fingers tightened on her shoulder, digging into her flesh so painfully that she almost cried out.

"You're hurting me," she said.

His grip loosened immediately. "I apologize," he said. "But a word of advice—or if you prefer, warning. Looking where you shouldn't has already cost you one eye. I'd be very careful I didn't lose the other one."

And he pushed her unceremoniously out of his hovel and slammed the door so loudly the sound reverberated through the entire Maverick like a shout.

Chapter 5

THERE WERE STILL OLD-TIMERS in Woodstock who could tell you about the April Fool's Day fire that consumed the old Overlook Mountain House in 1875— could spin with cackling irony the tale of the little girl who ran to tell the workman that a chimney had caught fire, only to be patted on the head and told to find a better April Fool's joke. The fate of the second hotel built two years later had not been much kinder.

"But what can you expect?" Stanton sighed, as he finally mercifully allowed his automobile to clank to a halt after a grinding, jolting trip up the Overlook Mountain road that had irritated Gavin as much as it had his old injury. "Henry Allen Tupper might have been a writer, but at least he was a staunch Protestant. Of course, he had no head for business, that was proved quickly enough. Now Newgold, who took over, he had a sharp head for business, I'll give you that. Just like the rest of his kind. Morris Newgold. Name says it all, I think. Always grasping. Not content to rake in the money hand over fist down among the actresses and lowlifes in Times Square, now he seeks to bleed the Catskills dry. But as I said, Newgold at least had a sharp head for business: he gave that nonsense up after a year. Realized Woodstock wanted no truck with their kind. But leasing it to the Unity Club, like he did? Now, that was just mean. They're not just Jews, they're anarchists and Communists! They don't even call it a hotel anymore. Unity House. I ask you, what kind of name is that?"

Not waiting for Gavin to reply—or to safely negotiate the edge of the running board—he turned his attention to the frame building, which had certainly seen better days. The pillars and arches of the broad porch that gazed out on the mountain views in all directions had been recently painted, but the timbers on the rest of the façade were faded and peeling from snow, wind, and rain. Gavin's bad leg felt in much the same condition as he finally managed to lower it gingerly to the ground.

"Can't see why the whole town is kicking up such a confounded fuss about another missing Bloomer Girl. You know how they are, always coming and going. But my aunt knew some of them back during that Suffrage nonsense— even went to jail with them—and so she feels an obligation. Of course, I drew the line at her coming up to investigate herself, but it's easier to humor her than argue. There's no denying that she's been under a strain as of late, and we all know the cause of that. As well as the cure. Any progress made on that front?"

He barked the last in a tone that would have been rude even in the heat of battle under heavy shelling, but Gavin refused to take umbrage.

"Mrs. Adams agreed to wait for me to present my report until I believe it is complete," he said, his tone far more even than the ground he limped across to the porch where a frightened knot of the so-called Bloomer Girls awaited—identical in their white sailor tops. The fear in their faces was also identical—and to Gavin's practiced eye, genuine. As was their instinctive hostility as Stanton strode up the steps and demanded, "Now what's all this about another girl gone missing?"

"Did you call the sheriff? Is anyone going to investigate?" the boldest among them, clearly the natural leader, demanded. "We've been waiting since morning. They sent down to Mead's Mountain House to telephone, but no one's said anything."

"No point in worrying about investigations until we know there's something to investigate—" Stanton began, but Gavin took one look at the fire burning in the girls' eyes and interrupted.

"I'm a special investigator up from New York City," he said. "An expert in these situations. They thought it advisable to consult me first."

The bold girl eyed him narrowly. "What kind of investigator? What kind of situations?" She shook her head in disgust. "Let me guess. You're some kind of specialist in nervous disorders?"

Well, given recent events, Gavin would be forced to allow that by all appearances, he had far more experience of such matters than this young lady with her feet planted firmly on the ground—but not from the specialists' point of view. "I'm a specialist in ghosties and ghoulies and things that go bump in the night," he allowed. "But mostly I specialize in making them go away."

Except in one glaring instance. He pushed the thought aside. "And the way I do that is by finding an explanation," he went on, mustering a firmness he didn't feel. "I have yet to discover an explanation that involved magic or monsters of any other than human variety. So, if you don't mind, I'd like to ask you a few questions. Get the details of the case while they're still fresh in your mind."

Stanton snorted expressively, but the girl trusted Gavin with a nod. "Go on then."

"This girl—"

"Essie," the bold one corrected him.

"Essie," Gavin amended himself. "You discovered she was missing this morning?"

"Gone," the other girls joined in an angry chorus.

"Vanished."

"Her bed wasn't slept in."

"It was like he snatched her out of thin air."

"He," Gavin repeated. "Are you sure of that? Did someone see him?"

"No one ever sees him," a new girl explained. "Not even the ones he's chosen."

"They just hear him calling," another girl chimed in. "He always calls during the dancing."

"Balderdash!" Stanton snorted. "Come Fellowes! We've wasted quite enough time on these shop girl fantasies."

Gavin ignored him and kept his attention on the girls. "So Essie heard him calling first? But he didn't take her until later?"

"He never takes them during the dancing," the girl said. "He only chooses them then—and calls to them, so they know he's coming. But he waits 'til the middle of the night to take them."

"That's always how it happens," another one said. "It was just the same with Miriam. And Rachel."

"Rachel and Miriam," Gavin repeated. "Those were the first two who vanished?"

The bold girl nodded.

"And how long ago was that?"

"Two months ago for Rachel. Last month it was Miriam. But no one was worried at first. It just seemed like … well, a lark. But then Judith died."

"So only one girl was harmed?"

"Judith was her name. And she was the last. She was different from the others. The first two came from the theatre. Rachel danced. Miriam sang. But Judith … Judith wanted to go to college. Get a degree. Become a teacher. Judith had plans." The bold girl's composure wavered, and she bit her lip. "Judith had more plans than the rest of us, but I guess she's done with planning now."

"Theatre!" Stanton huffed. "Who brings actresses to a decent establishment? Bad enough we have all those artists and dancers over at the Maverick doing God knows what, but I'll be damned if I allow it to penetrate this side of the town. I tell you, we should call the sheriff and have this place shut down."

Gavin suppressed a surge of irritation. For God's sake, the man couldn't do more to alienate these witnesses if he was trying to. Or was he trying to? Gavin filed that thought away for further consideration and forced himself to return to the more immediate line of questioning.

"Please allow me to repeat my question," Gavin said. "So Judith was different? She didn't follow the same pattern as the others?"

"What does it matter?" Stanton snapped. "These kinds of girls are always running off. The parents do what they can for them, but if they are determined to escape—"

"What do you mean, 'escape'? This is no House of Mercy. We aren't prisoners here. We are *paying guests*."

"Back in the day, respectable women didn't travel alone," Stanton huffed. "Still don't, if you ask me."

Which no one had, Gavin forbore to point out. "And Judith was the only one who was harmed?"

"Yes. The others just turned up down at the Maverick, saying they didn't remember what had happened to them. Then they disappeared back down to the city before the sheriff could question them properly. That's why we thought it must be just a prank."

"There you have it!" Stanton blustered. "What more evidence do you need? The girls did this to themselves— who knows for what purpose? Is it not inevitable that one of them would come to harm? Hoist on her own petard, I'd say. And many would say there's justice in that."

"Was that the only difference?" Gavin asked the girl.

"No. The others have happened regularly, once a month," she said. "The night of a full moon just like now."

It was a good, precise observation. Unfortunately, rituals beneath the full moon were so much a part of the standard wisdom on witchcraft that it made such precision suspect. Still, it was simple enough to check an almanac and determine whether the moon was in fact full last night.

"But Judith disappeared only a week ago," the girl went on. "And it wasn't at all the same. No calls. Not even dancing. Judith would rather read than dance, anyway."

"Instead, she just disappeared," another girl chimed in.

"From her bed in the middle of the night?" Gavin asked.

The girls shook their heads grimly. "No one knows. No one really even knew she was gone until they pulled her out of that bathing pool."

The bold girl's face set with anger. "They said she did it to herself—and that she should have been more thoughtful about bringing her troubles down on the heads of respectable folk. Told everyone she was no better than she ought to be. And now that's what they're saying now about Essie, too."

"What other explanation is there?" Stanton snorted. He looked up and down at the girls' outfits. "What else would you expect when you allow girls to gallivant unchaperoned. Small wonder a gentleman might feel entitled to take liberties. We should call the law on Newgold. Shut this place down in the name of decency."

Two bright red spots of color appeared on the bold girl's cheeks. "You tell me what kind of girl runs off with a man in the middle of the night when she was free to take the train back down to the city any time she pleased. And leaving all her clothes behind? No, there's only one reason one of us would leave like that: she was carried off." She turned her glare to Gavin. "And not by any fairies either. No matter what those artist types down at the Maverick want to believe."

Gavin was disposed to agree. More importantly, he was disposed to believe the girls. Their stories were consistent, as was their certainty in them. And their girls' dismissal of the fairy story had been immediate and practical-minded. On the other hand, Gavin had dealt with mass delusion before. "How can you be so sure of that?" he asked. "Especially if none of you has ever seen him."

The bold girl smiled shrewdly. "We never *saw* him," she said with careful emphasis. "But we've seen his picture."

"You have a picture?" The shock in Gavin's voice was matched only by the shock with which Stanton stiffened beside him.

"Yes, we do!" the bold girl said with a triumphant glance at Stanton. "And you can call us silly shop girls all you want, but pictures can't lie."

Having witnessed—and debunked—the best spirit photography had to offer, from astral spirits hovering above a bound medium's head to the winsome girls playing with the fairies at Cottingley, Gavin would beg to differ. Nonetheless, the Bloomer Girls' case had just improved significantly. "Do you have a copy here?" he asked.

"Of course! We keep an album."

A girl scurried back into the house and emerged with a cheap, cardboard scrapbook. Carefully, she turned the pages of photographs, pictures cut out from magazines, and pressed flowers until she came to a picture of Bloomer Girls paired hand in hand in a circle on the very lawn they overlooked, while an instructress called instructions from the center.

Gavin reach for the picture to remove it from the cardboard corners that held it in place, ready to see Ned Adams crouched in the shadows, his eyes glittering with the peculiar greed that lit his face when he spoke of the grimoire. No, not just ready, but eager, for it would bring a quick end to what was rapidly turning into a thoroughly unpleasant case. The only problem that would remain was calculating the mixture of delicacy and firmness needed to convince Mrs. Adams that her frankness might be crucial to saving a girl's life.

But then, he found himself blindsided. Hands shaking and pulse pounding at his temples, he carefully removed the picture from the book as Stanton let out an obvious sigh of relief. The shadow of the man the camera had caught watching from the edge of the woods was far too tall and lean to be Ned Adams. But, as for who he was … well, Gavin could reel off explanations for a score of impossibilities caught on film, but this one was truly impossible to explain.

"MacLeod?" he murmured. "It can't be … I closed your eyes myself. I clutched you to me as your life's blood spilled over me." He sucked in a breath. "I saw you die."

In the distance, the Gabriel Hounds howled.

Stanton's insistence on Gavin riding back down to Mead's Mountain House in his automobile rapidly approached the point of rudeness. Clearly the man was determined to have a say in exactly how Gavin might present these fresh developments to Mrs. Adams, but Gavin much preferred to use his time limping down the mountain road and attempting to marshal his own thoughts—especially about the event that had led Stanton to bundle him into the automobile so precipitously in the first place. And especially in light of the Bloomer Girl's photo.

For when Gavin had earlier returned to Mead's Mountain House in a cart hastily borrowed from Ker-Ys after his guided tour, the foreigner to whom Jean Adams had so violently objected slid down from the porch to introduce himself. "Josep Havel, Impresario," he said, then leaned closer, and dropped his voice confidentially. "Forgive my being forward, but I am a direct man. Did Ned

Adams do no more than arrange for your transportation? Does he not propose to accompany you himself?"

"I'm sure I couldn't say," Gavin said. "As you can see, I have only just arrived and have yet to inform myself fully about the situation."

"But surely Mrs. Adams would have informed you of this much!" Havel said in feigned surprise. "Surely she did not neglect to tell you that the two girls who vanished had both posed for Ned Adams' fairy pictures."

Gavin drew a deep breath. "I was unaware of that," he allowed—although in fact he was more dismayed than surprised. He had sensed Jean Storrs Adams had been holding something back from him—and maybe even from herself.

Havel's lips curled into a smile. "Then pray allow me to enlighten you, for I am certain that, as a psychic investigator, you will be more than a little intrigued by the details of Ned Adams' habit of photographing fairies. Or more precisely, of the young girls he invited to his colony in order to dance with them?"

"Like Cottingley," Gavin said, with a careful neutrality intended to close the topic.

"If you say so," Havel said with a smile that insinuated otherwise. "It is one of Adams' many obsessions, one that has consumed him since he claimed to have discovered a magical apparatus, a camera—"

"Fellowes! No time to tarry. We are leaving now!" Stanton had blustered out the front door, and Havel had slid into the shadows with a sly smile, leaving Gavin with no time to think any more of the incident until now. But Stanton's bullying the Bloomer Girls was all the proof he needed that something was amiss with the girls who came to Ker-Ys, something more dire than a mere drowning, accidental or otherwise. And Hollis Stanton knew all about it. The only question in Gavin's mind now was how much Mrs. Adams knew. It was an uncomfortable issue on which to press a lady he admired far more than he liked, but two girls had vanished, a third was dead, and now a fourth disappeared, and discomfort was a luxury available to no one. And there was the question of the photograph.

Gavin had no way of knowing whether the most recent girl was destined to be returned pixilated or a drowned corpse. But he was realist enough to know that the latter was by far the more likely possibility. That urgency allowed him to be more direct with Jean Adams than was strictly polite.

"A thousand apologies for the discourtesy, but urgency forces me to be frank," he accosted her. "I have just been made privy to some disturbing rumors, tales that would suggest your husband's obsession with Melisandre was not the sole reason that drove you to seek my aid. And so, I must ask you directly. What do you know about your husband's habit of photographing fairies?"

A pause during which he knew she was considering whether to lie to him. Then, she inclined her head and said, "I assume you are referring to that nonsense about these girls being his models."

"One dead girl is already more than nonsense," Gavin pointed out. "The possibility of two is … frankly unspeakable. So, I'm afraid I must insist you answer the question. Were Melisandre's supposed mediumistic abilities the only mystery you wished me to investigate at Ker-Ys? Or did you also hope I would uncover the truth about your husband's purported magical camera?"

Mrs. Adams drew herself up angrily, but after only a moment's internal struggle, she set aside her unwillingness along with her cup of tea and said, "The two are one and the same. For that is exactly how that woman seeks to manipulate him: through his art."

"Manipulate him how?" Gavin asked. "Is she using these girls to entrap your husband into some kind of criminal behavior?"

"My husband is incapable of criminal behavior! He is an artist!"

"Of course, of course," he said. "So, I am comfortable in assuming that these disappearances had nothing to do with your decision to seek my help?"

Mrs. Adams stiffened at being pressed, and, had not Gavin a lineage far longer and nobler than hers, he was certain he would have been dismissed for his impertinence. But eventually she conceded with a sigh, "Of course they did. But it is Melisandre who is at fault here, not my husband. Melisandre is the hand pulling the puppet strings, although I cannot prove it. The minx has been too clever for that."

"Do you have any idea to what purpose? Does she seek to trap him in a compromising position?"

"If she does, she will find herself sorely thwarted. My husband's only lust is for art. Not for the pleasures of such cheap, unwholesome flesh."

"Then I shall accept your word on the matter and press the issue no further," Gavin said, for there was clearly no point in doing so. But for the life of him, he could not explain why he did what he did next. Instead of courteously excusing himself from continuing to pursue the investigation as he had intended, he laid the photograph he had taken with him from the Bloomer Girls on the table between them. "If you will permit me just one more question, would you be as willing to attest to the motivations of this man?"

She raised an eyebrow in surprise as she studied the photograph, then her face lit with a beatific smile. "But there it is, Mr. Fellowes. You have identified the problem exactly. Bravo, Mr. Fellowes! You have proved yourself even more effective than your reputation suggests."

Gavin did his best to disguise his surprise. And his dismay. As well as his complete bewilderment at what imp of the perverse might have prodded him to behave as he just had. "You recognize this man, then?"

She immediately hesitated. "Well, of course it's difficult to say after all these years, and the man's face is in shadow, but the silhouette does bear a striking resemblance to an artist who joined us our very first summers at Ker-Ys."

"And that artist's name?" Gavin asked, willing the answer to be anything other than what he knew he was about to hear.

"Of course, it's impossible to identify him with any certainty after all this time, but I believe that is Duncan MacLeod."

Believe, Gavin repeated her words to himself, even as in the distance, a hound began to cry. Hard to recall. A striking resemblance. There was no reason that the fact Mrs. Adams thought she recognized the same man he recognized should bring fear to his heart. Instead, it should be reassurance indeed. He himself could bear witness to the fact that this was not the Duncan MacLeod he knew, for he had watched the man die beneath him in the muck at Belleau Wood. But clearly, the resemblance was close enough that it had fooled another as well. So, the question was, what would have brought such a man to Ker-Ys in the first place, and what could have brought him back now?

"And would you have any idea why he might have come here now?" Gavin forced himself to press. "Is it possible that he is assisting your husband with his photographic efforts?"

"Quite the contrary, I should say!" Mrs. Adams said. She shook her head. "Although I must say that I never thought a man capable of creating such beauty would be capable of such baseness."

"He was talented, then?"

"He was more than talented, just as he was more than an artist," Mrs. Adams said. "Indeed, one might fairly say Duncan MacLeod was a magician. The most gifted toymaker anyone had ever seen. He made the most cunning mechanisms: magic lanterns, stereopticons, dioramas, music boxes, tiny automata—all of them of such delicacy and grace that they gave the illusion of life."

A moment's pause warned him they were about to reach the heart of the matter before she added, "Alas, he left behind other, far crueler illusions as well."

"Your husband's magical camera," Gavin hazarded.

Her gaze grew far away. "Before MacLeod arrived, Ned had accepted that the muse disdained him and was content to serve his mistress in the only way left to him: by fostering those she had favored instead. But, yes, when MacLeod left, he left his camera behind. And my husband was tempted by the possibility that the magic lay in the camera, not the man." She sighed. "Alas, his artistic career could best be described as proof positive of quite the opposite."

"You refer, of course, to your husband's photographs of the fairies?"

"I always thought it an unwitting cruelty on MacLeod's part," she assented. She raised her gaze to Gavin's face in sudden determination. "But his presence in this photograph suggests otherwise. He left that camera deliberately to tempt my husband, and when that did nothing to serve whatever foul purpose he intended, he turned to colluding with Melisandre to destroy Ker-Ys completely! You must stop them at all costs!"

"Even if that cost is your family's good reputation?"

Her spine stiffened with almost as many centuries of breeding as Gavin suffered from. "Certainly, you don't think I suspect my husband of so much as laying hands on the girls he photographs," she said. "My husband may be a besotted innocent, but you have my word he would not touch such creatures with a ten-foot pole."

Chapter 6

"IMPOSSIBLE! I CANNOT ALLOW such a thing! I will not have it, do you hear me?"

The shouting from the lobby of Mead's Mountain House put an end to any further conversation, and Gavin and Jean Adams rose in unspoken accord to hurry inside where they found Stanton locked in furious argument with Josep Havel. "I don't care whether she proposes to find the missing girl or not," Stanton roared. "I will not tolerate the likes of such a woman as a guest at Ker-Ys."

"And I don't see how you are in a position to allow or disallow anything your uncle chooses to permit."

"My aunt has an interest in Ker-Ys, as well, and I assure you she will not stand by and allow my uncle's reputation to be ruined forever."

"Or perhaps," Havel suggested, "you are afraid of what she might reveal?"

Stanton stiffened. "You exceed yourself. You would do well to recollect that I have friends in high places."

"And *you* would do well to recollect that a girl is missing!"

"And Melisandre has the talent to find her, when a score of searchers and hunting dogs cannot?" Stanton sneered.

"Of course not. If there's one thing we can agree on, it's that the woman is nothing but a charlatan." Havel's mouth drew up in a sly smile. "But we were not speaking of Melisandre. We were speaking of her invited guest, Miss Kate Ames, the well-known children's book illustrator, whom Ned Adams has personally invited to enjoy an indefinite stay as his houseguest at Ker-Ys."

Mrs. Adams drew a sharp breath. In another woman, it would have been a shriek of horror. "Are you quite sure?"

"Oh, there can be no doubt. Miss Ames enjoys quite the reputation." Havel laid a pretty volume whose embossed covered read *The Flower Fairies* before them on the table. "And to judge from this, quite deservedly so."

Mrs. Adams opened the book with a worried frown, but her face relaxed as she turned a few pages. "Dear Kitty," she said with a sigh. "She always had such talent. What a proud moment for the settlement school to see it fulfilled."

"Another charlatan," Stanton dismissed her. "What care I, if that medium brings the entire monstrous regiment of her ilk to bear? I will not have them at Ker-Ys!"

"What choice do you have?" Havel asked—the sly undercurrent in his voice growing even more pronounced. "Miss Ames is already on her way. I believe her steamer has docked at Kingston in more than enough time for her to board the connecting train that arrives in West Hurley this afternoon."

"No," Mrs. Adams murmured. "No, we cannot allow this—"

"We will not allow it," her nephew assured her. He poked a finger into Havel's chest. "You will call off this farce now. If you do not, I will have you horsewhipped out of here. For believe me, I know your kind, and I know exactly how to deal with them."

Havel smiled, and Gavin recognized immediately that Stanton had just made a mistake. "A word of warning, Mr. Stanton," Havel said, his voice the more menacing for its quiet calm. "You may think you have friends in high places, but I assure you they will abandon you like the rats they truly are at a single word from me. You would do well to choose your enemies more wisely."

Having delivered his parting shot, Havel nodded at Gavin and withdrew into one of the private rooms the Meads had set aside for business, closing the door with elaborate courtesy behind him. Stanton's jaw flexed with rage, then he spun on his heel with an oath and stormed out the door. Jean Adams watched her nephew go, and then laid a hand on Gavin's arm, her face pale.

"Please, Mr. Fellowes," she breathed. "The regular wagon has already left to meet the guests at the railway station, and I am uncertain whether the office could reach the driver in time. Could you be so kind as to drive down to the station yourself and persuade Kitty to come and stay with us here, instead. Clearly, Melisandre and that … *mountebank* are conniving at something that involves her, and I will not see her corrupted by such creatures."

Gavin glanced down at the prim, white-gloved hand resting on his arm and thought it might as well have been an iron fist in a velvet gauntlet. "Of course," he agreed with a polite nod. Absently picking up the book from where everyone seemed to have abandoned it, he went out to the stable to do her bidding. The Mountain House's brochure proudly advertised that Meads boasted well-trained horses to accommodate guests who wished to enjoy the most scenic drives in the Catskills, and the pony cart Gavin engaged made good that promise. He accomplished the trip down to the West Hurley Railway Station quickly and easily, leaving him with almost an hour before the train arrived to satisfy his curiosity about the art of talented Miss Ames.

Just a glance at the illustrations was enough to explain her success—for her drawings could be described as nothing short of magical. Her illustrations of the flowers were as meticulously detailed as a herbarium could hope for, but only the slightest shift in perspective revealed the magical creature hidden within the botanical exactitude. The iris fairy was tall and stately as befitted the messenger of the gods; the buttercup fairy tumbled through the dairy, his round face alight with mischief. The rose and lily fairies lounged serenely in their own beauty. The dreamy lilac fairy wandered half-lost in memories evoked by her scent. The fiery snapdragon fairy, clad all in red, brandished his dragon's head staff. The aged crone that was the heather fairy beckoned with a mischievous twinkle in her eye. Then came the wilder fairies of the woods: The white lady who danced in the birch groves. The stately oak king. The rowan and alder fairies, first woman, first man, arm in arm. The ash fairy, hovering somewhere between man and woman. And the apple fairy smilingly offered everlasting youth and beauty along with her fruit.

It was not just the pixies that were unique. Kate Ames' effects varied as well—each one more skilled than the next: Gossamer wings woven out of a wash of color so light as to be nearly invisible; a mid-air cartwheel caught so deftly by only a pair of sketched lines that even a skeptic like Gavin caught himself blinking away the sensation that he had actually glimpsed something move. Yet beneath all the grace and technical expertise lay a sly wit and mischievous sense of humor. The rainbow that trailed the iris fairy tumbled topsy-turvy down from heaven, like an upended bucket of water. Her buttercup fairy worked the churn by gleefully spinning on his rear end. Her white lady did her best to keep the flustered-looking hunter she had enticed to dance from treading on her bare toes. And her rose fairy concealed her thorns carefully behind her back as she smiled sweetly at a pompous suitor. In short, nothing on the pages was exactly what it seemed and everything on the pages intrigued Gavin immensely.

Kate Ames, he concluded, as he shut the book with surprised respect, was not just a children's book illustrator. She was a genuinely talented artist with a vision to rival any of the masters in Paris ateliers. Small wonder Mrs. Adams could well believe that her dear Kitty had truly communed with the fairies.

But the woman who stepped down from the train could scarcely look less like one who could summon the Fair Folk. Small, dark, and attractive, with a quick smile and a clever face, she wore a sensibly cut traveling costume that allowed her to descend the metal steps pulled down by the porter with rapid ease.

"Miss Ames?" he asked as he stepped forward to greet her. "Gavin Fellowes. I've come to drive you to Woodstock."

She turned to him, and Gavin saw that Mrs. Adams was indeed correct: Kate Ames had the most extraordinary green eyes and they were gazing up at him with undisguised wariness. It was not a reaction Gavin was used to. Centuries of breeding had given him the look of a man who was not simply to be trusted but relied upon by both kings and their courts and damsels in distress. And while there was part of him that would freely admit he had forfeited that right in at Belleau Wood, he was still unaccustomed to a woman recoiling as if he were about to shanghai her from the docks.

"I was not expecting to be met," she said. "Did Melisandre send you?"

From her tone, it was clear that she would consider nothing less likely, and Fellowes offered her a tentative smile. "No, I was sent by an older friend than that. Mrs. Edward Storrs Adams."

He proffered Mrs. Adams' calling card with a message penned across the back as a bona fide. "Dear Kitty! Allow me to introduce Mr. Fellowes, whom I have taken the liberty of sending to collect you."

Kate studied it with the same wary indecision, prompting Fellowes to add, "I will be frank. She has sent me to persuade you to stay with her at Mead's Mountain House rather than joining Melisandre at Ker-Ys."

Her green eyes abruptly lit with wry humor. "So, it is as I suspected. Melisandre has been stirring up a hornet's nest?"

He hid an answering smile. "Perhaps it would be more discreet to allow you to observe the situation for yourself and draw your own conclusions," he said. "However, Mrs. Adams felt you might do that more comfortably from the distance of Mead's Mountain House and has taken the liberty of securing you a room. I am merely the emissary she sent to persuade you to change your plans. Along with her assurance that she alone will be responsible for any expenses you might accrue."

Kate inclined her head. "A generous offer."

"Mrs. Adams is a generous woman," he agreed. He gestured toward the pony trap he had driven down from the Mountain House. "At the very least, please allow me to offer you a ride to Woodstock. If, when we arrive, you still prefer to not to change your plans, I will take you to Ker-Ys directly. However, if I were to venture an opinion, I would suggest you accept Mrs. Adams' offer. I have only a brief experience of Ker-Ys but have already come to the conclusion that matters are somewhat likely to be ... draughty there. And it's said the water supply is irregular—except when it's raining."

"Then I'd be pleased to accept Mrs. Adams' offer," Kate said. "For I am, frankly, more than a little fond of running water myself."

But her wariness didn't vanish, even as she allowed him to help her up into the trap. "And what of you, Mr. Fellowes?" she asked. "What brought you to Woodstock? Are you interested in the arts as well?"

He considered prevaricating, if not lying outright—and immediately decided against it. "Mrs. Adams has solicited my aid in investigating several purported fairy kidnappings in the area."

"Ah." She drew a deep breath. "So now we come to it. This is Melisandre's current hornet's nest, I presume?"

"Several girls have gone missing," he said with careful neutrality. "It has been said that your friend Melisandre proposes to enlist your aid in questioning the Faerie Courts as to their whereabouts."

"Then you have my word she will find herself sorely disappointed." Kate shook her head with a smile. "I illustrate fairy tales, Mr. Fellowes. I don't believe in them."

"A person who has seen your work would be justified in thinking otherwise—myself among them. They are some of the most extraordinary pictures I have ever seen."

"You flatter me."

"Not in the least. A single perusal of your most recent book was enough to make even a cynic like me believe that fairies really do hide beneath fairy plants—and that you have been gifted with the grace to see them."

She smiled. "I write books for children, Mr. Fellowes. That is all."

"Books about fairies?"

"Books that sell. Even in these modern times, it is hard for a woman to earn an independent living, especially if she chooses not to wed. And since I have no urge to become a telephone operator or a typist, I choose to earn my living by my pen—or more accurately, my paintbox. I could, I suppose, write sentimental poems or sensation novels, but I admit I am more talented with pictures than words, and so I have resigned myself to fulfilling the publishing industry's idea of what is a decorous employment for a lady artist." She raised a shoulder. "If tastes change, so shall I. I assure you I can sketch a buccaneer astride a ship's prow or an Indian maiden's ghost haunting the cliff from which she threw herself for love with equal conviction."

He nodded, uncertain as to whether he believed her. "Then if I may be so bold, what led you to answer Melisandre's summons?"

He was braced against any reaction, but her only response was a troubled frown. "I may have known some of the girls who disappeared. It's possible that they modeled for the artist in whose atelier I learned my craft, Mr. Abbott Thayer."

"The dazzlepaint man?" Gavin asked, frankly startled.

"The credit for dazzlepaint proper must go to Everett Warner, but, yes, Warner's work made use of Mr.

Thayer's original theories of protective coloration and countershading." She raised an eyebrow. "But how strange for you to mention that first. Mr. Thayer's much-admired angel paintings are usually the first thing people refer to when they recognize his name."

She tried to hide a surprisingly impish smile. "Although I privately share your opinion and consider his efforts at dazzlepaint by far the more stunning aesthetic accomplishment. Skilled as they are, his angels belong only on a chocolate box."

Gavin gave an answering laugh, for he thoroughly agreed. "Whereas many would claim Mr. Thayer's theories of camouflage have revolutionized warfare as we know it," he said. "To which I can only join my personal opinion that they were decisive in ensuring the Allies' victory and bringing about an end to the recent war."

"Not to judge from the Allies' reaction when Mr. Thayer went to England to convince them of his theories," she countered. "Not even the fact that he was accompanied by no lesser a figure than John Singer Sargent was enough to convince the English they were not dealing with a madman who offered his proof in the form of a suitcase stuffed with his wife's hosiery. If it had not been for one spymaster who saw the potential in his work—" She clamped her jaw shut abruptly, as if aware she had said too much.

Gavin's mind returned to Mr. Havel's ill-concealed threat about Stanton's friends in high places and Stanton's reaction. Did what was going on here run deeper than just an errant husband with a taste for photographing fairies? And was Kate Ames the key to understanding how deep the roots of this suddenly menacing tangle might really run?

"So, you worked for the War Office, then?" he probed.

But it was too late. She raised one shoulder in a practiced shrug. "As did many artists. The War Office recruited experts in creating all kinds of illusions, from girls with angel wings to disguising ships with dazzlepaint."

Gavin nodded, for he knew only too well the lengths to which desperate men had gone to bring an end to an increasingly senseless war.

"Many of which were covered by the Official Secrets Act, I surmise," he said with an easy smile and pressed her no further—for the moment. He would find a subtler way to broach the matter later. For now, he was content to ride with her in surprisingly companionable silence across the rolling farmlands, past the occasional stone quarry hewn from a hillside, to the heart of Woodstock, where the white-spired Dutch Reformed Church presided gracefully over the Village Green. There, he turned the pony cart up the steep, twisting road that rose along the flank of Overlook Mountain, bringing them to the welcoming piazza of Mead's Mountain House.

But it was not Mrs. Adams who emerged to greet them. Instead, Josep Havel sprang from the rocking chair where he had been lounging, every inch the mountebank Mrs. Adams had accused him of being.

"Miss Ames?" he asked, with a faint, foreign lisp. A diamond flashed as he grasped her hand and raised it to his lips without waiting for a reply. "Josep Havel, Impresario. So pleased to finally make the pleasure of your acquaintance. For I trust you cannot help but be aware I have gone to no little effort to track you down."

She withdrew her hand, masking the sting of the gesture with a perfunctory smile. "My publisher forwarded your card to me," she said. "I am, of course, flattered, but I'm afraid I have no idea why you would go to such trouble."

"Then I hope you will take the time to hear the offer I propose to make you and give it serious consideration."

"I'm afraid my time here is not my own," she deferred with more grace than Gavin would have been able to muster. "Mrs. Adams has been generous enough to invite me to stay, and I must put myself entirely at her disposal."

"Of course, of course! But surely you do not propose to abandon the search for your friends!" Havel's tone grew insinuating. "For I am correct in stating that the poor girls who have vanished were your friends, am I not? Do correct me if I'm wrong, but is it not true that you were all models for Mr. Abbott Thayer's celebrated angel paintings?"

A flicker of humor twisted Kate's mouth, and Gavin recalled her comment about them being fit only for a chocolate box. But her voice remained carefully neutral, as she said, "Not precisely. The girls who vanished may have been models for Mr. Thayer, and that is something I traveled to Woodstock to ascertain. But I was merely an apprentice at his atelier."

Havel's greedy gaze never wavered. "Strange. I was certain I recognized your face."

"I can't imagine why," she said. "My place has always been behind the easel."

Havel began to press the issue with ungentlemanly determination, but at that moment the door to the Mountain House opened, and Jean Storrs Adams herself emerged, holding out her arms. "Kitty!" she cried. "I'd always wondered what had happened to you. How lovely to rediscover you—all grown up. And quite the career woman, I'm told." She smiled mischievously at Kate's murmured demurral. "Now, don't bother to deny it, because I give you fair warning, I intend to be absolutely ruthless in striving to convince you to share with us a few days each month teaching art to the girls in our settlement school."

Ever the cynic, Gavin thought that was not likely to be a difficult task, given that a settlement school had arguably saved Kate from an unimaginable life, and that Mrs. Adams had insisted on assuming full responsibility for Kate's board, which was equivalent to many laborers' weekly wages.

"But there will be time enough for that later," Mrs. Adams said. "Right now, I'm sure you want to do nothing more than get yourself settled in your room." She ignored the foreigner's presence and turned to Gavin. "Mr. Fellowes, may I implore you to assist my young friend with her bag?"

Kate accepted the dismissal with a grateful smile and allowed Gavin to escort her into the lobby's office to retrieve her room key from Mrs. Mead. But no sooner had they set foot through the door than the telephone began to ring, causing Mrs. Mead to excuse herself to answer it. Gavin watched as the woman listened intently, nodded once, then turned to Gavin and Kate with a worried frown.

"That was Mr. Rose down at the general store. He says someone saw the missing girl near the bathing pool at Ker-Ys—the self-same place the other girl drowned—and the sheriff is sending up a search party to investigate. He didn't want to bother Mrs. Adams, but seeing as Mr. Adams refuses to have modern conveniences such as telephones or automobiles at Ker-Ys, he had no choice but to telephone here with the news."

Beyond Ker-Ys

WHEN THEY FOUND JUDITH drowned, Essie knew she wanted no more part of the game. It was supposed to be a lark. Harmless fun. No one was going to get hurt. They were just making a daft old man happy. But that had all changed when someone had snatched Judith—bookish, short-sighted *Judith,* who should never have been asked to join the game in the first place.

And when Essie had told them she was through with the whole thing, they hadn't tried to stop her. Instead, they told her that of course she was entitled to make her own decisions, and she had every right to change her mind. After all, there were a dozen other girls up at the Unity Club who would be happy to take her place. They had no need to compel the unwilling, they said, and had even made her a gift of the money she had tried to give back.

So what was Essie doing *here*—if this place could even be described as some*where*? How had she found herself among these dank ruins that seeped with moss and stank with rot, shivering in her thin nightdress against the mist rising from the waters that lapped at her from every side, her feet bare and grass-stained, her head aching with vague dreams of horns and pointed ears and glittering cats' eyes, whirling and singing as they trampled out the fairy ring?

But *why*? And even more importantly, *how*? She didn't believe in fairies! It had only been a game!

"I … must have sleepwalked," she stammered to herself. "But that hasn't happened for a long, long time. I guess the country air.…"

But her reasoning rang hollow even to her own ears. What kind of sleepwalker could let herself down from her comfortable bed on the second story of the Overlook Hotel without raising the alarm with the other girls? What kind of dreamer could imagine the litany of names like Cobweb, Peaseblossom, Moth, and Mustardseed, Candide, Coulante, Miettes, Canari, and Violente? And what kind of trance must she have been in to traverse the water, which spread in every direction with no shore in sight, when Essie had never learned to swim? No, Essie had been brought here, and given what she knew about Judith, it didn't take much imagination to guess why.

They had lied to her! They had told her they understood. Had glanced anxiously at one of the summer squalls that rose in the Catskills as unexpectedly as dust storms in the desert and insisted Essie wait it out over a cup of tea. The tea must have been drugged, of course. She realized that now. The streets were full of cautionary tales of girls who had been kidnapped and held against their will as slaves in opium dens. But Essie had never heard any warnings about the impossible creatures who had borne her here on the backs of flying white steeds with bright red ears and eyes, as they bid her "Come away, come away, come away."

Essie's fists clenched in rage, but rage wasn't going to get her anywhere. She had to think. She had to figure out where she was and who had brought her here. One thing was certain; it wasn't fairies.

Drugged. That was the only explanation. Their kindness had been as false as the game they had tricked her into playing. And they had probably taken back her money before she'd been brought here—the two-faced cheats! What else besides drugs could explain this place? She must still be laboring under their influence. For this tiny island was a dreamscape itself. How could one hillock hold its head above the bottomless lake that washed to the horizon in every direction?

Curling her bare toes away from the waves that lapped ever closer, she walked carefully around the tiny knoll. There was nothing here but walls, most of them low and crumbling, a few high, with iron mullions and the remains of arched windows. All of them salt-stained and moss-covered, as if the earth and water were racing to see who could swallow them first. A creaking iron gate guarded the remains of a fountain that was the only dry place on the entire little island.

And in front of the fountain, as if laid there in offering, a glint in the muddy grass: a pair of broken eyeglasses, their steel frames twisted and broken.

"Judith," Essie breathed.

Then the fear seized her, and she glanced wildly around the abandoned ruins.

"Please," she moaned. "I said I wouldn't tell. I tried to give you the money back."

A footstep sounded, and she felt a brief surge of hope before she recognized one of the guests from the Mountain

House. Her betters, many would have it. Well, for all his fancy clothes and calling himself an impresario, the man who faced her now was nothing but a called bone-conjurer, his eyes gleaming with the infernal purpose of the Mad Monk, Rasputin himself, on whose name her family spat along with the Royal Family he had served and the Cossacks who had driven them from their homes.

"I wanted to give back the money," she protested.

He studied her with the dispassion of a butcher considering a carcass.

"You're no better than the last one," he said.

Now Essie knew exactly what had happened to Judith. She had been tossed aside as useless—like the scraps even the rag and bone men had no need of. And she knew with equal certainty that this was about to be her fate as well. But she was helpless to move as the sorcerer drew a strangely wrought knife set with a dull red carbuncle, and his lips began to move in a voiceless chant.

"Please," Essie whispered. "Help me. I don't want to die."

The sorcerer rose over her. The blade flashed against the sky.

And a great shout rang out, and the ruins crumbled into a stream of sand, as the floodwaters of the Ashokan began spilling over the broken walls, sweeping the sorcerer with them.

Chapter 7

THE NEWS OF ANOTHER missing girl had spread
from farm to farm, so that now there was a search party
gathered at what was the *de facto* town hall, a collection of
battered chairs and wooden benches gathered around the
big, white-bellied stove in the middle of the General Store
on the Village Green. Up at Mead's Mountain House, the
wagon driver who had ferried the newest boarders up from
the railway station waited to drive another group down to
the village and on to Ker-Ys for the search. While cooks
packed a hamper with bread, meat, and cheese for the
search party to enjoy afterward, Stanton, impatient with
the delay, called for his motorcar.

"You'll come with me, Fellowes."

Gavin took a moment to fight down an unreasoning
surge of anger toward Stanton. "I believe it would be
preferable for me to travel down to the village with the
others. Strictly in order to assure my objectivity when I
make my report, of course."

Stanton's jaw set, but before he could press the issue,
Havel cut in. "I, on the other hand, would have no such

scruples about accepting your invitation," he announced in a pompous tone.

"You, sir?" Stanton sneered in disbelief. "Ride with me? I would think you might do better to leave town before that search party turns into a mob bent on hanging a man for murder."

"Murder?" Havel response was all exaggerated surprise mirroring Stanton's. "Who, dare I ask, would you accuse of such a crime?"

"Do not bandy words with me! I give you fair warning. Woodstock has a reputation for Bohemians, yes, but under the surface it is a very old-fashioned town, indeed."

Havel raised an eyebrow. "If you have an accusation to make, I would prefer you make it directly."

"Then allow me to be frank. Girls have been disappearing for months now. But it was not until you appeared in Woodstock that one of them died. And not just any girl, but the girl you came to Woodstock to find. Or would you deny that you came specifically to seek out the poor girl later found drowned?"

"Why would I deny the truth?" Havel asked with an elaborate shrug. "Yes, I came to Woodstock to seek out Judith Shattuck."

"Why seek out such a girl if not to murder her?" Stanton demanded.

"It is certainly no business of yours, but I had the honor of serving with her uncle as a clerk on Lord Kitchener's ill-fated diplomatic delegation aboard the H.M.S. *Hampshire*—"

Gavin's hearing and vision clouded.

"—and was one of the fortunate few to survive the U-Boat attack that sank it. Miss Shattuck's uncle was not. I came to Woodstock to share my condolences and to convey a last message from her uncle."

Gavin grasped the railing of the wagon bed to steady himself.

"And what message is that?" Stanton demanded.

Havel stared at Stanton. "A confidential message."

"A girl is dead," Gavin managed to say as he pushed aside thoughts of the H.M.S. *Hampshire* and the 737 souls drowned beneath the icy waves of the North Sea—souls whose blood was on his hands. "And another is missing." He fought to keep the quavering from his voice. "If there is any possibility this message has a bearing on either case—"

"Of course, it has no bearing!" Stanton snapped, then whirled back on Havel. "Spare us your tales of a war we would all do best to forget! Instead, heed me well. If I urge you to leave town as quickly as possible, it is strictly out of concern for your own safety. The good farmers of Woodstock are hardly as tolerant of outsiders as one might presume, and if you continue to meddle in their affairs, you are likely to find yourself hanged!"

"I sincerely hope not," Havel responded with a sly smile. "For I can assure you that such an unfortunate outcome would trouble certain of our mutual friends in New York City for it would place them in a very awkward position, indeed."

"I sincerely doubt we have any mutual friends." Stanton voice was cold as ice. "But if we do, my friends—"

"Are hardly as loyal as you presume," Havel finished the sentence for him.

The silence that followed would have presaged a duel in more primitive times—and still might, had not Mrs. Adams stepped forward. "Please, Hollis! Have done with such wild talk! There can be no question of murder or hangings. I'm certain the poor girl who vanished simply grew bored and skipped back to Manhattan. I can address a few inquiries … And you," she turned to Kate as if struck with sudden inspiration, "can help me! You always had such a lovely hand."

Gavin frowned. Mention of the H.M.S. *Hampshire* had thrown him off balance, but he was not so far gone as to resent Mrs. Adam's privileged presumption on Kate Ames' behalf. On top of everything else, the idea that the price of Kate's board at Mead's Mountain House would be using her talents to serve as an unpaid amanuensis soured his mood even further.

Kate, on the other hand, responded with a calm smile, as if the argument between Stanton and Havel had never happened. "I would be delighted to help in any way I can," she answered Mrs. Adams, then added, "*after* we return from Ker-Ys. For we must be reasonable. Melisandre was the one who invited me here, another girl is missing, and it is inevitable that I must go to Ker-Ys sooner or later. So why not put the unpleasantness behind us as quickly as we can?"

Her point, Gavin allowed with admiration, was inarguable, and Mrs. Adams could do nothing but concede. Then, when the engine on Stanton's motorcar refused to start, Gavin even managed a grim smile as he climbed into the back of the wagon to take his place as a member of their ad hoc search party. He stretched out a hand to help Kate up to sit beside him and watched as Havel hoisted his bulk up to take his place opposite. Stanton, grumbling under his breath about scandal and search parties and unshod villagers nosing about family property, climbed in as well, and when the luncheon baskets were packed and handed up to be secured in the wagon, two gardeners, a young groom, and a handyman climbed up to join the party. With a flick of the wrist, the driver got the horses started on the journey down the steep mountain road to collect the small band of farmers, farriers, and hangers on corralled by the Presiding Elder of the Dutch Reformed Church on direction of the county sheriff to conduct the search. Once everyone was packed in, the motley search party headed up the winding road to Mt. Guardian, Overlook's smaller, less assuming brother. When they reached Ker-Ys, the driver halted his wagon on the broad stretch of road by the dormitories, not trusting his sturdy draft horse to navigate the narrow road up to the Great House. The searchers disembarked and walked the rest of the way, led by the imposing Elder himself. When they reached the crest of the road, he pointed toward the bathing pool that nestled by the edge of the woods.

"You said you saw her by the spring house? Over there?" he asked the farmhand who swore he had glimpsed a Bloomer Girl as he was delivering the milk that morning. But before the man could manage an answer, the doors of the Great House burst open, and Ned Adams raced across the lawn to block their way, clutching an inlaid Turkish sword that had clearly seen no more active service than being a prop for a model posed as an Odalisque.

"Stay back! I'll not have strangers traipsing about my property!" he yelled, waving the sword at the newcomers.

Stanton broke away from the group with a curse. "Put that down at once, and come with me, Uncle! I will not allow you to humiliate my aunt further with your nonsense."

Ned's jaw squared, but before he could say anything else, a graceful silhouette emerged behind him.

"Kitty!" Melisandre cried. She swept forward, arms thrown wide for an embrace. "Why, Kitty! Is that really you?" She looked from Kitty to the group of men and back to Kitty. "But how did you come here? And when? We have been expecting you at Ker-Ys. Why did you not come to us directly?"

"Mrs. Adams sent a messenger to fetch me from the railway station and was kind enough to invite me to stay with her instead," Kate said, making no move to return Melisandre's affection.

Gavin watched Melisandre's face darken as she dropped her arms. "Oh, Kitty, tell me that woman does not seek to turn you against me."

"I am here to aid in the search for the missing girls," Kate said. "Nothing more. Nothing less."

"You always were so stern, so purposeful," Melisandre sighed, before she turned to the knot of searchers with a clap of her hands. "Gentlemen, Kitty is here now, and that is all that matters. I thank you for bringing her to us, but there is no need to further inconvenience yourselves. Once she is settled in, we will continue the search together, and all will be well."

"Ha! You mean to conduct a thorough search by your vaunted psychical means? Not likely, so long as I have voice to speak." Stanton dismissed her and turned back to the group from the village, seizing the opportunity to be rid of them. "But the lady is right about one thing," he said, "There is no further need for you to inconvenience yourselves any longer. I pray you have done with this madness and allow us to handle things from here."

The searchers muttered among themselves, clearly torn between their desire to have nothing to do with the

scandalous artists that had invaded their quiet village—
beyond taking their money, of course—and a stubborn
Dutch dislike of newcomers issuing orders to those
descended from the oldest families in the county.

"Oh, no, gentlemen! Pray do not leave!" Havel
insinuated himself into the conversation. "If these ladies
propose to find the lost girls by communicating with the
spirit world through 'vaunted psychical means', what
better proof could there be than a score of upstanding
witnesses?"

"By all that's holy!" Stanton exploded, turning on Havel
in a fury. "You seek to turn this into a circus sideshow, but
I tell you I will not tolerate the humiliation of my aunt."

Havel raised an eyebrow. "Your desire to protect your
aunt is naturally admirable, but the fact remains that a girl
is missing, and time may be running short for her."

The restive muttering that had been swelling among
the villagers finally gave way to the booming voice of the
Presiding Elder as if proclaiming God's own truth from
the pulpit. "Gentlemen! Gentlemen!" he protested. "Such
quarrels are more properly conducted in private. We are
here merely to search around the spring house for the
missing girl on the word of one of our own upstanding
citizens, so let's have done with it, and then we can leave
you to your own concerns. But first, if I can just get down a
few notes and names in case the sheriff asks for any future
inquiry ..."

He broke off, embarrassed to realize he had brought
neither paper nor pen with him.

"I can help on that score," Kate said with a quick smile,
and began rummaging in the artist's satchel she carried in
place of a purse.

"In the meantime, Mr. Adams, if you could just stand aside, it won't take these lads but a moment to search the—"

"Nooo," Melisandre moaned, her hand clasped over her mouth in horror. "You cannot. The spirits will not allow it…" She slumped to the ground, stretched out elegantly in the path of the few men who had started toward the spring house. Ned brandished his sword in a fury.

"Stand back! She's gone into a trance! Disturb her and she will die!"

A couple of the searchers' eyes narrowed skeptically, but the others acquiesced with shrugs that suggested they would not care if a newly-awakened Rip van Winkle was hiding in the spring house in the company of the Catskill witch herself. It was time for them to get back to their white-bellied stove and tobacco.

"Damnit, if no one else will put an end to this farce, I will!" Stanton lunged for Melisandre and grabbed her by one of her flowing sleeves. "Woman, have done with this playacting at once!"

Ned cried out, and several of the searchers murmured a protest, just as Melisandre's lips began to move. "It was all just a game," she murmured. "All just a game until someone told. Someone told and someone looked. Now, she is beneath the water, beneath the water with the rest of them…"

Stanton paled. "This is infamous! You will cease and desist, or I will swear out a writ that will have you in prison!"

"She is scarcely strong enough to bear this," Ned cried, springing between them. "You will withdraw yourself at once. You will *all* withdraw yourselves."

If only they all could, Gavin thought, weary of the entire performance. Only a fool such as Ned Adams could be taken in by such clumsy effects, but he knew too well that some men had a peculiar gift of seeing only what they wanted to see. On the other hand, he was very curious about what Melisandre clearly did *not* want people to see in the spring house.

"Someone told!" Melisandre's eyes flared wide open and her voice rose. "And someone looked. Someone spied upon secrets they were never meant to see. Someone told and someone looked, and now they must all sink beneath the sea."

She collapsed back to the ground, her chest heaving beneath the thin white fabric of her gown. Her lips parted, as if she was calling for air, and petals began to emerge: Pansies, violets, nasturtiums, and roses. Ned fell to his knees, rapt, but Gavin had seen better effects on vaudeville stages.

"My dear!" Ned cried. "You must not exercise yourself. Lie still! Lie still!"

Melisandre refocused her gaze on Ned, pushed herself to one elbow, and blinked uncertainly at the petals surrounding her. "What happened? Did they come? Did they tell you why they took Essie?"

Stanton planted his hands on his hips. "You mean to say you do not recall a single thing?"

"I never do." She drew in a long breath and shook her head sadly. I am a simple vessel, nothing more."

Which was a very convenient way to fling around accusations without having a shred of evidence, Gavin thought—albeit with a shiver of foreboding. He pushed it aside. *La commedia e finita.* All that remained was for him to make his report to Mrs. Adams and return to exposing mediums possessed of at least a modicum of finesse. He made a show of studying the petals that lay on the grass, poking at one or two of them with the tip of his walking stick.

"Roses and violets," he commented. "Lavender and honeysuckle. All fairy plants, are they not?"

"All plants are fairy plants." Melisandre responded as Ned painstakingly helped her to her feet.

Gavin conceded the point with a curt nod and turned back to studying the plants. "And yet there is no foxglove. Strange, is it not? For is not foxglove a fairy plant?"

"As I said, all plants are fairy plants." Melisandre brushed the dust from her gown. "As dear Kitty has so delightfully demonstrated in her pictures."

"No hellebore either," Gavin pressed. "Nor monkshood. Daffodils. Or lilies of the valley. Instead, I wonder whether it is customary for fairies to be so thoughtful as to cause you to ingest only non-poisonous plants?" He could barely hide the contempt in his voice. "As an expert in fairy plants, perhaps Miss Ames could weigh in on this question."

But Kate Ames said nothing. Gavin turned to see that she had moved away from the knot of searchers and had fallen to her knees at the edge of the bathing pool. Sketch pad on her lap, pencil gripped tight, her eyes were focused on the depths as her hand moved quickly this way and that, seemingly pushed and pulled by invisible forces.

Damnation. So the curtain was not set to come down on the comedy after all, Gavin thought, with an unexpected surge of irritation. His disappointment in Melisandre's performance did not matter, for she was only the *amuse-bouche*. Apparently, green-eyed Kitty was to be the sumptuous main course.

"Miss Ames," he said sharply. "Are you feeling quite yourself?"

Kate's eyes snapped away from whatever vision had enraptured her and spared only a swift glance at her drawing, before looking up. "It was just a moment's dizziness. I'm afraid I'm not used to the mountain air quite yet."

Gavin strode toward her as she, with another troubled glance at the sketch, tore the page from the book and made to crumple it. But Gavin stopped her, snatching it away with ungentlemanly force. "Oh, no," he said. "If the Fair Folk have gone to such efforts to smuggle a message across the astral plane, it would be the height of rudeness to refuse to read it. Pray allow me."

Disillusionment had made him harsh, and the day's events had put him in a foul mood, but still he was surprised by the violence of his emotions. He had liked Kate Ames. Even more, he had imagined her above such trumpery parlor tricks.

"There has been no spirit communication," she said, reaching out for the paper even as he lifted it away from her. She held his gaze. "There has been nothing but an embarrassing moment's distraction on my part. I confess, I was taken by surprise and consumed by a childhood memory. It will not happen again."

Her words immediately made Gavin feel small. It mattered not whether what had happened at this pool was truly the fault of the Fair Folk. *Something* had happened to her here. That was obvious. Would his own behavior have been any more rational if he had found himself thrust back into the mud at Belleau Wood? "Apologies, Miss Ames, he said with a slight bow. "This is of course a delicate moment for you."

She held out her hand again and continued to hold his gaze. "Then please, Mr. Fellowes, return that unfortunate sketch, and let us waste no more time on these foolish games."

It would have been boorish to refuse, and despite his disillusionment with Miss Ames, Gavin found himself reluctant to risk her bad opinion. He lowered his hand … but then stopped. For the shock that twisted Melisandre's face as she caught a glimpse of the drawing instilled in him an irrational surge of hope. Melisandre was clearly surprised by the drawing, and although it was nothing close to a complete exoneration of Kate's participation in the ongoing nonsense, it was, at least, proof positive that whatever they may or may not have planned between them, this was not part of the scheme. And once he realized that much, he was determined to know more. So, instead of answering Miss Ames, he turned to Melisandre and suggested, "Why do we not leave it to the medium herself to decide?"

Uncertainty twisted Melisandre's face, confirming his instincts. She had been caught wrong-footed and had lost control of her own creation, even if only momentarily. She had no more idea what Kate might be up to than he did. Then, the smooth, medium's mask slid back into place, and she said, "Of course, Kitty must show us what she's seen. Please Kitty, there's no need to be ashamed. The fairies called to you because they want to help. We must accept the gifts they freely offer, and humble ourselves when they choose us for their vehicles."

"As you will," Gavin said. Too much of a coward to meet Kate's now furious glare, he smoothed open the crumpled paper for all to see. And was stunned.

"Do most of your dizzy spells produce work of this caliber, Miss Ames?" he asked, when at last he trusted himself to speak. For it mattered not whether she had done so consciously or unconsciously; what Kate Ames had created was a work of art of such quality he had rarely seen before. With only a few deft strokes, she had drawn the surface of a lake, rippling and restless. But the storm that had disturbed the water did not descend from the sky. Instead, it rumbled up from the lost city that seethed with life in its depths, its dreamy spires crawling with drowned spirits that clambered over one another in a futile struggle to reach the surface, their long fingers grasping greedily for the life and light they had forfeited long ago.

"Lost beneath the waves," Havel murmured over his shoulder. "Just as the voices said."

"There are no voices!" Stanton snapped. "There is simply a plot to profit from my uncle's guilelessness."

"Do not insult a gift you cannot hope to understand," Ned retorted. He gazed upon Kate with an avidity every bit as disturbing as Havel's earlier interest had been. "My child, you cannot allow them to keep you mewed up at Meads. You and Melisandre are possessed of great powers individually; how much greater will that power be when you work in tandem. You must stay with us here at Ker-Ys, and we will continue the great work the two of you began as girls so many years ago."

Kate spun away with decidedly unladylike impatience. "I am here to help search for the missing girl, nothing more. And I suggest that we waste no more time in this foolishness and instead do what we came to do. Namely, examine the spring house."

"No!" Melisandre cried. "Even our skeptical Mr. Fellowes must admit you have sustained a dreadful shock. You must not throw yourself headlong into further exertion. Would you not concur, Mr. Fellowes?"

Gavin was unable to reply. For the water Kate Ames had sketched with such force that she had stabbed through the paper with the soft charcoal began to ripple in front of his eyes. The lost city vanished, and now the waves formed the pattern of a face, trapped beneath the surface, crying out for release. Gavin shuddered as he remembered a man shouting in fierce joy from the depths of the mud and the blood, answering the Gabriel Hounds that roiled across the sky in full fury, and then the thought struck him that it must be the same agonized soul that was said to haunt the mossy pool at Ker-Ys. But where had such a thought come from?

He shook his head to dispel the ridiculous notion, as a tide of disappointment in Kate Ames flooded through him, deafening him to the surrounding conversation. Automatic writing was the most obvious of mediumistic tricks. Yet Gavin would have sworn on the strength of all his years of experience that Kate Ames' face was not the face of a fraud. She was obviously disturbed by what happened when she knelt beside the bathing pool, her vivid green eyes bright against her sudden pallor in a way that made him recall Jean Adams' saying, "Now, if it had been the other one, I might have been given to at least wonder…" Now, for the first time in a life that had always been rooted in skepticism, if not the outright cynicism the Great War had taught him, Gavin was, himself, wondering.

How could the sketch pad she had so conveniently to hand have been anything but a ruse? How did she come to draw such a compelling image in so few stylized strokes? And so quickly? He had already seen her genius in the children's book she'd illustrated, but this … this was something altogether different.

He shut his eyes to erase the vision when a shout rang out, and he flinched with superstitious dread. But it was no lost soul that screamed. It was the farmhand who had summoned them in the first place.

"There she is!" he cried. "She's right there! The Bloomer Girl. She's hiding out there in the woods."

He pointed at a flash of white visible beyond the brambles. The searchers all tensed to give chase, but the brush parted, and the flash of white expanded into a Bloomer Girl striding purposefully toward them. But it was not the one they called Essie, the one missing. It was the one Gavin had spoken to on the porch of the Overlook Hotel, her bold eyes now narrowed in defiance, her hands clutching an oilskin-wrapped parcel.

"Yes!" she said. "Yes, I am a Bloomer Girl, and I am done with hiding. I am who I am, and I am here for only one reason. I will see justice done for Judith Shattuck."

"Justice? Hollis Stanton roared. "For trespassing and burgling?" "Did you not learn anything from the fate of your friend? Perhaps a night spent in the county jail will convince you of the error of your ways."

She brandished the oilskin-wrapped packet. "Oh, I'm happy to go to the authorities," she said. "It's about time they saw *this*."

It was only in retrospect that Gavin might have allowed that the rush of foreboding he felt was because he understood immediately what the oilskin parcel might hold—no, what it *must* hold.

"And what is that?" the Elder asked.

"The reason Judith died," the girl spat.

Chapter 8

EVEN THOUGH BONFIRES crackled across the Maverick, as they had since Beltane and would continue to do until the witches' cutting of the first fruits on Lammas, one man's fire had yet to be lit. He was still busy hauling wooden trays of glass slides to pile on top of the kindling. Gipsy Sarah fought down a surge of disappointment at the sight. It was exactly as she had known it would be even though she had willed him to set aside his cowardice.

She had been summoned on Beltane—called on St. John's Eve, the day the Devil walked the Earth—and would linger no longer herself. But first, before she went, she had to try to change his mind. She thrust herself between the stranger and his makeshift pyre, and in a jangle of beads and bracelets, planted her hands on her hips and stared up at him. "Stop this! Now."

The stranger studied her with an incurious look on his face. "And who are you to stop me?"

"I am Gipsy Sarah." She brandished the enameled knife she always carried in her left boot. "And this is the knife with which my father taught me to gut a fish or slice the throat of a traitor. And I'm as quick with it as any of my people. Just ask any man who denied my people a dram of whiskey or a bit of bread when they begged the age-old courtesy of hospitality. Then you might want to ask them who my father was and how many men he gutted with nothing sharper than a table knife before they hanged him."

To her surprise, he threw back his head and roared out a laugh. "Oh, well done! Straight out of *The Secrets of the Gipsy Horde.*" He fished a whiskey bottle from amidst the wooden trays and pulled the stopper. "A word of advice, though. Don't go stealing lines from the nickelodeons when you're dealing with a man who photographs them."

"And is about to burn them," she pointed out.

He shrugged. "I created them. I have a right to destroy them." He took a healthy drink from the neck of the bottle before he moved to pour the rest on the pyre, but Gipsy Sarah was too fast for him. Her knife flashed. The bottle fell to the ground and the whiskey oozed harmlessly into the dirt.

"And what of the girls?" she demanded. "Do you have the right to destroy them as well?"

He watched the whiskey as it seeped off into the ground. "So, there's another one vanished."

It was not a question. "Her name is Essie," she confirmed. "Snatched from her bed in the middle of the night. Just like Miriam and Rachel before her."

"Girls vanish," he said. "Both in the middle of the night and in the middle of the day. Some take a new name and go on the stage. Some run off to Europe with a lover. Others turn penitent in a House of Mercy. They all have their reasons."

"After Miriam and Rachel came Judith," she went on. "But Judith did not vanish. Judith died. And now it's Essie's turn."

"Is it not more likely that this Essie disappeared for her own reasons? Or have you already scryed that answer in your crystal ball like any self-respecting Gipsy?"

"Do not play the fool with me," she said with a dangerous glare. "There has been entirely too much foolishness already—right from the very start." She shook her head angrily enough to rattle her earrings. "A prank, they called it. A lark. A simple matter of humoring a harmless old man in his dotage. But all that changed when Judith died. And Essie saw it at once."

"Then she must have been a very foolish girl indeed to continue with the game."

"She tried to stop it, you fool! She tried to give them back their money, but they wouldn't take it."

Something kindled—albeit briefly—in his eyes. Then his face hardened, and he turned his attention back to lifting the trays of slides onto the growing pile. "I'm sorry for your friend, but I have nothing to do with her fate."

"Do not lie to me!" she spat. "For you well know your kind cannot."

He raised an eyebrow. "Then perhaps you should assume I'm telling the truth."

"Oh, you can never tell a lie any more than you can refuse a bargain already struck, but the truth you tell is never what it seems. Your kind knows how to twist the threads of a story until the truth is no longer recognizable." She stamped a booted heel. "They were my *friends*."

"Then they're luckier than most," he allowed. "But a smart girl would be more concerned about her own luck right now—and doing what she can to make sure that it isn't about to run out."

"And what about Essie?"

His jaw set. "Your friend is gone to the fairies. You are here. I would suggest you strive to keep it that way. What can you hope to accomplish?"

"More than you," she said, casting a critical gaze at the funeral pyre. "The pictures don't matter. Not so long as there remains a camera that can take new ones."

"The camera is safe in the hands of a harmless fool who seeks a talent he can never possess. He will never penetrate its secrets."

"No, but he is surrounded by those with the ruthlessness to seize it and the penetration to bend it to their purposes, as you clearly have seen for yourself—even if you persist in denying it. For if your kind cannot lie to others, you certainly can't lie to yourself."

Abruptly, his eyes went bright with menace. "You think you're very clever, don't you, Gipsy Sarah? Sharp as a tack. Well, I warned you once, and I'll not warn you again. The most likely one to be cut by such an edge is you."

She tossed her head and stood her ground, the challenge in her single eye more than a match for his own. "I know who you are," she said. "And I know *what* you are. I gave my right eye for that knowledge."

"And I know who you are," he replied with a laugh. "The one-eyed girl with a nose for getting herself in places she shouldn't. The girl who is too simple or stubborn to learn her lesson even when she discovered the cost of a peep at the pixies for herself."

She stepped forward. "And I know why you're hiding."

The stranger fell into a silence so absolute that even the raucous revelers around the more distant fires seemed to have fallen silent. Then he shrugged and his defenses slipped. "If you truly knew that, you'd see that hiding is the only way."

It was a plea for understanding that would have had her sympathy under ordinary circumstances. But these were no such thing. "Hiding is no more choice than burning the pictures. For she has found you once more, and once more, she has named you true."

"True naming?" he snorted, his defenses sliding swiftly back into place. "What is that? Another Gipsy talent, to go with your crystal balls and palm reading?"

"A true name speaks a being's true nature," Gipsy Sarah said. "And woe betide any creature so foolish as to unthinkingly betray it, for one's true name wields the most tremendous power there can be. Our great queen Isis spoke the true name of Ra and placed her son Horus on the throne in his stead. The peasant girl commanded the dwarf who spun gold, just as St. Olaf commanded the troll, all because they knew their true name. A Nix can be defeated, a Boggart unleashed, if you call them by their true name. A magician cannot control a demon if the demon knows his true name...."

He snorted again. "Begone with you and leave me to my task."

Arms akimbo, booted heels splayed, she stood her ground. "I know what happened," she said. "I knew it the very moment it happened. Because I felt it just the same as you when she named you true."

"Begone!" he snapped, turning back toward the pyre. "I have no time for fairy tales. I have work to do."

"I was not alone to see her name you true," Gipsy Sarah went on. "They all did. I alone understand what I truly saw, but soon the scales will fall from their eyes, and it will be too late. They will seek to claim the secret of true naming for themselves, just as the one did before—"

The stranger stiffened and eyed her narrowly. "Which one?" he asked.

"The one who will stop at nothing to destroy it now," she said. "While the other will stop at nothing to possess it."

He contemplated that for only a moment. "And what would you have me do?"

"You must answer the summons, and you must claim back your own. For Essie."

"You have no idea what you ask."

"On the contrary," she said. "I have every idea. And I can help you."

"Fat lot of good a Gipsy brat will do me."

"I am no common Gipsy brat! I am the girl who dared gaze on fairy land." She waved her knife contemptuously at the slides on the pyre. "And I have seen not magical pictures but magic itself. I have gazed upon it. I touched its true power. And I have learned by my own efforts how dangerous that power would prove in the hands of those who seek it now. Did you not see enough of what they did in the last war, over nothing more than a dead archduke, and a handful of promises scribbled on paper? Only imagine what this world might be like if those same armies were to fight to win a power such as this?"

Silence fell, and his gaze grew so distant he might have fallen into a trance.

"And if I do not? If I *cannot*?" he finally asked.

"Then more girls will vanish. And more girls will wash up on the shores of lakes and pools, rivers and oceans, all of them drowned beneath the waves you were meant to protect," she told him. "And it will not end with dead girls. Not until you answer the summons and defend what you are called upon to defend."

Chapter 9

"INFAMOUS!" STANTON EXPLODED at the defiant Bloomer Girl, still standing her ground. "Do you accuse my uncle of murder now?"

At least, that might have been what he said. Gavin's mind, still brooding on Kate Ames and her drawing, was now overwhelmed with the foreboding that gripped him when he considered the oilskin package the Bloomer Girl wielded like a shield. What was in the package? What part did this girl play in Kate's plans? Was she a fly in the ointment, or were they all in it together?

"I have found out *why* she was killed," the bold-eyed girl challenged Stanton. "I leave it to others to discover *who* killed her."

Stanton whirled on the searchers. "Do you hear the insolence? I insist these creatures be run out of town immediately."

The Presiding Elder's jaw set as stonily as the sturdy Dutch walls that criss-crossed the neighboring farmlands. "Now, sir, I don't think that's quite possible. At least not until what we hear what the young lady has to say." Ignoring

Stanton's protest with the same stoicism that his forbears had faced everything from being captured by Indians to the Down-Rent Wars, the Elder turned to the girl. "Now, Miss, you are making some serious accusations here. Supposing you tell us straight out what you mean."

The girl held the oilskin aloft. "I mean, Judith came here to look for this," she said, then added flatly, "and that's why she's dead."

"So, you admit that the dead girl was a thief who died for her pains, and you yourself are no better," Stanton snorted. "This girl should be charged with trespass and breaking and entering! The spring house is private property. And locked."

"Aha! And you admit you knew she was searching for something in the spring house before she died!" the bold girl cried. "Judith was no thief, and besides, thieving isn't a hanging offense, at least not anymore! She saw what happened to Rachel. She saw what happened to Miriam. She was trying to put an end to it."

The girl's lip began to tremble, and she bit down on it. "Instead, they put an end to her."

It was the first hint of weakness in this unlikely warrior, and Gavin was moved to rise to her defense in much the same way he felt with Kate Ames—although he freely admitted neither might welcome, or even have need of—his rescue. But the Elder had already supplanted him with careful common sense.

"Now, it may be difficult, but plain speaking is what we all need right now," the Elder said. "So, tell it to us all plainly, if you will. Your friend was trying to put an end to what exactly?"

"Photographs!" she spat, recovering her anger, and with it, her composure. "Photographs of them dancing with the fairies. Photos that would ruin them if anyone ever saw. Small wonder they ran away."

Ned, who had sunk down to sit on a rough-hewn log with Melisandre recovering by his side, sprang to his feet. "MacLeod sent you! He sent you to steal back his camera."

Gavin sucked in a breath.

"Say one more word, Uncle, and I will have you carted off to the lunatic asylum at once!" Stanton snapped.

But Stanton was too late. The bold-eyed girl turned her fierce gaze on Ned. "It was not your camera. It was never your camera. And that's why he came back to look for it."

"Who came back?" the Elder asked.

"Duncan MacLeod," the girl said. "The one that's been watching the girls as they dance."

In the distance, the Gabriel Hounds howled. It was impossible. Duncan MacLeod was dead. Gavin had watched him die. "Is?" he stammered. "Surely, you mean 'was.'"

"It is said he has returned to Woodstock after a considerable absence," Havel burst into the conversation, his eyes shining with the same avaricious interest as when he had first been introduced to Kate Ames. "They also say that unlike the first time he came to Woodstock, when he resided in Ker-Ys under the especial patronage of the Adamses, he has grown quite the Wildman and creates his enchantments in a cabin no better than a hovel."

There must be some mistake. Gavin forced himself to swallow. No. No, no mistake, He blinked and called himself back from the edge of madness. A simple coincidence. Duncan MacLeod was a common enough Scots name. Jean Adams had pointed out the resemblance between the man the girls had photographed and the artist she had known years ago. Perhaps the Duncan MacLeod Gavin had watched die and this artist resembled each other because they were related. Stranger things had happened.

"So do you suspect this MacLeod is responsible for these pictures?" the sensible Elder asked. "To what purpose?"

"Must you have it laid out for you like one of your plowed fields, when it is perfectly clear to all of us that more than the eye was naked in those pictures!" Stanton snapped.

"Sir, there are ladies present!" Gavin said sharply.

"Not ladies." Stanton snorted. "Artist's models,"

"You will withdraw that remark at once—"

"Yes, they were models, but they never would have posed like that!" the girl cut over Gavin. "Not if they were in their right minds at least. He must have given them strong drink or drugs. Opium. Morphine."

"No!" Ned's face twisted in anguish. "No, there were no drugs. There was only fairy dust. Fairy dust sprinkled in our eyes, so we could behold the wonders of fairy land for ourselves."

"Enough!" Stanton threw up his hands. "There can be no further point to this conversation! I want all of you gone! It's clear that the dairyman mistook this ... thief for the missing girl, who has long since run back to the city in shame! So, gentlemen, you have no further purpose here."

The searchers looked to the Elder and shifted restlessly, less in concession than in a desire to be done with such shenanigans and return to their tobacco around the warmth of the white-bellied stove. But Gavin was still staring at the package the bold girl clutched.

"No. Not yet. Not before we all see what Judith was searching for," he said. He addressed himself to the bold-eyed girl with conscious formality. "Would you please show us what you found in the spring house? Will you please show us the book you have concealed in that package?"

"How did you know…" she began, then shook off her suspicions with a defiant shrug. "What does it matter? Yes, there was a book, just as Judith said. Some kind of magic book. A Book of Shadows, he called it."

"He?" Gavin asked, trying to keep his voice even. "Who exactly called it that?"

The girl turned and glared at Havel. "Judith never said his name. Just called him the gentleman from Budapest. But *he* was the one who told her where to look for the pictures. Just as he told her that she was also to look for this." She pulled the item from the oilskin parcel, and Gavin shivered with a thrill of recognition. An Ariosophic ritual. *The Most Sacred Protocols of the Germanenorden Walvater of the Holy Grail*, richly bound in leather and brass as befitted the occult riches it was meant to contain.

All eyes turned to Havel. "Is this true?" the Elder asked. "Did you send the drowned girl to steal the book?"

Havel raised a shoulder. "Rather let us say it was I who told her it was valuable," he said, his eyes focused greedily on the volume. "I held such a volume once, and I freely admit it is a lifelong quest of mine to once again hold a copy in my own hands."

"So, you sent the dead girl to steal it?" Stanton demanded.

"I sought only to ascertain its existence and authenticity, so that I could know to whom to address a suitable offer."

"Impossible," Ned cried. "The Book of Shadows is not for sale! The ritual it contains is beyond price!"

"No!" Kate Ames threw herself unexpectedly between them. "There can be no question of a sale. There can be no question of doing anything with this book other than burning it. For it is not valuable. It is dangerous! It has already been responsible for scores of deaths—"

"Through witchcraft?" Stanton scoffed.

"No," Gavin heard himself say, as if from a vast distance. "Through spycraft. And not scores of deaths. Hundreds—737 souls to be precise, including that of Lord Kitchener and Judith Shattuck's uncle, if Mr. Havel is to be believed." Gavin did not look at Kate Ames, although he felt as though she was appraising him as much as he had been appraising her.

"Mr. Fellowes speaks of the sinking of the H.M.S. *Hampshire*," Havel agreed, his greedy gaze never moving from the book. "And Kitchener's clandestine mission to bolster the Russian cause by any means he could, no matter how unscrupulous."

"I know nothing of the uses to which it was put," Kate said firmly, moving to stand next to the Bloomer Girl who now clutched the book to her bosom. "I know only that the War Office should not have meddled with such matters. They thought magic was a joke. A plaything they could bend to their own uses just as they bent the talents of those like me."

And those like Andrew Piper, whose words Kate so eerily echoed? Between the appearance of the book and Kate's words, Gavin did not know where to look or what to think.

"Is this another sort of trance?" Stanton demanded. "Would you have us believe the American government stooped to employing mediums during the recent war effort?"

Kate offered him a decidedly untrancelike smile. "Desperate men will resort to desperate measures," she said. "And there were many desperate men during the recent war.

The English were desperate for America to enter the war. Most in America were desperate to stay out. But as I have already told you, I make no claim of mediumistic skills. No, I am speaking of a different sort of magic. I am speaking of artists. And writers. Weavers of dreams and creators of illusion. I am speaking of men like Abbott Thayer."

Havel turned to Kate, his gaze every bit as greedy as it had been when he laid eyes on the Book of Shadows. "What a happy coincidence. For I have long wanted to talk to someone who is personally acquainted with Abbott Thayer's methods. There are many who would describe Mr. Thayer's angel paintings as nothing short of the work of a magician."

This time, Kate's attempt to suppress her emotions was genuinely comic—and Gavin could only sympathize. For Thayer's angel paintings were a vogue that defied explanation. Their bodies culled from the flying draperies of Hellenistic statues, their faces idealized from the children that surrounded him, their massive feathery wings best explained by incipient madness, Kate's tart dismissal of them was more than deserved. Although, Gavin had to admit that the man's technical brilliance was such that there could be no question of where Kate had learned how to create her illusions of the impossible.

"Mr. Thayer is an acknowledged genius," she allowed.

"And what would an artist's model possibly know about that?" Stanton asked, not bothering to hide his contempt.

Gavin's fist balled at the rudeness, but Kate took no apparent umbrage. "As I have already explained, I was one of Mr. Thayer's apprentices, not a model. However, what I neglected to point out at the time was that Mr. Thayer's studio also was significantly involved in the American war effort."

"Doing what?" Stanton asked with a laugh. "Selling war bonds?"

"Not exactly—although persuading people to buy them was part of my remit—along with every other possible form of persuasion." She paused only briefly to collect her thoughts, then looked around at those gathered. With a soft sigh of resignation—or resolve— she said, "Mr. Stanton, have you ever heard of dazzlepaint?"

"It was a way to camouflage ships, was it not?"

"Not camouflage exactly," she corrected. "It would be more accurate to describe it as misdirection, which is actually something quite different. Camouflage attempts to hide an object by disguising it as something it is not. Whereas dazzlepaint makes it impossible for you to know what you are truly seeing. Take, for example, the first people who strove to make use of Mr. Thayer's theories of protective coloration and countershading," she went on, seemingly oblivious to Stanton's rising impatience. "They quite naturally turned their efforts to creating an invisible ship, but the camouflage only made the vessel more obvious, and it fell off before the ship had even left the harbor. So they turned their attention to devising a method that made no attempts to hide the vessels; instead, it was designed to make it impossible to see the ships clearly, no matter how carefully you tried to focus. But you see, dazzlepaint could not be mass produced. Each dazzlepaint not only needed to be suited to the type of vessel it was meant to disguise, but it also needed to be unique so the Germans wouldn't eventually discover the pattern and compensate for it. So, the War Office hired art students—women, mostly—to design the dazzlepaint on models of each vessel." Kate hesitated only briefly before she continued," She paused and glanced at Ned and Melisandre. "Rather like the truth of the Fair Folk," she added, with small smile, "dazzlepaint is always pointing somewhere other than where you think you're looking. The U-boats were well aware a ship was there, but the paint made it impossible to determine its speed or direction in order to fire a torpedo."

Kate had caught the attention of everyone standing in the clearing, but Gavin was riveted. Yes, he agreed, dazzlepaint was rather like the truth of the Fair Folk, but even closer to their magic. He still remembered his wonder at that first demonstration—a photograph of the model of a steamship against a background of ocean and sky, and then that same photograph, but covered with a kaleidoscope of slashing diagonals and mismatched chevrons that seemed to give a boat a thousand prows and no stern. The jagged zigzag along its side made it impossible to tell where the water ended and the ship began, just as the backwards slanting on the smokestacks seemed to be at once part of the sky.

Stanton looked down his nose at Kate and said with a sneer, "Well, grateful as I am for that little art lesson, I have no more time to waste on irrelevancies, no matter how charming."

"I would remind you that you're talking to a lady," Gavin said, but Kate waved off his interference.

"Unfortunately, this is no irrelevancy," she said. "Although I admit I thought it was, and that was why I neglected to mention the connection at first. But now I fear it is quite germane."

"Germane to what?" Stanton stomped his booted foot as if he were a spoiled child. "My time is as short as my temper, and you have gone on quite long enough."

Gavin took a step forward, but Kate ignored him and continued. "The point of all this is that there were other kinds of … misdirection used as weapons. And other kinds of experts in deception that the War Office hired."

"More artists?" Stanton snorted.

"Yes, more artists. And authors and stage magicians. Makers of moving pictures and the actresses that played in them. And thieves and con men. Carnival barkers and impresarios. All of them experts in misdirection and illusion. Why such puzzlement, Mr. Stanton?" she dismissed his obvious disbelief with a laugh. "Surely, the recent machinations of Mr. Creel's Committee on Public Information is no secret. He persuaded President Wilson to systematically reach every person in the United States multiple times with patriotic information about how the individual could contribute to the war effort. They papered this country, with innumerable copies of pamphlets, newspaper releases, magazine advertisements, films. They conducted campaigns in the schools, as well as in the moving picture theatres, recruiting patriots to deliver speeches during the time it took to change a movie reel."

"That's why they were called Four Minute Men," one of the farmers in the search party murmured to his friend.

"Mere propaganda. No different than the Krauts dropping leaflets behind enemy lines."

"According to Mr. Creel, it was not propaganda as the Germans defined it, but propaganda in the true sense of the word, meaning the 'propagation of faith.'" Her eyes went to the copy of the *Protocols*. "Which many of us with experience of such efforts, might argue is a far more dangerous prospect."

"Be that as it may. Surely you would not have it said that this book is one of Mr. Creel's creations."

"Of course, it was not." Kate frowned at him. "This book was an English spymaster's creation. The only Englishman who bothered to listen when Mr. Thayer risked the journey to England to offer his theories about camouflage to support the Allied war effort."

"And did this spymaster have a name?" Stanton asked. "Perhaps one Duncan MacLeod?"

Gavin drew in a sharp breath, but Kate was already shaking her head. "He was known only as the Magician. A fanciful enough nickname, one must admit, but a fitting one, for even the effects of such failures like this could only be described as magical."

Stanton's eyes narrowed. "And exactly what effects was this volume intended to produce?"

"The only effect the English were dedicated to accomplishing as those last years of the war dragged on," Kate said. "To bring the Americans into the war effort by fair means or foul. This Book of Shadows was meant to convince the Americans that a powerful and dangerous German secret society had already infiltrated the highest echelons of the American government."

"It was also a ruse to help Lord Kitchener bolster the Tsar's wavering support by convincing him the same society was funding the Bolshevik's," Havel seconded her, his eyes still greedily on the book. "I know. I was there the night Kitchener opened it. But he raised a U-Boat, instead of the Russian Army."

The Gabriel Hounds swelled full throated, as memories threatened to flood in from every direction. When their howling finally receded and Gavin was once more able to make sense of the words buzzing back and forth around him, Kate had retaken the thread of the conversation and several in the search party had lost interest and wandered back toward the waiting wagon.

"The English would have to wait another year to create a ruse that worked. Or does anyone really think that the Americans simply stumbled across the Zimmerman telegram?"

"Oh, come now!" Stanton scoffed. "You would have us believe you created the Zimmerman telegram—along with this book?"

"I did not create this grimoire," she evaded the question with a faint smile. "But I knew the man who did. It was another of Mr. Thayer's apprentices. A man named Andrew Piper. Quite a talented artist in his own way, if you consider forgery an art. Before the war, he had confined his talents largely to checks and banknotes, but the threat of a lengthy prison sentence inculcated in him a sudden patriotic desire to serve his country instead."

"Are you suggesting our government recruited criminals to the war effort?" Stanton demanded.

"Does that surprise you?" She raised an eyebrow. "In peacetime, we call such people liars, thieves, murderers, and wantons. In wartime, we call them spies. Bad men doing bad things to serve the greater good. And when a country is desperate, the ends always seem to justify the means—at least at the time. But one never pauses to remember those means can be just as easily subverted to other ends." She met Stanton's eyes squarely. "Again, much like the Fair Folk. As the old legends would have it, the Fair Folk are neither fallen nor saved. They are the Unfallen, the angels that did not take sides. In Dante, you see them in the vestibule of

Hell, rushing after any banner that rises to lead them. In folklore, they are instead confined here on earth, but they are still creatures without free will, and so can make no choices of their own but must only follow those who dare to lead them."

Stanton snorted. "Do you seriously believe that this book has magic powers?"

"I believe if you asked Mr. Piper, he would attest to the fact. For the poor man went quite mad after he finished forging it. Pixilated, was the only word to describe it. He became obsessed with the idea that it actually had the power to raise the Fair Folk and bend them to the will of the summoner, and he claimed the Fair Folk were hounding him, demanding their release."

"Well, if we have the common good sense not to ascribe such nonsensical powers to a book, I believe we need not fear such a terrible fate." Stanton waved the idea away as if it were a buzzing fly. "I wish I could say as much for my uncle." He turned a piteous gaze toward Ned and Melisandre, who still sat on the log listening intently to Kate's every word. When he turned back to Kate, he froze at the look etched on her face.

"A power does not need to be magical to be uncontrollable when placed in the wrong hands, and I very much fear this book has very dangerous powers indeed." Her voice was low, edged with fear and danger. "It should be destroyed, and the other copies hunted down and destroyed as well, before anyone else can seek to turn them to their own uses."

And in the distance, Gavin heard the hounds baying as in warning of the looming danger.

Stanton sprang into action as if he had heard them, too. "And you have my word I shall do exactly that." He yanked the book away from the Bloomer Girl. "I am confiscating all of this, which you already have admitted is stolen property, and you should count yourself lucky that I have a concern for my uncle's reputation—or else I would have the whole lot of you thrown out as the cheats and thieves that you have just demonstrated yourselves to be. Instead, I will persuade the sheriff to see this matter closed quietly and will leave it to your common sense to choose when to depart of your own accord."

Ned jumped up again, jaw set. "You can't do that! You can't take that book. Lammas approaches, and we must complete the working then."

"Of all the arrant nonsense!" Stanton spun to face his uncle. "You have gone too far this time, Uncle Ned, and you have my word I will take steps to save you from yourself! I am taking this cursed book and those foul photographs. And I demand you rid this place of the woman who is nothing but a trumpery charlatan that would hardly fool even the most casual visitor to a vaudeville hall," he railed. "Now, I am willing to handle this quietly for my aunt's sake, but if you do not dismiss this woman immediately and place the entire control of the family's assets into your rightful wife's hands, I will not flinch at having you declared mad."

Melisandre's languid beauty grew as fiery as her hair. "I would be very careful, Mr. Stanton, before you make an enemy of me," she breathed, then turned to Ned Adams, as magnificently imploring as if she had been on the stage. "Tell them, Ned. Tell them we will not stand for being threatened like this!"

But Ned Adams had sunk down into himself, cringing with a supplicating smile like a chastened child. "Now, nephew, the summer will soon end, and we'll all be home then. Jean will forgive me as she always has. She knows I have my little lapses, but I never mean any harm."

"You never mean harm, but you always do harm! And I intend to make sure it never happens again—for my aunt's sake. And for yours, although you probably will never see that." Stanton snapped his fingers at Ned as the others began to disperse. "Pack your bags, Uncle. You are coming home with me."

Chapter 10

KATE COULD NOT HAVE EXPLAINED what
had happened to her at the bathing pool at Ker-Ys, but
she could certainly tell you that *something* had happened
when she gazed into the depths of the water. Something
that brought long-buried memories bubbling back to the
surface. She had tried to push them away. Such memories
had taught her to trust only herself, but the incident had
unnerved her. She needed to confide in someone. The
question was, who? Certainly not Havel, who clearly had
ulterior motives for wanting the book. Hollis Stanton was
nothing but a bully, and his uncle a besotted fool. Which
left the singular Mr. Gavin Fellowes, whom Kate no more
trusted than he apparently trusted her.

He appeared to be a conventional enough English
gentleman, handsome in his own way and lean with a
faintly military bearing, his clothing both well-cut and
well-worn—in the way of an aristocrat who gave his newly
tailored items to a manservant to wear first to break them
in. His behavior, however, was anything but conventional.
Surely, she had not been the only one to notice the way his

eyes had gone distant when he saw her drawing and when the Book of Shadows had been produced by the Bloomer Girl. He looked as if he were being snatched away just like the vanished girls. And the mere mention of the name Duncan MacLeod had caused him to pale as if he had indeed seen a ghost.

Unfortunately for Kate, she had every reason to believe that a ghost was exactly what Mr. Fellowes had seen, for she had cause to know there was no better way to describe Duncan MacLeod. He was a phantom. A chimera. A will-o'-the-wisp. A rumor. But first, she had to be certain. And if Havel was correct, the proof she needed lay across the village in the Maverick, and so the next morning she set off to find answers.

Kate had had considerable experience of artists' colonies, from the cheerful tumble of Abbott Thayer's atelier, where the children were never formally enrolled in school, and the family slept out of doors year-round, to the Bohemian poets in Greenwich Village. But the freethinkers that populated the Maverick made the unsung geniuses of Greenwich Village look as artificially picturesque as a production of *La Boheme* at the Metropolitan Opera House. Shacks were scattered across what once had been farm fields. Musicians in shirtsleeves were rehearsing in the timbered concert hall, before an impromptu audience of passersby, children, and pets, while a frantic search was being held for two champion wrestlers who were supposed to be putting on an exhibition, but had been last seen sitting beneath a tree listening to Hervey White reading them poetry.

No one paid much attention to Kate as she wandered through the colony, inquiring whether anyone knew Duncan MacLeod. But theirs was not the hurried indifference of New Yorkers to her carefully cultivated camouflage as just another career girl in shirtwaist and sensible skirt, hurrying toward her typewriter or telephone switchboard. In the Maverick, her questions were answered with the cheerful forthrightness of people who assumed she had her own reasons for asking and paid them no further mind.

Nonetheless, after an hour of searching, she found Duncan MacLeod to be as much of a phantom as ever. Some thought they recalled the name, others remembered a stranger who was said to create the most extraordinary illusions. Some gestured vaguely toward where they thought they remembered his cabin to be. Some spoke of a cavern hewn out beneath one of the quarries. Others assured her he was a hobo and pitched his tent where he chose. Still others said he slept in a bearskin hammock deep in the woods.

Many offered her soups, stews, and teas from iron pots steaming on tripods over the open fires—as if in compensation for their lack of knowledge, but Kate kindly refused them. Instead, she found a wooden bench just outside the music hall, where she fell into a brown study. So absorbed she was by her thoughts and the strains of chamber music that wafted through the air that she did not notice the approach of Josep Havel until the heavy scent he affected assailed her, and she had no choice but to acknowledge his presence with a frozen smile.

"Miss Ames," he cried as if coming upon her was a sudden surprise. "What a fortunate coincidence to find you here for I have been longing to convey my sincerest compliments. I am entranced by your way with a pencil. If anything could make me believe in the existence of fairies, it would be your … art."

She murmured a polite demurral and made to take her leave, but he stopped her and glanced around theatrically, as if only just then becoming aware of his surroundings. "But what brings you here? Am I to believe you are a collector of Psychical Art, as well as a creator?"

"Psychical Art? I'm afraid I've never heard the term before," she said.

"And yet you are one of the most talented Psychical Artists I have ever seen." He drew closer, confidingly. "You may not know that in addition to being an impresario, I am in the way of being a collector—even a bit of a connoisseur. And I would claim that I have seen no finer examples of the art than your own work—with only the possible exception of the man who brings us both here, Duncan MacLeod. For am I correct in assuming you have come here to find him as well?"

She drew a deep breath, determined not to give away her dismay. "If I am, it must be for far different reasons than yours," she prevaricated. "For I'm afraid I remain a skeptic about the very existence of psychical abilities—including my own. My drawings are at best cleverly constructed illusions, Mr. Havel. Nothing more. Now, if you would please excuse me, I'm afraid I have seen no trace of Duncan MacLeod here, and was just about to return to the Mountain House."

"Then this is a doubly fortunate coincidence, for we can continue our search together." Once more he leaned closer to confide, "And I do think you would be much wiser not to continue your search unescorted. Of course, I am accusing you of no impropriety, but I would counsel you against any appearance of having anything to do with those foul pictures."

"Appearances can be deceiving," she said with a calm she did not feel, "but if that truly is your purpose in seeking Duncan MacLeod, you have my word that he could never have had anything to do with such pictures. I am certain of it."

Raising an eyebrow, he studied her. "Then pray let us be frank with one another," he said. "Why do you seek him?"

She met his gaze unflinchingly. "I might ask the same of you."

A moment's pause before he conceded the point with a brief nod. "Very well, then, Miss Ames. Let us have complete honesty between us. And I shall offer you the truth first, as a token of my good faith. I am a collector of Psychical Art, yes. But I am also a collector of psychical illusions. And while my interest in Psychical Art is simply aesthetic, my pursuit of psychical illusions is purely practical. In certain circles, the illusions woven by Duncan MacLeod in the recent war are already the stuff of legend, and I make no secret of the fact I wish to obtain them for myself, before others can."

His face darkened. "Unfortunately, many of my competitors are less scrupulous than I, and will stop at nothing to win MacLeod's arts for themselves. And I very much fear that when they discovered it would be impossible to bend him to their will, they turned their attention to finding others who might help them in that task. Others such as yourself." His voice lowered gravely. "Allow me to be frank, Miss Ames. I fear you may be in considerable danger now that you have arrived in Woodstock."

In truth, she was beginning to fear as much herself, and had not Melisandre's letter insinuated the same as well? But she betrayed nothing but calm indifference as she answered, "As I do not believe in psychical abilities or fairy kidnappings, I must protest that I have no idea why you would believe that."

"Pray do not be disingenuous, Miss Ames! Three girls have vanished and one is dead—for no more reason than they may have modeled for MacLeod. What dastardly efforts might my enemies not scruple to employ in order to command a lady whose ability to weave those illusions is equal to MacLeod's own?"

Especially after she had given an inadvertent public demonstration of those talents as soon as she arrived in Woodstock? There was reason enough to admit the truth of his assertion—however unwillingly. But she offered Havel nothing but a tightly ironic smile as she asked, "And what illusions are you suggesting I have woven? I believe you were the one who brought up the torpedoing of the HMS *Hampshire*?"

Havel sobered immediately. "As a survivor of that catastrophe, I can give you my word that it was no illusion," he assured her. "In fact, it was nothing short of premeditated murder by the American government—"

"That is a serious accusation to make without evidence," she said, her voice low.

"A serious accusation I am not afraid to make," Havel said. "Nor am I afraid to say that it is in fact only one of a thousand such plots and lies that poisoned the war ever since the angels descended from heaven to save the British at the Battle of Mons—some even said, with St. George charging at their head."

"Just as others have said that these miraculous rescuers were the English bowmen who took Agincourt for Henry V, and that the first report of their intervention was a tale published by Arthur Machen in the London *Evening News* in 1914," she pointed out drily. "A tale, Mr. Havel. Pure fiction."

"Or, if you prefer, pure illusion." His voice lowered. "Or *pseudos,* the Greek word for fiction—and lies. Come, Miss Ames, you know as well as I that the war was fought with lies and that it was won with lies—many of them woven by you.. And by that very spymaster you mentioned yesterday. The Magician."

She froze, suddenly aware they were about to embark on dangerous ground. She had made a mistake in bringing up the name at Ker-Ys for very few people knew of the Magician, and even fewer knew of her connection to the man. When Abbott Thayer's visit to England to convince them that his theories of camouflage could help them bring an end to the Great War, the English had openly derided him as a madman. At best, they were bewildered by a man who had fled his appointment with tears streaming down his face, leaving behind as proofs of his system a paint-stained Norfolk jacket pinned with scraps of fabric and several ladies' stockings. But one Englishman had listened. One Englishman had contacted the studio and invited Thayer and his acolytes to place their preternatural skills at creating illusions into the service of bringing an end to the holocaust that threatened to extirpate an entire generation. One Englishman so vested in the power of illusion that—

A gasp, an explosion of laughter, and then a burst of applause interrupted her thoughts, as a busker completed her performance and bowed elaborately to her impromptu knot of admirers before she passed a silken pouch for coins. Once she had tucked it securely in her belt, she abruptly departed in a series of cartwheels and handsprings that brought her up squarely in front of Kate.

"You're the one what's looking for Duncan MacLeod," she accused Kate, arms akimbo.

She was an extraordinary creature even in this camp of outlandishly costumed artists—kitted out in a parti-colored riding skirt that swirled out from a lavishly embroidered vest before it was tucked into high-heeled riding boots, whose spurs clinked as merrily as her beads. A silken headscarf was tied low across her forehead, and its bells chimed a music that accompanied her wherever she strode. Indeed, her clothing and acrobatics were so extravagant that the last thing you noticed about her was the spangled red patch that covered one eye.

"That is so. I have made no secret of it," Kate agreed. "My name is Kate Ames. And you are?"

The girl laid a finger against her nose, then cast a long look at Havel from her one good eye. "A true name's a dangerous thing to say on first acquaintance—especially before ones like *him*." She cocked her head at Havel. "But you may call me Gipsy Sarah."

"Pleased to meet you, Gipsy Sarah," Kate said with instinctive formality.

But Havel cut impatiently between them. "We both seek Duncan MacLeod. Do know where to find him?"

Gipsy Sarah tossed her head toward Kate with a laugh, and a gold tooth glinted in the sunlight. "*She* knows she will find him in the same places she found him before. The times and places in between. At daybreak, at sundown, neither day nor night. On the strand, with one foot in the sea and one on the sand. In the lone oak that marks the portals between worlds: its roots touching the underworld, its branches, the sky, and its trunk in the middle world with us. At the crossroads that lead both nowhere and in all directions at once. In the fens, neither earth nor water—"

"Enough fortune-telling!" Havel snapped. "If all this is a ploy to make sure we will cross your palm with silver, you shall have it, but when we have found him. Tell us where he is, and there's money in it for you."

"Fah on your tarnished silver. My kind trades in the gold of truth and nothing less," she laughed, her teeth gleaming with malice. "And here is your truth. You need not look for Duncan MacLeod. He will come for you— and he will come soon. He will shout for you when the sun rises at break of day. And a wise man would close his ears and bury his head back beneath his pillow. But a fool will find himself believing that he is strong enough to risk a peek into a world he was never meant to profane with his eyes."

Then she looked off into the distance, again put a finger to the side of her nose, and promptly tumbled away from them in a rush of flips and twists.

Chapter 11

MEAD'S MOUNTAIN HOUSE proudly advertised the
reliability of its communications for those summer boarders
who could not afford to neglect their business affairs even
for a week. Mail was delivered twice a day, and those
guests who needed speedier communications need not
inconvenience themselves with a trip down the mountain
to the lone operator in the Village. Instead, any cables sent
to the Kingston telegraph office were immediately relayed
by telephone directly to the Mountain House Office. But
the information Gavin wished to request from New York
City was too urgent and sensitive to trust to the vagaries
of a party line, so instead of returning straight to the
Mountain House from Ker-Ys with the others, he had
climbed down from the Meads wagon along with the rest
of the search party being dropped off at the General Store
and proceeded to dictate a few cables away from the prying
eyes of Mr. Havel or Mr. Stanton. Gavin had requested that
the replies be addressed to the General Store as well and
had ridden back down to the village to retrieve them the
next morning. Upon exiting with the messages that had

arrived by courier just after the store had opened, Gavin saw Kate Ames hurrying across the Millstream down the road toward West Hurley and the Maverick and was helpless to resist the instinct to follow her.

His stomach had clenched with embarrassment as he, like the vilest of Pinkertons, crouched behind the Maverick's Music Hall to eavesdrop on Kate and Havel's conversation. And that was even before the motley-clad busker's one eye focused squarely on him. She'd laid one finger against her nose with exaggerated wink, before she vanished in a merry series of handsprings whereupon Gavin fled back to Mead's, urging the placid cob as mercilessly as if the Hounds were hard on his heels. He arrived at Mead's weary but purged and retreated to his room to open the several packets marked "Private" and "Confidential" in bold black ink that had awaited him at the General Store.

The first files he opened were straightforward enough. The first contained ledgers and numbers that mapped out the business interests of the Adams and Stanton families, a landscape that was much as he suspected. The family fortune Ned Adams struggled so valiantly to repudiate had been forged in the Yorkshire steel mills, while his wife's family, the Storrs, had roots deep in the Pennsylvania steel industry. Both Adams and his wife had eschewed their industrial heritages—although not the income they derived from them. But in recent years, Hollis Stanton had begun to manage the family holdings, and was aggressively seeking to forge partnerships between the family's steel interests and the arms magnates that now ruled America with an iron fist, to judge from their handling of Gompers and his trade unionists.

The second, Havel's file, was at once more problematic and more suggestive. A self-described aristocrat and refugee, who claimed to have lost all his personal papers in the sinking of H.M.S. *Hampshire*, he had arrived in New York City armed with nothing but his calling cards, which he had left in the offices of steel magnates, arms manufacturers, financiers, and the more select gentlemen's clubs. Men who moved in the same circles as Hollis Stanton, Gavin noted. It appeared Havel had been admitted wherever he had called—both at the clubs and at the offices of those in the same circles to which Stanton claimed admittance. Why? How were his visits connected to his presence here in the same hotel as Stanton, despite Jean Storrs Adams' unconcealed dislike of the man?

The third parcel brought unhappy, but not unexpected, news of Andrew Piper. The patient had done himself mortal violence, awakening with a shriek from the torpor into which he had sunk after Gavin's visit and running out naked to plunge into a neighboring millpond. It was no use, he warned those who sought to rescue him. The Seelie Prince had been summoned, and the waters had been loosed. "*Sauve qui peut*," Piper sighed, as he sank beneath the surface for the last time.

The third packet also contained a folded sheet of foolscap—drawn by Piper, Gavin had always assumed, especially since that extraordinary scene in the madhouse. Stiffened by dried bloodstains, the map cracked in protest as he spread it out on his desk. Like so many others he had pored over to debate strategy during the war, it was carefully detailed and beautifully illustrated, but instead of the cruel litany of Ypres, Verdun, Soissons and Arras, the names penned in elegant calligraphy over the battlefields were of another war altogether—a fairy war that had raged invisibly around the men that fell, died, and were buried in the muck and mud of Europe.

The troops that were sketched in the cunning cut-outs that annotated each battle were no Germans or French or Englishmen. A miniature Erlkonig thundered at the head of his terrible horde, while the circling Valkyries shrieked with joy at the promise of carnage below. A determined detachment of brownies and Piksies marched beneath a fairy lord's banner. The Gentry, the Shining Ones, rode their red-eared, red-eyed white horses behind St. George, while gems tumbled from the clouds where their hooves struck. Gwyn ap Nudd led the Wild Ride forth from Wales, spreading death in equal parts to the Hun and the hated English.

In the seas that surrounded the lands, the U-Boats and battleships did not war with torpedos and guns. Instead it was the fantastical figures out of ancient maps that reached greedily to drown the vessels beneath the waves: Selkies, Leviathan, the white horses of Mananaan mac Lir. Sea serpents, the Kraken, Scylla and Charybdis. Capricorn, Cetus, Hydra, Proteus. And there were the rivers Glein, Dubglass, Bassas and Tribruit. The wood of Cat Coit Celidon. Castle Guinnion. The City of the Legion. Mount Agned. Mount Badon. And finally, above Belleau Wood, almost obscured by Duncan MacLeod's life blood, Camlann.

As he bent over the map and studied it closely, he saw proof of what he should have realized from the moment he first laid eyes on Kate Ames' work. Andrew Piper may have created the Book of Shadows, but he had not drawn the map. Kate Ames had. And Gavin Fellowes was not going to rest until she told him exactly what it meant.

He turned to the window, trying to marshal his restless thoughts, and there she was. Kate Ames completing the brisk walk up the mountain from the village, moving with surprising athleticism in her shortened skirt and sturdy boots. Gavin's stomach clenched. He no longer had any excuse to put off confronting her.

His hesitation was unusual, for he flattered himself that he was the last man on the planet to be taken in by a pretty face. And if he were being brutally honest, Miss Ames was not pretty—at least in any conventional sense of the word. So how was a man who had sent more than one beautiful woman to prison without a trace of regret to explain this sudden surge of reluctance?

Carefully folding the map and taking up his cane, he set out to confront the singular green-eyed artist and to find an answer to that question. He found her in the nearly-deserted dining room, sipping a cup of tea. He slid into the chair opposite her at the table, leaving her no opportunity to refuse his perfunctory apologies for intruding upon her privacy.

"I can only plead my eagerness to speak with you candidly about the recent events at Ker-Ys," he excused himself.

From her expression, she was decidedly less than eager to do the same, but she offered little resistance beyond a polite shrug. "I am not sure I am in a position to tell you anything more than what you witnessed with your own eyes. Indeed, it is more than likely I can tell you less than what you saw for yourself."

"Ah, yes. Your trance-like state." He raised an eyebrow. "Is this common in the practice of automatic writing?"

"I'm afraid I couldn't tell you," she repeated. "I am not an expert on the matter. I can speak solely to my personal experience, and attest that I have no memory of the event at all."

"As is so often the case with mediumistic communication," Gavin said.

"I lay no claim to be a medium!"

He studied her appraisingly. Could a woman speak with such vehemence and not be sincere? An accomplished actress, perhaps, but theatrical effects seemed more a stock in trade of Melisandre. "My apologies," he said. "I did not mean to place words in your mouth. I was merely referring to what I witnessed with my own eyes—along with many of Woodstock's most upstanding citizens. Did I not see a disembodied spirit communicate through you?"

She set her cup down carefully. "I have no idea what you saw."

"But what of you, Miss Ames? What in fact did *you* see?" he pressed. "The self-same fairies with whom Melisandre purported to commune?"

Her jaw set. "At the risk of repeating myself," she said, "I write about fairies and I draw fairies; I do not believe in them. However, on occasion, I have been known to suffer from … spells. It is a problem that I thought I had left behind me in my childhood, but apparently, it has resurged."

She made a show of returning to her tea, and although many would have missed the tremor she sought to conceal in her hands, Gavin had too much experience with that struggle not to notice. And suddenly he found himself overwhelmed with an emotion he never thought he'd feel again. The urge to protect her. The appalling need to charge in like some white knight and rescue her, from what, he had no idea. And the even more appalling tremor in his voice as he struggled to cast aside the vision of wrapping his arms around her and pulling her close as he heard himself say, "Miss Ames, if you are in some kind of difficulty, I beg you to confide in me and allow me to assist by any means I have to offer."

For a moment, her cool mask slipped, and the look that crossed her face removed Gavin to another time, another self. Like an alley cat flattening its ears as it slunk away from the trash bin where it had hoped to find a bite to eat, she sought to minimize herself and stay out of trouble. If Gavin had been another man at another time, he would have said it broke his heart.

And then the calm smile was back in place, and she said, "Well, most people would agree that demonic possession is some kind of difficulty, would they not?"

"Is that your explanation of what happened?"

"That is, I believe, the received explanation in the Church. Personally, I'm more comfortable saying I have no idea."

"And do you not care to seek the truth?"

"No," she said simply.

He drew a deep breath, furious with himself for the momentary lapse. If she was determined to rebuff his sincerely offered aid, the only choice left to him was to steel himself to attack. "Then what other reason did you have to spend so much time down at the Maverick, inquiring after a photographer named Duncan MacLeod?"

Her expression darkened. "Spying on me, Mr. Fellowes?"

"Doing my job. Which, I warn you, I do very, very well. I have been hired to get to the bottom of these hauntings, and I promise you that I will."

"Then perhaps you would be better served by investigating them instead of the necessities of my career."

She shook her head. "I owe you no explanation. But in the interests of expediency, I can only repeat the explanation I have already offered everyone. I made Mr. MacLeod's acquaintance at Mr. Thayer's studio. As I am certain that at least two of the missing girls served as models for Mr. Thayer, is it so unreasonable to wish to speak with Mr. MacLeod to make certain that the connection is entirely coincidental?"

If Gavin hadn't overheard her conversation with Havel with his own ears, he would have believed her—and fallen over himself to apologize for his clumsiness. Instead, he was flooded with disappointment at this proof of how smoothly she could lie, and the bitterness made him ache somewhere deep inside—and it made him bold.

"As I said, in my opinion your sketch drawn hastily by the pool was among the finest I have ever seen. In fact, I can think of only one other specimen that even approaches being its equal." He pulled out the bloodstained map of the fairy battles and opened it across the table. "This one."

Her eyes went to the bloodstain and she recoiled. It was only a momentary flicker of uncertainty that crossed her face, but it was enough to tell him he had struck a nerve. "What is that?"

"I was hoping you would tell me. Is this an example of dazzlepaint, as you call it?"

She recovered herself and pushed the map back to him with a faint smile. "Painting dazzlepaint on paper would have been entirely useless, for the whole point was to disguise the vessel's geometry in three dimensions. Therefore, dazzlepaint was painted on three-dimensional models of ships. And I can assure you, the designs I painted were considerably less fanciful. Lines and angles were best for most of our purposes, with the occasional whorl or circle when we felt adventurous."

He made no move to reach for the map. Instead, he changed the topic entirely. "Are you aware that considerable scholarly debate rages about the authorship of the *Iliad* and the *Odyssey*? Was there really a blind poet named Homer, or was it ever anything but a convenient name? For does it not seem nearly impossible that the same man could have written two such dissimilar works as the great war poem and the tender paean to family and home? Yet most scholars believe in the single blind bard, even though there is only one argument to support that position—and that is the quality of the works. Was it at all likely that two such geniuses could exist at once?"

She sipped at her tea carefully. "I'm afraid I lack the erudition to venture an opinion. I was not afforded the benefits of a classical education."

"It was merely an analogy. For I would venture the same argument about these two pieces." He lay her sketch of the drowned city with its anguished guardian beside the map. "Although their style and subject matter are dissimilar, would you deny these two are by the same hand?"

She closed her eyes briefly, then conceded, "Upon cursory examination, it would appear to be so. But I am scarcely an expert."

"And would you deny you drew the sketch on your left?"

"Why would I? There are apparently a dozen witnesses willing to swear they'd watched me draw exactly such a thing. Including you."

"Indeed, why should you?"

And suddenly he was furious—as furious at himself as he was at her. The woman had reduced him to a callow schoolboy. When he could find his tongue to speak, he delivered the syllables with clipped precision. "Miss Ames, I beg you heed me, and heed me well. Whatever it is you seek to hide, I will find out—sooner, rather than later. So, for your own sake, I beg you to confide in me completely. Because I can assure you that you would rather have me as a friend than an enemy."

"Alas, like you, Mr. Fellowes, I believe in very little. And I have long since given up believing in friends. Now if you have no more questions...."

She rose to go. And Gavin was left with no resort but to fire one last, blind shot. "Only one, Miss Ames. Were you looking for Duncan MacLeod because you believe he was the English spymaster known as the Magician?"

It was a wild gambit, flung with the desperation of a man preferring to die on the barbed wire than endure another hour in the trenches. But it hit its mark. She froze, then subsided back into her chair. "Do you accuse me of nigromancy, now?"

No, he could never accuse her of the black arts of Hell, for there was an air about her of purity, if not innocence, which put paid to such a possibility. But the unfortunate truth was that the magic arts of the Middle Kingdom, or, as others might put it, the lying illusions wrought on earth by mankind, were far more difficult to define—as he, who of all people bore no claim to innocence, had good cause to know.

"Miss Ames, forgive me if I offend your sensibilities, but I must convince you of the seriousness of the situation. The blood that stains this sketch was that of a dying man who fled to Belleau Wood to evade those who sought the Magician. That man was also named Duncan MacLeod, just like the man you seek, and I am increasingly unable to believe that is any coincidence. So, forgive me for pressing you to answer directly. Do you believe this man was the Magician?"

She paused for so long that he began to fear she would simply refuse to answer him. Then she conceded and began, "If you propose to pursue either the Magician or Duncan MacLeod, I would warn you that you might as well pursue the will-o'-the-wisp. For you have my word that they are both nothing but fairytales. Still, I suppose the easiest way to convince you of that is by telling you the truth."

"Then, I would beg you do just that," Gavin said.

She met his eyes. "Even if I warn you that they are the self-same fairytales that drove Andrew Piper mad?"

"Then I will have to be stronger than he," Gavin replied with a calm he did not feel.

She studied him briefly, as if assessing her belief in that possibility, before she said, "Yesterday, Mr. Stanton asked whether the War Office employed mediums in the recent war. He might have more profitably asked whether they employed magic."

Gavin raised an eyebrow toward the sketch that lay between them. "Then am I to assume those means include automatic writing?"

"Does that surprise you, Mr. Fellowes?" she asked. "The battlefields boasted almost as many miracles as illusions. The Angels of Mons. King Arthur rising to save Britain in the form of Lord Kitchener."

And the Wild Ride charging across the night sky to the tune of the Gabriel Hounds, as Gavin held a dying man in his arms? "What of miracles that were in fact nothing but illusions?" he asked.

"Many who worked for the Magician would claim the two are one and the same," she allowed. She paused, then added, "And that was Andrew Piper's fatal mistake. He began to believe in the power of his own illusions. He came to believe that the books he forged were not a simple exercise in disinformation, but in fact contained the power to bend the Fair Folk to the summoner's will."

"The summoner in this case being the War Office?" Gavin asked with a laugh.

"Our business was illusion," she said. "Could there be any better masters of illusion than fairies who could spin lavish feasts out of acorns and bark and gold out of dirt and leaves?"

Gavin managed a half-hearted smile as he steeled himself to broach the question he knew he must ask next. "And what of Duncan MacLeod? What part does he play in this sorry tale?"

"Duncan MacLeod was the form in which Piper claimed to have raised the Fair Folk. I believe Piper's version of the tale was that MacLeod was a High Prince of the Seelie Court trapped in a drowned city and condemned to eternal servitude to any who summoned him to atone for betraying the Fair Folk."

Just as she had drawn it—in the sketch she was studiously avoiding looking at. "And do you believe that was the case?" he pressed.

Her face set in a way that he had already learned meant she was prevaricating—or at least withholding part of the truth. "It matters not what I believe any more than it matters what Andrew Piper believed. What matters is what Andrew Piper sought to make others believe. For Piper's folly was not to believe in the power of the book he had forged. His unforgivable crime was to offer its power to the highest bidder—for in the wrong hands, such power is the most destructive force the world can know."

Her voice trembled with true conviction. But conviction in what? "And so you would have me believe in the Faerie Rade?" he asked with deliberate cynicism. "In the Wild Hunt? In the magical creatures you have drawn here?"

Her fingers trailed across the surface of the map, as her eyes grew far away. "It matters not what name you give them. You served in the Great War. You have seen the results for yourself. Call them Fair Folk, call them propaganda and innuendo, call them the hysteria of the Mob, would you deny that they roamed the battlefields knowing no master other than chaos, sowing panic in their wake?"

"Belief," Gavin said, "and the terrible force of true believers."

"No! Quite on the contrary, the catastrophic power of such forces is they know no belief, but, instead, like the Ronin, the masterless samurai, they must follow any banner raised in front of them. And the banner raised by the men to whom Piper sold his secrets was the most terrifying banner of all. We Americans are quick to decry the destructive power of blind loyalty to such masters as church and monarch, but can there be any force more truly destructive as those who believe in nothing but the power of money?" She met his eyes. "Unless, it is those who cannot believe in anything at all?"

He looked back down at the map, avoiding the question.

"You have yet to tell me what you believed, Miss Ames," he said. "Did you believe Piper's book to have real power? Could you have drawn such a map if you did not believe such a tale was true?"

"I can only repeat that I often do not remember what I sketch or why. But I would venture that, from the looks of this map, someone believed such a story and believed it with all their heart."

She had neither confirmed nor denied she was the author of the blood-stained map. Yes, she was definitely hiding something; he was certain of it. But the question was what? And how important could it be? "Someone like the man who created it? The Magician?" he asked. "Do you believe he was possessed of supernatural powers? That he was a Prince of the Seelie Court?"

She shook her head with a wry smile. "If you are at all versed in the Lore of the Fair Folk, you must understand he cannot possibly be both. For whatever else the Magician may or may not have been, he was a consummate liar. And surely a skeptic as well-read in the occult as you are knows that the Fair Folk must always tell the truth, no matter how deceptive their words. For it is said that they are the Unfallen Angels, the ones who did not choose sides and are thus creatures neither of heaven nor of hell, but of this Earth. And while the Prince of Hell may spawn an infinitude of falsehoods in his realm, here in the Middle Kingdom, it is only men who can lie."

Chapter 12

SHE HAD GIVEN THE FOOL fair warning, but he was powerless to resist the bait. Gipsy Sarah was not surprised. She had seen too many of his kind—magi, necromancers, scholars, and scientists—blinded by their belief in their own powers into daring to command forces far beyond their ken. At the heart of their arrogance was their pathetic faith that the truth could be captured and prisoned in books like so many insects pinned to the taxidermist's boards. When in fact, the truth was a thing of gossamer wings and half-glimpsed flutters. And even then, the truth you saw was rarely the truth that you thought you had seen. But there he was, crouched over Hollis Stanton's desk, stuffing the Book of Shadows and a stack of photographic plates into a cloth satchel.

"Stop!" she said, announcing herself in a rattle of spurs. "Such things are not for you."

"And who are you to tell me what I can and cannot do?" he sneered. "Do you think a thief and a liar can command a man like me?"

"I am neither thief nor liar," she said. "And I am not

here to command. I am here to warn you against stealing what is not rightly yours."

"And whose rightly is this Book of Shadows?" he demanded. "The man who stole it in the first place? The Bloomer Girl who sought to betray her betters? Or to the one who has borne witness to its powers, and now dares to risk all to command them?"

"Judith did not betray you. Rather, she saved you—no matter how unworthy that exchange might seem to me," Gipsy Sarah spat. "Judith is dead, and nothing can change that. But her sacrifice could still save your life and maybe even your soul—if you would only give ear to her lesson and learn from her fate."

"Judith was a fool," he snapped. "My only mistake was trusting her with such a momentous task."

"Judith was an innocent who put her friends before your promises," Gipsy Sarah retorted. "And that is why she is dead. How much more cruelly will the man who sought to make her his cat's-paw be judged?"

His face set. "I was not responsible for her death."

"Perhaps you didn't kill her," Gipsy Sarah allowed. "But you are responsible for her death."

He frowned and Gipsy Sarah wondered if maybe this one would be different, maybe this one heeded the dark wasp of truth he glimpsed out of the corner of his eye. But then he shook his head and turned back to his task. "You play with words. It's what your kind always does." He slid the grimoire into his satchel. "Then again, that's all you can do, isn't it?"

"You'd best beware who you insult." She drew herself to her full height, spangles, beads, and spurs quivering with portent. "For you are right! My kind can only speak the truth—and by the time you see that truth with your own eyes, it will be too late. So heed my warning—and heed it well. It is not for you to look on fairy land. It is not for you to taste its fruits."

Once again, a moment's hesitation suggested that a warning had buzzed past one ear. "It will take more than a child's poem to frighten me."

"Then behold!" she said. "Behold the truth for yourself. Gaze upon fairy land with my eye."

And she drew off her eyepatch and allowed him to see what lay beneath.

"Get out. Now."

MacLeod's voice echoed through the empty hut, ringing off the barren shelves that had been stripped of his wondrous playthings.

"Would you then refuse me the sacred obligation of your hospitality?" Gipsy Sarah asked.

"What hospitality would you have me share?" he asked, throwing open his cupboard to display only empty shelves.

"I beg you for apples and quinces, lemons and oranges, plump unpeck'd cherries, melons and raspberries, bloom-down-cheek'd peaches, swart-headed mulberries, wild free-born cranberries, crab-apples, dewberries, pine-apples, blackberries, apricots, strawberries, all ripe together in summer weather." She smiled, her gold tooth flashing. "And you will give them to me, for it is unwise to turn the stranger from one's door, for one never knows when they might be a god in disguise."

"Are you a god?" MacLeod snorted.

"I am but a poor traveler without a home. One of the lost race, long ago driven from their lands, willing to mend your pots and pans or tell your fortune for a scrap of bread and a taste of milk." She tossed her head proudly. "And I am the girl who dared to buy from the fairy men and taste their fruits. And I have sucked on every last one of them and drained their magic to claim it as my own. For I am the girl who gave an eye to gaze upon fairy land."

The silence hung as emptily as the barren cupboard. "By all that's holy or unholy, by all the creatures of the day or night, what have you done?" MacLeod finally asked.

"What you were too afraid to do for yourself," she retorted. And opening the satchel she carried slung over one shoulder, she pulled out the slides and stacked them carefully beside the dusty and broken magic lantern that was the only furnishing that remained in the hut.

"What is this?" MacLeod hissed, his face clouding with fear.

"You have been called by your True Name. The time is come for you to answer the summons," she said, as, one by one, she slid the plates into the machine, where they fitted perfectly. "Behold, I give you the True Tale of Ker-Ys. It is a tragic tale, at once nobler and more craven than the one the ballads would have you believe. For the true tale of Ker-Ys is not that of a doomed city led into sin by a wicked princess. No, the true tale is the song of the Weakness of Gradlon."

A touch of her finger, and the machine flared to life. But MacLeod did not so much as glance at the pictures shimmering on the wall. His gaze never wavering from hers, he listened as if hypnotized.

"Once the greatest of the Princes of the Seelie Court, Gradlon abandoned his kingdom for love of the Sorceress of the North, Malgven, and laid all his powers at her feet. For Malgven was waging bitter war with her husband, the King of the North, who, since the Christian saints had taught him to fear her pagan powers, sought to put her aside. Ensorcelled by her pleas for succor, Gradlon led the Faerie Rade to win back the North for the Old Ways. Instead, they met with a bitter and humiliating defeat.

"The Old Ways were thrown over, and the cross and Christian King prevailed. The Seelie Court was banished, and Gradlon and Malgven were forced to flee the wrath of the both the Christian King and the Seelie Court. Away they galloped on the back of Morvarc'h, Malgven's black-coated horse, who breathed fire through his nostrils and could run across the waves as if they were turf. And on they galloped and galloped. For they could find no refuge, neither with humans nor with the Fair Folk, so much did both hate and fear Malgven's power. And so, for many weary years they did naught but wander, until Malgven gave birth to their daughter, Dahut, and died of exhaustion and sorrow.

"Alone and abandoned with a babe in arms, Gradlon turned to the city of Ker-Ys as his last hope of refuge. The High Court of the Unseelie, where selkies and mermaids, water sprites, salamanders, gnomes, brownies and tommy-knockers ruled, it had risen and fallen beneath the tides that washed the sea strand for two thousand years. But Gradlon was a proud Seelie Prince, and so would not bend the knee to the Unseelie Court. Instead of thanking them for the hospitality they freely offered, he dammed the city to drive out the Unseelie, locking it with a gate to which only he had the key, and exiled its first inhabitants beneath the waves.

"It was a deed unworthy of either House of the Fair Folk, but Gradlon had tarried too long with Men and was corrupted by their Ways." Her sole eye hardened with the accusation of two. "Mercifully, his daughter was not, half-breed though she was. As Princess Dahut grew older, she heard the voices of her fellow creatures, pleading for her to return to them what was rightly theirs. And she strove to do, only to be denounced as a wanton and a traitor by the Christian holy man Winwaloe, who had curried her father's favor and so made complete his corruption by men and their Ways.

"Now, as the ballads would have it, one day, a knight dressed in red armor arrived in Ker-Ys and Dahut became besotted with him. He persuaded her to steal the key to the gate from her father, and on a stormy night when the tide was high, they opened the gate and the city was flooded and sank into the sea. King Gradlon snatched his daughter and escaped the city on Morvarc'h, the Christian saint hard on their heels. But as they rode over the tempestuous sea Gradlon heard a mighty voice cry out, 'Throw the demon thou carriest into the sea, if thou dost not desire to perish.'"

Her face hardened. "And so he did, murdering his own daughter to save himself. And all pronounced him justified, for what more fitting end to a woman so debauched that she took a new lover every night, only to kill them with an enchanted silken mask after they had pleasured her? Just as they said that the Red Knight was the Devil himself, the Prince of Lies."

Once more, she pinned MacLeod with her implacable gaze. "But those who say either are themselves the liars. For the Red Knight was the Champion of the Unseelie Court whom Dahut had invited to reclaim the city for its rightful citizens."

Her final words echoed across the empty hut, then died away, along with the light of the magic lantern. And MacLeod's face set. "Is there a point to this tale?"

"There is more than a point. There is *truth*. There is the truth of why these girls have disappeared—and will continue to vanish until the summons is answered. For the men who seek to call forth Gradlon and command his powers have tethered these girls on the sea strand like a goat set out as bait to trap a leopard. That is why the girls disappeared, and that is why they will continue to disappear until Gradlon finally answers the call and atones for the betrayal of his daughter."

Gipsy Sarah met his eyes with the full force of her lone one. "Essie is trapped upon the strand, just as her sisters were before her. And time runs short for her, the tide is rising fast. But it is not yet too late. There is still one that can outrun the sea."

"You?" MacLeod asked.

"You know very well that one is not me. I have done what I can. I have finished what Judith could not. I have retrieved and hidden the Book of Shadows from those who were not destined to command its powers. But I am not the one to outrun the sea."

MacLeod's face hardened. "I cannot help you. Or your vanished friends."

"You must," she said. "You have been called by your true name."

"By whom?" he asked sharply.

"The magus who seeks to summon the power of the Fair Folk and enslave them to his purposes."

"And who am I to stand up against such a man?"

"You are the only one who can." Her face softened and she held out her hand in a flurry of bangles. "Fear not. I am not one to outrun the sea, but I can stand with you. And I shall. Just take my hand. And do not fear to dance with me."

"Enough!" MacLeod dismissed her. "For all my sins, I have no taste for bedding children."

"I said I would stand with you, not bed you. This is not the tale of the Debaucheries of Dahut. It is the true tale of the Weakness of Gradlon."

With a toss of her head, she whirled on her heel and strode out of the hut, ignoring the furious curses as he shouted after her.

Beyond Ker-Ys

ESSIE WAS NOTHING but flotsam and jetsam, the sea's plaything now. The waves of the Ashokan floodwaters pulled her greedily from the shore, sweeping her choking and gasping into their embrace, only to spit her back onto the strand as they drew back into the horizon. But they ebbed only to return with greater force, a wall of water that blotted out the sky and sent her scrambling in a hopeless attempt to outrun it … only to feel the cold tentacles coil around her ankles again and again and again.

She had no idea how many times she had been swept away and washed back. It could have been the eternity of Hell, just like those missionaries that she'd ignored with a toss of her curls kept preaching would be her fate if she did not turn to Jesus. All she knew was that she lay gasping on the sand once more, and the waves were already crashing closer. And this time, she was too tired to outrun them. Too tired of trying to believe there might be some place she was safe. No! As long as there was breath in her, life would not be denied. She lurched to her hands and knees and began to crawl wearily across the packed sand, scrabbling until her fingernails were broken and bloody, as the tide pounded ever closer...

She looked around. This was not the pounding of the tide that shook the earth beneath her and threatened to overtake her. This was louder, harder. And closer and faster than the water, upon her with a sheet of flame and a clap of thunder. Too tired to care any longer, Essie rolled onto her back to at least have the final dignity of meeting Death face to face.

But she saw not a pale horse like the missionaries were ever describing. Rather, a coal black stallion that breathed flames with every stride bore down on her. And if that much were not impossibility enough, its hooves did not pound against the earth, but rather skimmed across the water, as lightly as if it was sound Irish turf.

The horse's rider was no less extraordinary. For he glowed with light as if he consisted of flame himself. His pale skin gleamed like alabaster, his blue eyes had the brilliance of sapphires, his armor shimmered with silver and golden scales, the silken cloak that streamed behind him glittered with all the colors of the rainbow, as did his swirling, inky hair.

"Help me," Essie breathed.

The rider skimmed ever closer, galloping atop the tide. Then just as the fingers of the lake closed around her ankles to drag her back into their heart, he swooped low and seized her from the waves' cruel grasp. Lofting her across the horse's pulsing shoulders, he bore her away across the strand, pounding through another eternity until they reached a distant shore, bounded by another sea. And as the water-horse galloped toward it, waterspouts began to swirl and rise into spires that stretched ever skyward.

They were followed by domes with silvery scales and arches carved from coral that spanned stairwells and grottos lined with shells. At last the walls of the sunken city emerged, as massive as the wall of water behind them, with a mighty bronze gate stained green by its years beneath the surface.

With a triumphant cry, the prince plunged his mount back into the sea. And Essie began to thrash in terror. "But I don't believe in fairies," she cried. "I don't want to go to fairy land!"

The rider smiled. "Peace," he said, as he lay his finger in the middle of her forehead. "It will only be a little while."

He spurred his horse forward, but another waterspout swelled in front of them, and an arm thrust through the surf to seize the horse's bridle. "Throw down the girl!" the sorcerer commanded. "And ride with me."

"The Seelie prince rides with no man!" the rider cried, as his mount reared, then plunged beneath the surface of the water, its black coat smoothing into a silver dolphin's hide. As he dove, he pulled both water and city with him, drawing them away to the distant horizon. And Essie was tossed up back on the strand where it had all begun—cowering between the prince and the sorcerer who brandished the horse's empty bridle angrily. "What trickery do you play at?" he demanded. "You are Named. You must ride at my command."

"I ride with the girl," the prince said. "I will not abandon her."

The sorcerer's eyes flared red. "That is not your choice to make. I have discovered the ancient compact you signed in fire when you first betrayed your kind over the love of a woman. It is my compact now, and you are bound to honor it."

"And so I shall," the prince said. "For the Fair Folk always keep their word and honor any bargain they have sealed. But only if you are strong enough to face me and Name me, as the compact itself dictates."

A moment's hesitation from the sorcerer. Then his voice grew soft and wheedling. "But why such trouble over trifles? Why not ride with me? I will forgive you even your preferring the girl over me. Gift her to you as your concubine, if you will. You will find I am an easy master and will reward your faithful service with pleasures well beyond this barren strip of sand."

"I will strike no bargain until you prove yourself worthy of being my master. I will obey no man until I am truly Named."

"But you will not survive a third Naming, as you well know!" the sorcerer protested. "For the first Naming was in the Beginning. The second you sacrificed when you fell for the love of the daughters of Man. The third Naming is saved for the Apocalypse, when all hidden worlds will be revealed, and the Lord will judge you as he sees fit."

The prince's glow wavered—but only for a moment. "I am under no obligation to offer you reasons," he told the sorcerer. "Only terms. I will ride with you when you Name me."

"Folly! You know as well as I do that you will be destroyed." The sorcerer cast a long look at the city that shimmered faintly in the distance. "Or do you hope they will come forth to save you," he asked slyly. "For that would be a foolish hope indeed. The gates have been sealed against the rising sea and they will not unlock them to save you. And why should they? Why should they save the prince who betrayed them so cruelly?"

"I look for no help from that quarter," the prince said.

"Then perhaps you have hopes of your own kind?" the sorcerer sneered. "Perhaps this time the Gentry will muster to the aid of a traitor who sold their secrets for a quick taste of life snatched from a woman's flesh? What has changed that now they would send a champion to rescue you from your humiliating captivity after all these years?"

"I hope for no champion," the fairy prince said. "I will defend myself."

"And you will lose all," the sorcerer cried. "And when your Name is inscribed on the Book of Doom, it will disappear—and so will you. No hope of heaven. Simply oblivion. It will be as if you never were. So, it is written in the stars."

"If I die, my powers die with me, and you can no longer command them. I will have to be satisfied with that," the prince said. "And that is my choice to make. I hereby claim my ancient right. Meet me at the moment the sun first peeks over the Devil's Path tomorrow morning, the moment when it is neither day nor night, just as this place is neither real nor imagined—as am I. Then Name me if you dare."

"The time is set. I will not fail to meet you." The sorcerer hesitated, then cast a puzzled frown at Essie. "You would truly choose oblivion for one such as her? What are those of her kind but will o' the wisps? Fireflies. Tiny flames of magic flickering out almost as quickly as they spark to life. While yours is the great magick, the Old Magick. Why should a creature like you humble yourself for them, when heaven granted you endless youth and pleasure here on Earth?"

The prince's brilliant eyes dimmed, as if he were gazing on a loss too enormous to comprehend—but only briefly. "I need not justify myself to you," he said. "My only obligation is to fulfill the terms of the ancient compact. I will ride across the waves once more at sunrise, and you will Name me if you dare. Until then, the girl is under my protection. I failed her friend. I will not fail her."

Chapter 13

WHEN THE SHOUT RANG OUT across Woodstock, echoing from Overlook, across the Village Green to Tonshi and Tycetoneyck Mountains beyond, and then back to Guardian, everyone could tell you they heard something— even if no one could agree on what it was they heard. The wives of the quarrymen cast an anxious eye up the cliffs and braced themselves against the foreman knocking on the door with a sad and sympathetic expression. Longyear, who ran the livery stable, cursed whatever fool had frightened the horses. Miss Anita Smith, whose herb samples were widely regarded as more efficacious than any doctor's remedies, murmured the old tale of the Catskill Witch, who Mr. Irving said, *lived on the highest peak of the Catskills, and had charge of the doors of day and night to open and shut them at the proper hour. She hung up the new moon in the skies, and cut up the old ones into stars. In times of drought, if properly propitiated, she would spin light summer clouds out of cobwebs and morning dew, and send them off from the crest of the mountain, flake after flake, like flakes of carded cotton, to float in the air; until, dissolved by the heat of the sun, they would fall in gentle showers, causing the grass to spring, the fruits to ripen, and the corn to grow an inch an hour. If displeased, however, she would brew up clouds black as ink, sitting in the midst of them like a bottle-bellied spider in the midst of its web; and when these clouds broke, woe betide the valleys!*

The good people enjoying the balmy breeze on the piazza of the Mead's Mountain House cast a baleful eye at the road that led to the Overlook Hotel above them and muttered darkly about anarchist plots and Bloomer Girls, then gasped in horror as an answering shriek rang down from the upper floors of their very own hotel. Surely, this sort of thing never happened before the Jews came to the Catskills and took over all the hotels that once catered to decent people. Only Kate Ames, who had made no secret of her attempts to avoid any further conversation with Gavin, sprang to her feet and hurried indoors to help.

"Miss Ames, no!" Gavin cried. "At least, allow me to accompany you!"

His concern lessened when he saw she had been joined in short order by a stout knot of indoor staff, and he allowed himself to slow his pace and favor his aching leg as he climbed the staircase. And so he was the last to be confronted with the extraordinary spectacle of Mrs. Adams murmuring in dismay over a maid who had arrived so pale and thin from traveling steerage that the officials at Ellis Island had tried to send her straight back to Killarney. The girl had collapsed outside the door to Hollis Stanton's room, her rosary clutched in one hand, and the spilled coal scuttle in the other, sobbing that she had heard the Banshee, just as her grandma had done the night before she died. Death was coming to Mead's Mountain House, she warned. There was no denying it once the Banshee called.

The stout Irish quarryman's widow who Mrs. Mead had taken on for extra housekeeping help during the summer months, made to send the girl downstairs with a cuff and a flea in her ear about troubling her betters, but Mrs. Adams intervened kindly, explaining that a girl could not be held responsible for the ignorant superstitions instilled by her Papish upbringing, and the war in the housekeeper's breast between respect for her betters and respect for the parish priest waged only briefly before she gentled her tone and told the maid she could have the rest of the afternoon off to recover from the shock.

The girl safely seen to, the housekeeper only glanced at Mrs. Adams for permission, before she tapped briskly on the door and asked Mr. Stanton to come out and explain himself, for in truth she considered it her personal prerogative to mistreat her girls, and would defend them like a mother bear against any gentleman who would venture to insult them. When there was no response forthcoming to a third and even a fourth knock, she sought Mrs. Adams' permission more deferentially before she unlocked the door—and opened it upon chaos.

Something had shaken the room; every picture, knick-knack and curio had been knocked off center as if rifled by unseen hands. The gentleman's desk had been the hardest hit—papers, letters, and files scattered by the force of the blow that had overturned the chair and knocked the poor gentleman clean to the ground, where he lay in a dark liquid pool that plastered his hair and clothing to his skin.

"Hollis!" Mrs. Adams cried, collapsing against Kate. "Quick, sound the alarm! My nephew has been murdered!"

But Gavin immediately saw that it was not Hollis Stanton who lay there insensate. It was Josep Havel. He knelt swiftly by the man's side and saw that his chest was rising and falling beneath his soaked shirt.

"This is not your nephew," Gavin said. "This is Josep Havel. And he is not dead."

He touched the soaked shirtfront with a frown that deepened as he sniffed the liquid, then tasted it. For it was in fact not blood, but rather a sheen of sweat so profuse that the man might have been doused with an entire bucket of water.

"I think he may have had some kind of fit," he said as he climbed awkwardly back to his feet.

"A fit! And in my nephew's room?" Mrs. Adams straightened out of Kate's arms in dismay. "I will speak with the Meads immediately. That man must be removed, or I will not stay here another day. He has brought us nothing but trouble since he arrived. And now… this. This sort of thing never happened before his kind came to the Catskills."

By all that was holy, the woman sounded more like Havel had spilled wine on the carpet instead of possibly choking out his last breath. "We need to summon a doctor," Gavin said, as levelly as he could.

"A doctor!" Mrs. Adams cried. "We should summon the law! This man was caught in the act of thieving!"

"And met with some considerable violence along with the rest of this room," Gavin pointed out. "It might be wiser to ask Mr. Stanton whether he can throw any light on the matter before you involved the authorities."

"You dare suggest my nephew is responsible for this?"

"It would seem a natural enough reaction in a man who had caught a thief rifling his property."

"Impossible," Mrs. Adams sniffed. "My nephew would not so much as touch such a foreigner with a ten-foot pole."

"Nonetheless," the housekeeper intervened with a level-headedness Gavin admired, "it would be best for everyone if the gentleman does not die. Especially for the Meads. Hotels develop a reputation for scandal when a guest dies on the premises. And they rarely survive it."

But just as she began to issue orders for one girl to fetch water and sherry and another to find blankets, Havel shifted with a massive groan, as if bestirred by the commotion. His eyes blinked open and studied the ceiling with bloodshot bewilderment. Then he recollected himself with an angry gasp and heaved his girth onto one elbow with such force that he snapped one of his embroidered braces. "That bitch!" he moaned. "That thieving little bitch…"

"Sir!" Gavin said, "I understand that you are in some distress, but it would be best if you remained quiet until the doctor arrives."

"What care I for a doctor?" Havel snapped. "Call the Pinkertons! I will see that murdering bitch hanged!"

"Before we take any such drastic step, I must point out that you have been found in a highly compromising position," Gavin said with a quick glance at Mrs. Adams. "Might you not prefer to explain your motives for breaking into Mr. Stanton's room privately."

"I broke into no room!" Havel protested. "It was that gypsy bitch."

"That little waif? From the Maverick?" Gavin cast a quick glance up at Kate Ames, not bothering to hide his disbelief. For Havel was a large man, and heavy with the results of good living. Yet his hair was wild and tangled with dirt. His carefully trimmed beard was matted with bile; his eyes were reddened as if with hard drink. It was impossible to imagine how the skinny busker could have done this to him.

"I heard her in here as I passed in the hall, and I tried to stop her. Instead she attacked me!"

"Attacked you how?"

"A poisoned dart. A stiletto in the back. The Evil Eye. The Curse of the Black Hand. Who knows?" Havel spat. "Their kind learn their dirty tricks early on the streets."

"A dart did not knock those pictures off the wall," Gavin said. "Nor did a curse."

"It matters not how she managed it," Havel snorted as he attempted to raise himself to a sitting position. "I will see that bitch hanged."

Gavin frowned. The man's fury was all out of proportion, even for one who had been violently assaulted. Something had happened in this room; something that had frightened him—perhaps into an apoplectic fit. But what? It had to be something far more than some broken pictures and stolen pages.

"Have you long been prone to these spells, Mr. Havel?" he attempted a different tactic.

Havel's face set with sly cunning.

But before Gavin could press Havel to determine why, the front door slammed and a fresh uproar rose from downstairs. Moments later, Hollis Stanton crashed into the room, jabbing an accusing finger at Kate Ames.

"And so is it now up to you to try where your confederates have failed?" he demanded. "Who sent you to search my papers? Answer me now, if you do not wish to give your answers in a jail cell."

"I would beg you to recall your manners in front of a lady," Gavin snapped.

"She is no lady," he sneered. "She is a charlatan and now a thief!"

Kate paled, but her voice remained carefully civil as she said, "I'm afraid you are mistaken. Mr. Havel was assaulted as he attempted to prevent your room from being robbed. Not me."

"Mistaken am I? A search of your room should reveal the truth quickly enough."

"Then search it if you must—" Kate began, but Gavin laid a hand on her arm to silence her.

"And what is Miss Ames accused of stealing?" he asked. "What is it you are so jealous to protect? The photographs with which you sought to blackmail your uncle, perhaps?"

Mrs. Adams gasped, and Stanton's angry flush suggested that Gavin's wild shot had hit its mark squarely.

"That statement is actionable," he spat.

"Then I shall see you in court," Gavin said calmly. "Along with your filthy pictures."

"That is scarcely necessary," Kate protested.

"Mr. Fellowes, you forget yourself!" Mrs. Adams cried.

Stanton raised an eyebrow. "For once, it is the fair sex that brings the voice of reason to this conversation."

"Voice of reason, be hanged! I will not stand by and hear a lady insulted."

"Mr. Fellowes!" Kate cut him off. "I appreciate your chivalry, but I assure you, there is no need to defend me in a court of law, when a simple search of my room will easily suffice."

Gavin Fellowes froze at the sudden realization that his own reactions were at least as out of proportion as Havel's. Had he just proposed to pursue a courtroom scandal solely to defend a lady's good name that by her own account needed no defending? Why not go all the way and slap Stanton across the face with a glove and challenge him to a duel?

"Apologies, Miss Ames," he said with a curt nod. "You are, of course, correct."

Just then footsteps rattled up the stairs again, and a maid burst in, heedless of the housekeeper's startled admonition that the service stairs lay around the back. "They've just sent a boy from Ker-Ys!" she cried. "They've found the girl. They found her floating in the fairy pool!"

Chapter 14

"THIS IS ALL YOUR FAULT, Aunt Jean!" Stanton's accusation rang across the uproar that erupted in the wake of the maid's announcement. "If you had allowed me to compel my uncle to accompany us immediately—"

"And cause a scene? Not unlike the scene you are causing now?" Mrs. Adams quelled him. She then turned to the anxious maid who had brought the news. "If Mrs. Mead has bid you be discreet, I beg you to be direct instead. Have they found that unfortunate girl at Ker-Ys, then?"

"Yes, ma'am," the maid said, straightening to nearly military attention.

"Dead?" Mrs. Adams asked, her voice not betraying the faintest flicker of emotion, "or alive?"

The maid hesitated, before deciding, "More like 'dreadful queer.' That's what Mr. Ned's message said. Something's come over her dreadful queer."

Mrs. Adams smiled with exasperated indulgence—whether at the maid or her husband was impossible to say. "And is it too much to hope that Mr. Ned offered any more precise symptoms than that?"

The maid's face twisted. "I'm sure he didn't say, ma'am."

"Forgive me," Mrs. Adams said immediately. "It was unkind to be ironic at your expense. You are a good girl, and you have delivered your message faithfully. Mr. Stanton will see to it that you are suitably rewarded—as I am certain no one else in this house has remembered to do."

The command underlying those last words was such that Hollis Stanton reached into his pocket and tossed the girl a coin, before he instructed her to inform the office that his car would be required immediately at the front door.

"Come!" he ordered Gavin. "There is no need to trouble Mr. Mead for transport this time."

Gavin merely stared at him, making no attempt to hide the rising fury simmering just beneath his icily polite syllables. "First and foremost, I believe Miss Ames is owed an apology."

"Hardly necessary," Kate intervened hastily. "Mr. Stanton was understandably subject to considerable shock and spoke in the heat of the moment. So, may I suggest that we focus our immediate attention on seeing to this poor girl once again?"

"Our attention?" Mrs. Adams asked, aghast. "Dear me, Kate, you cannot possibly be suggesting a return trip to the bathing pool?"

"I forbid it!" Stanton cried. "I will not allow you to involve or humiliate my aunt in this way any further!"

Kate met his gaze. "Surely there can be no humiliation in seeking to fulfill our responsibility to those less fortunate than ourselves."

"What responsibility? How dare you suggest that my family has any connection with those sordid suffragists! You, who have partaken of my aunt's misplaced generosity—"

"How dare *you* impugn a lady who has inconvenienced herself considerably only in order to help these missing girls?" Gavin snapped.

"There is no need—" Kate began, only to be smoothly cut off by Mrs. Adams.

"Come, now, gentlemen! Let us not fight amongst ourselves. Kitty is quite right. The unfortunate girl can be our only concern here. While I appreciate your concern, Hollis, I am scarcely some child who needs to be hidden away from the world's unpleasantness. That role belongs to my husband." But Mrs. Adams' ironic smile did little to hide the flicker of exasperation that marred the cool serenity of her face, as she turned away to go to the office to arrange transportation.

"By all that's holy, Ned," she murmured. "What have you done now?"

It was the sum total of the woman's Gethsemane, but it was enough to make Kate feel ashamed to have witnessed it.

The sight of Ned Adams crouched over a limp, wet girl by the side of the bathing pool brought in its wake a flood of memories Kate had hoped to lock away forever. Memories of Mr. Adams' breath suddenly warm against her ear as he came upon her in the Ker-Ys library. Memories of Mellie rousing her ruthlessly from her bed. Memories of repeating her mother's lullaby faster and faster, weaving the rhymes around her to ward away the creatures that peeped and leered from the surrounding woods, rat-faced and wombat-tailed, leaving pearlescent trails of slime across the leaf-strewn forest floor whenever they moved. But no words she uttered could stop Mellie from posing daintily on the stone edge of the pool, then sliding a slender white foot into the water.

And then the swirling verses had coalesced into a single, agonized cry that swept Kate away and tossed her onto a distant strand, where the pounding of the waves slowly changed to the pounding of hoofbeats that drew closer and closer until a black stallion with fire spouting from its nostrils loomed over her and she felt herself snatched away.

When she had come back to herself, Ned had been slipping Mellie's thin, white shift back into place with just the same eager tenderness as he now stroked Essie's wet hair with his pocket handkerchief. And now, just as then, Kate could not fight down the certainty that this was all her fault. She should have told. She should have told. She should have told.

"*Twilight is not good for maidens,*" she murmured. "*Should not loiter in the glen. In the haunts of goblin men.*"

"Perhaps you would prefer to return to the Great House and await the results of our search there?" Gavin Fellowes' voice interrupted her thoughts. "There does appear to be some kind of rockfall in the path."

He offered the excuse with smooth courtesy, but his eyes, when he had thought she was not looking, had been all too knowing.

"It does look a bit perilous, doesn't it?" she agreed blandly. For something had loosened several of the stones that dammed the pool and cracked open the strangely carved wellhead, so that muddy water now flowed down the mossy walls. "But I believe there remains enough room for us to safely negotiate our way."

"You shall keep me safe, Kitty," Mrs. Adams said, taking her arm. "You shall be the rock to which I must cling as I venture down that slope."

And cling to Kate she did, her fingers hardening painfully into Kate's flesh as Ned Adams scrambled to his feet too slowly to hide the furtive caress with which he tucked the handkerchief into the canvas sack that slipped from one shoulder. "It was nothing! An unfortunate accident. The stones must have fallen, and she struck her head while bathing," he protested. "You can ask anyone. They heard the fall. And I was not even the one to find her! The boy pulled her from the water; I just stayed here to watch over her and keep her warm. I swear to you that was all—"

Stanton pushed him aside with a muffled curse and bent to feel the girl's pulse. He straightened only moments later. "She's alive," he announced. "Thank God for at least that much. She just seems to have been subject to some kind of … fit."

"What do you mean, fit? She has been attacked," Ned cried. He pointed a trembling finger at the cracked relief. "And with that!"

"If I might…" Gavin Fellowes said. He knelt awkwardly by the girl, whose bright blue eyes stared at the sky unseeingly, even though her chest rose and fell as regularly as if she had merely been slumbering. His fingers gently probed her head and neck, and a moment later, he stood, shaking his head at the broken stone. "We of course need to wait for an informed medical opinion, but it seems unlikely this was caused by a blow from that stone or any other. There's no sign of blood or bruising."

"Just as with Mr. Havel," Kate was forced to point out. "The two cases are not dissimilar. Both laid out insensate with no visible wound. And both found soaking wet."

"Why are you muddying the waters with useless speculation?" Stanton snapped. "What possible connection could there be between Ker-Ys and that thieving bounder?"

Beyond Ned Adam's extremely unpleasant taste in photography, of course.

"You must admit the coincidence of two such attacks in such a short period is suggestive," Gavin said, before Kate's hot tongue could get the better of her.

"Suggestive of what?" Stanton demanded. "Be careful, sir, be very careful what you are insinuating if you do not want to see me in court."

"Suggestive of what we might need to do now," Mrs. Adams once more moved to smooth the waters. "We were able to rouse Mr. Havel. Perhaps we should attempt to rouse her as well."

"And have her run straight down to the village, screaming her accusations?" Stanton snapped. "We'll do nothing of the kind. It's bad enough the girl must be found here. We can do nothing to suggest any further involvement of the Ker-Ys Colony. We must remove her to the appropriate authorities as quickly and quietly as possible."

"I believe there is an order of nursing sisters nearby in Kingston," Mrs. Adams agreed. "They are known for their discretion."

"With all due respect, the girl needs medical, not spiritual, attention," Gavin protested.

"And we will do our Christian duty and ensure she receives it," Stanton snapped. "Although by rights, this should be the responsibility of her friends the Bloomer

Girls, who seem to be making it happy to wander onto Ker-Ys' property to stage their dramas. But we dare not trust those feckless suffragists to handle the matter quietly."

Kate's stomach clenched, as another corner of the walls she had carefully built against her memories crumbled. She knew only too well the ways the Adamses handled uncomfortable matters as quietly as possible—especially those matters associated with the greedy gaze Ned Adams cast upon girls he determined had won the favor of the Fair Folk. Mrs. Adams had of course insisted that her only concern was protecting the girls from the vulgar press, but even Kate's young brain had rapidly perceived it was something altogether different Mrs. Adams was protecting. Especially, during those sessions in the settlement house in the parish basement, where an endless series of clergymen and teachers questioned her, all of them intent on forcing her to admit one sole point—that her drawings were the product of an unhealthy imagination, most likely caused by the influence of an unfortunate mother she no longer even remembered—and not any depiction of her actual experience at the bathing pool. Over time, she had reconciled herself to believing that was in fact the case—for she herself wished the problem to go away as much as any of them.

And in that way, Kate had long ago made her peace. But could she honestly stand by and watch them make Essie—and the problem she represented—simply go away, just as they had proposed she should?

"There can be no question of handling the girl—quietly or otherwise—until she has been seen to by a competent man of medicine." Gavin returned to his careful examination of the stricken girl. "For although it seems unlikely she was injured by the rockfall, there may be a hidden injury that could prove fatal if we move her. And we have yet to rule out the possibility of some kind of drug, an opiate, most likely—"

"Or perhaps one of Miss Ames' fairy plants?" Stanton sneered.

Gavin's sudden silence was as ominous as the air stilling before one of the Catskills sudden storms. But the explosion it heralded was delivered in clipped, measured syllables. "First, assaulting Mr. Havel and now ensorcelling this poor girl. It would behoove you to at least be more decisive about the means you are accusing Miss Ames of employing if not the actual crimes she is accused of committing. Or do you seek to make Miss Ames a scapegoat for something or some*one* else?"

Kate glanced up sharply at his obvious anger. From the beginning, Gavin Fellowes had not struck her as the type to play white knight, so why had he repeatedly galloped to her defense? Simple dislike of Stanton or disgust at the truth he thought he may have guessed about Ned Adams' proclivities?

What did it matter? Another word, and a scene would be inevitable. In order to change the subject Kate turned to the farm boy who had first discovered Essie floating in the pond. "Were you the boy Mr. Adams said found the girl?"

"Yes'm," he said. "Yes'm I did."

"I know you've had quite a shock, but are you able to answer just a few questions?"

Gavin recovered himself immediately and chimed in. "And can you tell us exactly what you saw?" he asked. "It could be very important."

"Now, now. I doubt there's any need to pressure the child with any kind of formal statement," Mrs. Adams said. "Children can be prone to misinterpret—"

"Children lie!" Stanton seconded her firmly.

The boy's face grew worried. "All I did was pull her out," he said. "And then I ran for help. I thought it the best thing. I don't know anything about what to do when people drown. I swear to you I'm not lying about that."

"Of course, you're not," Kate said, with a quelling glance at Stanton. "And you did quite right. In fact, you probably saved her life. But now can you tell us what you saw?"

The boy's face twisted. "I didn't exactly see anything. I heard. First a crash."

"A crash like the sound of that breaking away from the wall?" Gavin asked, pointing toward the broken stone.

"Maybe," the boy agreed uncertainly. "Although it sounded a lot louder to me. Like lightning when it splits a tree right down the middle."

"Or the crack of the hiding you'll be getting if you're lying," Stanton warned.

Ignoring Stanton, Kate encouraged the boy. "And then what did you hear?"

He licked his lips with a justifiably uneasy glance first at Stanton, and then at Mrs. Adams. "Hoofbeats pounding … hard, like at the racetrack," he admitted hesitantly. "And dogs barking."

"Arrant nonsense," Stanton snapped. "The lad is fantasizing. Just look around you. The place is dense with trees. There's no room here for some hunt to ride past."

"No one's accusing you of lying, my dear," Mrs. Adams prodded the boy more gently. "But are you quite sure? For it does seem unlikely. There are no organized hunts in Woodstock."

"There's the Wild Hunt," Ned countered. "And there's room enough for them to ride. For they ride invisibly on the wind."

"Enough of this madness!" Stanton cried. "Summon a doctor if you must, but she cannot remain here a moment longer than necessary. She must be gone before she recovers consciousness and offers the most lurid of accusations." He realized his statement was a fatal misstep as his aunt's face froze and she locked her gaze on him.

"I am uncertain what you mean by lurid allegations, but I can assure you that when it comes to a creature such as this, my husband would no more touch her than he would Mr. Havel."

"Of course not ... no ... I just meant ..." Stanton backtracked, but it was too late. "One must keep in mind how it might appear to the vulgar. You and I are aware of your husband's unworldliness, but as for the masses ... Ker-Ys, like Caesar's wife, must be above suspicion."

"Better a suspicion of impropriety than a certainty of murder," Gavin growled. "And moving this girl in her present condition would be tantamount to nothing less. For all you know, her spine is damaged and you might kill her. There can be no question of moving this child until a doctor has examined her—and it is very likely a doctor will recommend against subjecting her to travel by carriage in the strongest possible terms." He turned to the boy, to cut off any further objections. "Thank you for your statement. It will prove most helpful. But now, will you please instruct our driver to take you down to the village to summon a doctor. In the meantime, we need to fetch some blankets to make her as comfortable as possible where she is."

Stanton once more began to protest, but Mrs. Adams overrode him. "Mr. Fellowes is quite correct. We will, of course, take responsibility for this poor girl," she said. Her gaze darkened as she studied her husband. "Although it would be wise to summon a female companion along with the doctor. Do you know Miss Anita Smith in the stone house near the foot of Mead's Mountain Road? She is an artist rather than a nurse, but it is said she has gathered considerable skill as an herbalist in her pursuit of folklore and history. The locals quite rely on her. Perhaps she could be prevailed upon to attend this … poor unfortunate during her stay at Ker-Ys."

"But why not prevail upon Melisandre to stay and care for this child?" Ned protested. He cast a crafty eye at Stanton. "She is of a forgiving nature and will overlook the mortal insults you have cast upon her gifts. There is a disused nursery adjoining her room, and I assure you Melisandre will attend to the poor creature with her own hands—just as if she were watching over her own child."

A shadow of pain crossed Mrs. Adams' face—only to be replaced by the mounting exasperation she was either unable or unwilling to hide. "She cannot possibly stay at the main house. That would occasion the vilest sort of rumor. We will have to find a place for her and Miss Smith in one of the artists' cottages if the doctor recommends a lengthy stay."

"Far too dangerous!" Ned cried. "Duncan MacLeod haunts the Spring House cottage, and it is the only one available at the moment."

"Mr. MacLeod has long since left us," she answered him, more than a little severely. "As have most of the artists who have taken cottages. Honestly, Ned. There are already far too many foolish rumors swirling about Ker-Ys for you to be adding ghost stories to the mix."

Ned shook his head. "I speak not of a ghost, but of a real man—flesh and blood! And he has returned to Spring House to reclaim what is his. Melisandre saw him—"

"She saw him on this plane or on one of the more astral ones where she prefers to receive her visions?" Mrs. Adams asked with ill-concealed skepticism.

Ned's jaw set. "It was more than a vision. He forced a window open and laid hands on everything he could."

"My dear, that was that unfortunate girl who drowned," Mrs. Adams reminded him. "And it was several weeks ago."

"I'm not talking about *her*! I'm talking about *him*! And he was here last night—smashing everything that was left in there and soaking what he could not destroy."

Just as it had happened with Havel. One look at Gavin's face was enough to assure Kate that he had the same thought.

"If you don't believe me, see for yourself. I was gathering the remains when the boy found me." Ned pulled several shards of glass from the canvas bag that he had dropped onto the grass. He held them up, and their reflection set the grass and the girl's face dancing, as if they had been sprinkled with pixie dust.

"Not more of those wretched photographs," Mrs. Adams sighed.

"Give those to me! I will see to their immediate disposal." Stanton lunged to grab the sack from Ned, and the broken slides spilled across the grass and Essie's tangle of wet hair.

"Please!" Kate cried, kneeling to brush them away. "This is doing her no good. Why worry about where she will sleep tonight, when we should be thinking of making her comfortable now. At the very least, we should find a blanket to keep her warm, for surely she has been chilled by the water. Would you not agree, Mr. Fellowes?"

But Gavin made no answer. His eyes were suddenly as far away as Melisandre's in the most theatrical of her trances—just as it always seemed to happen at any mention of Duncan MacLeod. "Mr. Fellowes," she said sharply. "Are you quite well?"

He whirled, his skin pallid, his eyes still focused on the horror only he seemed to have witnessed. "I apologize, Miss Ames. My mind seemed to have ... wandered."

"As always, Kitty is quite right! We must see to the girl's comfort while we await the doctor," Mrs. Adams cut in over him. Now that she had come to a decision, she sprang into action, and in no time two of the farm girls who served as housemaids had fetched blankets out to the pool and tucked Essie in as securely as if the damp lawn was a cradle.

Mrs. Adams surveyed her handiwork with a nod of satisfaction, then said, "Now that she is comfortable, there is no use to our all crowding over her. For I can imagine nothing that could be more calculated to terrorize the poor girl if she does in fact awaken. It would be far better if we left one person to watch over her—someone with whom she would feel comfortable, someone of her own kind," she decided briskly. "Perhaps Miss Ames…"

Kate's brows knit over her green eyes. Her own kind— or as Mrs. Adams had so recently put it, someone an Adams would not touch with a ten-foot pole. But what was the use of taking umbrage? It might appear that Mrs. Adams' words conveyed nothing more than a gentle suggestion, but

Kate was well aware it was in fact a command from the woman paying her hotel board.

"I will of course be happy to help in whatever way I can. The girl's health and safety must be our only consideration," Kate said—earning a beneficent smile from Mrs. Adams, just like when she had bestowed a book prize on a deserving student.

Snapping out of his trance, Gavin cast a long look at Stanton, as he and Mrs. Adams converged on Ned like a pair of constables intent on escorting a prisoner to gaol. "I will stay with the ladies as well," he decided. "It would be unsafe to leave them alone and unprotected, when the girl's attacker might come back at any moment."

Stanton opened his mouth to protest, but Mrs. Adams nodded, settling the matter. "Quite sensible," she agreed, and turned her attention back to her husband.

"Please, Mr. Fellowes," Kate protested in an undertone as the others began to pick their way back up the rock-strewn path, "While I appreciate your concern, I can assure you that I am more than capable—"

"If there is one thing I do not doubt, Miss Ames, it is your capability," he assured her. He knelt with only some slight awkwardness and began to gather the shards of the photographic plates from where they had spilled on the grass. "What I am concerned about is who might return for these."

She raised an eyebrow. "Has a confirmed skeptic such as yourself suddenly been converted to the cause of the ghost of Duncan MacLeod?"

If she had meant to test his reaction at the mention of the name, it had no effect. "My concern is not for ghosts, but rather for flesh and blood men," Gavin said, without a trace of further emotion.

"You speak of Mr. Stanton," she said, with a quick glance at the man's retreating back.

"Not only of him, unfortunately. Stanton is a fool and a bully. Yet, however unscrupulous his means, he only wishes to protect the family name and fortune. Perhaps not the most honorable of motivations, but sterling in comparison to what might drive others to possess those photographs."

"And what might motivate these others?" she prodded, when he seemed disposed not to say anything further.

"You yourself have already suggested that Duncan MacLeod's magic might have been used to win a war." He hesitated only briefly, then drew a deep breath and went on. "I myself have enough experience of such methods to believe you are not in the least exaggerating. And as with any weapon of such catastrophic power, there are many men—and arguably more than a few women—who would stop at nothing to get their hands on it."

Was this then, the cause of his obsession with Duncan MacLeod? A very real and rational concern, rather than any fear of ghosts? "Including Mr. Havel?" she asked. "Is that what you believe he was seeking in Mr. Stanton's room?"

Instead of answering her directly, Gavin mused, "Incriminating photographs are very much like your description of the Fair Folk, are they not? Possessed of incredible powers, but subject to serve whatever banner claims them—regardless of the rightness of their cause."

"And you question the rightness of our cause in the recent war?" she asked.

"It is perhaps simpler to say that I question the rightness of our methods," he answered carefully. "The war is over, and the cause of justice prevailed—or so those of us on this side of the lines believe. But the power of such photographs to destroy lives remains undiminished. Like Piper's wretched Book of Shadows, they should have been destroyed the moment peace was made—if, in fact, they ever should have been created in the first place."

Chapter 15

ALTHOUGH SHE HAD BEEN described as an artist as well as an intrepid folklorist, Miss Anita Smith displayed none of the Bohemian eccentricities that most denizens of Woodstock sported as accessories. Instead, she exhibited the calm competence of a seasoned lady traveler, briskly instructing the farmgirls in the correct method of folding hospital corners and improvising a stretcher out of two oak branches and a pair of Ned Adams' homespun shirts. Only when the doctor finally pronounced it safe to move the girl, did Miss Smith dust off her hands, both physically and metaphorically, and apologize to Jean Adams for not taking the time to introduce herself properly.

"For if I am not mistaken, our mothers were at school together down in Philadelphia."

"Of course!" Jean said with a delighted smile. "How could I have possibly overlooked the connection?"

But as soon as Miss Smith turned back to supervise the sturdy farm lads as they lifted the girl onto the stretcher, Jean turned to Kate in dismay. "Oh, dear," she breathed. "I was unaware she was *that* Anita Smith."

"Do you know her?" Stanton asked.

"Well, I know *of* her," Jean said. "As one does. She's one of the Torresdale Smiths—their line runs all the way back to Giles Knight who sailed with William Penn. Of course, the family always had a bit of a Bohemian streak. It's said her mother educated Frieda and Anita in Europe to avoid the expense of maintaining the familial estate. Still, Anita made her debut into Philadelphia's Inner Assembly." Mrs. Adams turned to Kate in horrified appeal. "One simply cannot ask a lady such as that to act as a *paid nurse*."

She bowed her head with the furious concentration of a hostess confronted with a thirteenth guest at dinner. "Kitty," she said, "I'm afraid I have a dreadful favor to ask of you."

"Whatever I can do to help," Kate replied once again.

"Bless your kind soul," Mrs. Adams said, without any irony. She lowered her voice and leaned closer. "For I know if the poor girl awakens, you will be admirably suited to calm any mad fancies she might have about fairy kidnappings or midnight thieves, and I'm sure you're quite sensible enough not to jump at shadows."

Indeed Kate was sensible enough to know that mad fancies and jumping at shadows had little to do with the instructions Mrs. Adams issued. Once Mrs. Adams, Anita Smith, the good doctor, and Mr. Fellowes—the last having gone to fetch her bags from Mead House—had taken their leave, she looked around the room to get her bearings. The interior of the Spring House had been transformed, thanks to Anita, into a tidy sickroom, complete with jars of healing tinctures lined on the windowsill behind the enamel sink, and sprigs of lavender strewn across the floor to banish evil influences as well as infection. Even the steady rise and fall of Essie's chest was a calm relief after the day's fraught confrontations. Nibbling on one of the pastries Miss Smith had thoughtfully left folded in a napkin, Kate finally began to relax and felt at ease enough to turn her attention to examining the rest of the cottage.

There was little enough to examine in the two rooms. Duncan MacLeod's camera might have captured fairy land, but this cabin was devoid of any sort of magic. A couple of enamel pots and pans languished in a drying rack beside the sink. A few cracked photographic plates lay forgotten on the shelves. A stained oilskin and mud boots had been abandoned on the coatrack. In short, the ordinary debris found in any abandoned cabin. Nothing to indicate anything about its occupant or his personality.

Which was entirely consistent with what Kate already knew about Duncan MacLeod. She hadn't been lying to Gavin Fellowes when she had described him as a will o' the wisp. She had only seen the man three times, and at least one of those had been in a dream—and frankly she couldn't be entirely certain about the other two encounters.

She shook her head and looked around the little spring house turned cottage. She didn't want to be in this place, and she didn't want to think about Duncan MacLeod, so she sat down at the small table and did what she always did when her thoughts became too much to bear. She pulled out her sketch pad. She looked over at Essie, at the gentle rise and fall of her chest, and hoped the girl was not dreaming. Turning back to the blank page, she selected a charcoal and began to sketch the room. Mr. Fellowes would be back soon enough, and in the meantime, she might as well keep herself occupied.

The first time she had come face to face with Duncan MacLeod had been in the wake of Abbott Thayer's disastrous trip to England. When Thayer fled back to America, humiliated at having completely failed to convince the Allies of his theories of camouflage, he had taken to his studio with all the grace of a wounded beast, painting obsessively all day, only to scrape off his work in a nighttime fury and begin again in the morning. Models, family, and apprentices had tiptoed past his shuttered door, only occasionally venturing to knock and offer him some food or drink. The situation rapidly grew insupportable, and more than one person had raised the possibility of a rest cure, when Duncan MacLeod had appeared as the unlikeliest of *deus ex machina*. He brought with him the offer of a private commission: An English patron who preferred to remain anonymous wanted Thayer's atelier to design an array of extraordinary maps and models: A bristling gunner's nest disguised as a fairy mound. A troop of cavalry that appeared to be a drove of oxen from the air. A ship that travelled in no direction and in every direction at once. An entire French village masquerading as a field full of haystacks. In short, although the English War Office had remained unconvinced, there were interested parties in England that were desperate enough to put Abbott Thayer's theories to the test.

Thayer accepted this vindication eagerly, only to be overwhelmed by his customary self-doubt. The frantic overpainting and midnight scraping returned. He created one design after another, only to reject them immediately. After his assistants were driven to packing up his work while he was taking dinner and sending it off on the milk train, Thayer simply sneaked down to the railway station to uncrate the package and redo his work there. It was Kate who finally came up with a simple solution: while Thayer was occupied with destroying his work, she reproduced it from memory, and sent it down on the milk train instead. In very little time, she discovered that her talent equaled— and perhaps even exceeded—Thayer's, and her career as a dazzlepaint artist flourished.

The second time she had met Duncan MacLeod had been the night Piper's increasing anxiety finally spilled over into madness. She had found the forger, like Thayer, destroying his own work, crouched above a burnt pile of the *Protocols* he had so artfully created, muttering supplications to the Dybbuk to at last give him some peace. Kate had tried to do for Piper what she had done for Thayer, gathering up what remained of the damaged pages and trying to repair the damage before the milk train left in the morning. She worked late into the night, her pen moving of its own accord, its steady scratching so resembling the invisible spirit Piper claimed was dogging him, that she heard no footsteps approaching, but instead just turned to find MacLeod studying her work with sad blue eyes. "'Tis beautiful," he allowed. "But you must burn it at once. They are allowed their twelve copies, and I must answer to my own kind for that. But the Unseelie Court bears no part of this burden. Twelve copies for the twelve Seelie tribes; they must be content with that, no more."

Then he himself had slipped away, vanishing into the dusk as completely as if he had never been there.

The last time she had seen Duncan MacLeod, she had been drawing a map at the behest of an order the men in Washington would never acknowledge they had issued. They required a complete map of the invisible paths that connected the Magician's webs of deception, such as only one with Kate's peculiar talents could create. She was working unconsciously, aware of nothing beyond chasing a phantom from barbed wire to trench, from battalion to hospital, from lumbering tanks to swooping biplanes, until the phantom turned, and she saw it was MacLeod.

"You have done your part, lassie," he said. "and all I ask is that you grant me one last boon. You have the power of true naming, yes. But you have another power that I do not. You also have the power to lie. And lie you must about this map. You must paper over your talent with charming pictures meant for children, and frivolous fancies of worlds the common folk cannot imagine. And I will weave curtains of riddles so perplexing they will never know truth from lie. I will plant a forest of illusion so twisted and dark that any who dare follow the course you chart will wander astray and remain lost for the rest of their lives. So, I have sworn, and so it will be. After you finish, you will owe them no more. Go and forget what happened, and whatever you do, do not trust them. Do not trust any of them, for they will lie to trap you just as they lied to trap me. For you have the talent of true naming, and that is a power too many men will kill to possess."

And the weary soldiers and bloodstained battlefields had rapidly blossomed into drawings of magical oceans, where krakens and mermen guarded long-drowned cities, and miraculous vessels sailed in mid-air, drawn by horses whose hooves skimmed the waves. Kate had no idea how long she gamboled in the wake of those magical creatures, before she at last came back to the place where their merry chase had begun: Abbott Thayer's studio, where MacLeod was facing a grim tribunal of financiers, generals, and politicians, who all looked like Hollis Stanton. And MacLeod had turned to the men from Washington, who were bent over the last map she had ever drawn, and said, "Well, gentlemen, you have found what you're looking for. Now the question comes …"

"What do you propose to do?"

At once remembered and real, the words echoed through an open window, and snapped Kate from her trance.

"What do you propose to do?" Hollis Stanton repeated.

"What you have been too much a coward to do yourself," Melisandre's voice floated on the summer breeze after his. "I will do what I must to awaken her."

"Why? She can tell no tales when she is asleep."

"And if she awakens when we're not there and tells those tales to someone else?" Melisandre demanded. "If I rouse her before she is ready, she will be more likely to follow my lead."

"And if you kill her instead?"

A moment's ghastly pause before Melisandre replied with a laugh, "Well, that would solve our problems rather neatly, wouldn't you say?"

Solve our problems rather neatly? What did that mean? Could it be possible? Could Mellie and Stanton be responsible for Judith's death? Could the whole thing have gone that far? Although she must not reveal her suspicions, she could not keep silent. The words were like a slap in the face, and sent Kate flying out the door, stomach and fists clenched equally with rage. "Whatever you are going on about, I beg you to keep your voices down," she hissed, "for you are apparently unaware how well they carry and might disturb the patient."

Of the pair, Stanton proved himself better equipped to address the awkward moment. "Just as I was saying myself, Miss Ames. But Melisandre was so very insistent of coming down here to see to the girl's comfort. I hope our slight disagreement gave you no cause for any further misinterpretation."

"No, no. Your worry for Essie's comfort is laudable," Kate said forging ahead with her ruse, "but Miss Smith recommended complete peace and quiet as conducive to this poor girl's rest and recovery, and I must insist you both abide her wishes."

"I quite agree," Stanton said with ill-disguised relief, and reached to take Melisandre's arm.

"Rest assured," Kate went on, "that Miss Smith is quite the seasoned traveler and has set us up as tidily as if we were on an excursion on the Nile. So, although I'm certain you are both acting out of the kindest of motives, it is best if you went back to the main house."

"But she has called me!" Melisandre cried, shaking him off impatiently. "Essie summoned me from beyond. She has chosen to speak through me and her message is most urgent. I must commune with her now!"

And what message was that? What tales did Melisandre think Essie might tell? Tales of the hang-dog expression on Ned Adams' face when his wife had found him dancing with 'his girls,' clad as Cupid? Of his lectures on the Greeks' honest appreciation of the human body and their habits of competing in the Olympics in the nude? Of the dais in the middle of the studio where he had arranged his "Living Tableaux"? Of Mrs. Adams shaking her head in dismay as she crumpled the decidedly improper drawings Kate had no memory of sketching, and murmuring to her offended teacher, "I don't know where these children will pick up such things, but then again, we have no idea the horrors they might have suffered before they landed on our shores"?

Or perhaps these were the tales Melisandre *wanted* Essie to tell? Tales she wanted to plant in Essie's mind? But *why*? How could that possibly benefit anyone? Anyone, that is, other than…

Kate's heart hammered against her ribcage. "I'm sorry, but it's quite simply out of the question," Kate informed Melisandre, with a sidelong gaze at Hollis Stanton. Had the two of them truly been conspiring? Had she overheard a falling out among thieves—and murderers? "It was not just Miss Smith who insisted Essie be allowed to rest," she said, keeping her voice even. "The doctor also gave strict orders she not be disturbed, and you would have to agree that a séance is nothing if not a disturbance."

A woman who would use a stricken girl as a prop in a séance beggared description, but Melisandre was impervious to shame, and simply changed tactics.

"I know I'm being dreadfully selfish, Kitty. But I'm just so worried for Ned. They will take him away, you see. Force him back to that wretched wife of his. Even Hollis takes their side." She paused to glare at Stanton before she pleaded, "The only thing that will save poor Ned from the dire fate they have decreed for him is if Essie can tell us what really happened. But there are those who will not allow it to happen. Those who cannot bear to have the truth brought to light—"

Stanton stiffened. "Be very careful," he warned. "Be very careful about what you say next. I will not stand by idly and watch you drag my uncle's reputation through the mud."

"I speak not of poor Ned," Melisandre said with a toss of her head. "He is a victim here as much as anyone. No, I speak of dreadful powers no man should dare to command. I speak of Havel and Duncan MacLeod."

"Oh, come now!" Stanton snapped. "We are not here to chase ghosts!"

"Oh, Duncan MacLeod is no ghost," Melisandre's voice lowered. "And summoned or not, he will come back for this girl, for he cannot leave her—any more than he could ever leave Kitty."

Kate's face froze. "I think it's time for you to go. Now."

"I quite agree." Stanton moved to take Melisandre's arm, less gently this time. But Melisandre gasped and flung a shaking finger in the direction of the mountain laurels that clustered on the stony outcropping just above the Spring House. "I warned you he would come for her!" she breathed. "And now it is too late. *He is already here!*"

The laurels rustled and parted, and a shadow stepped out. "Leave her," Duncan MacLeod said to Stanton. "This one is not for you."

"Who are you?" Stanton recoiled, stammering. "What do you want?"

"I think you know," MacLeod said. He turned to Kate, and his voice gentled. "Have no fear for the girl. She will come back to you at sunrise."

"And she will have much to answer for!" Stanton snapped, recovering immediately from his spluttered protests. "As will you! I have no idea what farce you persuaded her to play at here, but I assure you there will be consequences. I will see her punished."

"You will see no such thing," MacLeod told him, his eyes piercing. "The girl is an innocent, but you are most certainly not. For nothing could excuse severing a girl from this world and trapping her in another solely to coax a creature from beneath the waves like tethering a goat to catch a jaguar…"

A moment's silence fell, as Stanton stared at him blankly. "I have no idea what you are talking about," he said finally.

A flicker of doubt dulled those piercing blue eyes, but then MacLeod shook his head. "Then it can only go the worse for you. For a debt is owed, and a debt will be repaid."

"No!" Melisandre burst in, and this time, there could be no mistaking that her fear was genuine. "No, it wasn't anything like that! The drops … they were only to encourage them—to help them see wonders that they could never imagine on their own—"

But her furious protest was cut off by another cry—this one sharper and more horrified—and accompanied by the heavy thud of something landing in the grass. All whirled to find Gavin Fellowes transfixed, the bags he had fetched down from Mead's Mountain House for Kate fallen forgotten to the grass.

"No," he gasped, his eyes fastened on MacLeod. "This cannot be! I saw you die!"

"Hello, Captain Fellowes," MacLeod said with an understanding smile as he held out his hand. It took another frozen moment before Gavin summoned the will to limp across the lawn and touch him—only to snatch his fingers back with a cry of dismay. "But … how?"

MacLeod shrugged. "Dazzlepaint." And then, as quickly as he had appeared, he faded back into the clustering laurels and was gone.

Chapter 16

IT TOOK ALL OF GAVIN'S self-discipline not to press his mount up the steep road to Mead's as savagely as he pressed his mind to erase the memory of what he had just witnessed—of what he could not possibly have witnessed. The stunned tide of disbelief carried him straight to the quiet corner of the porch where he found Havel still recovering from his ordeal over a flask of brandy. Havel proffered a half-hearted invitation with a wave of his cigar, but Gavin refused to sit. "A young girl has been discovered insensate and soaked at Ker-Ys in much the same circumstances as you were. And a man has returned from the dead," he said without preamble.

"Do I now stand accused of being a sorcerer?" Havel raised an eyebrow. "I know that the Americans assume that we poor refugees from the Empire are nothing but a band of witches and warlocks, but I thought an Englishman would be more cosmopolitan."

"The dead man was Duncan MacLeod, and he proceeded to threaten Stanton with retribution over what has happened to the girl," Gavin continued, his calmly clipped syllables at odds with the fire raging through both his flesh and his soul. "And given that you're the closest thing we have to an eyewitness right now, I think the time has come for you to set aside your tales of thieving Gypsy girls and tell me the truth about what happened to you in his room."

"My dear sir, if I could explain it I would. But as matters stand, I might venture to argue that I am the one who deserves an explanation."

"You went into that room for a reason, and I, for one, do not believe it was to catch a thief," Gavin persisted calmly, even if it cost him several deeply drawn breaths. "I need the truth of what you were seeking, and I will not leave until I have it."

Havel raised one shoulder with elaborate disinterest. "And I, for one, believe you. But could I at least prevail upon to please sit down rather than looming over me in a manner than can make neither of us comfortable?"

Havel waited pointedly for Gavin to settle into a chair before he began. "Very well then. You demand an answer, and an answer you shall have. If, perhaps, I broke into Hollis Stanton's room, there could only be one reason that motivated such folly, and that is that I was seeking what everyone in this place is seeking: the truth about Duncan MacLeod."

Gavin drew another deep, steadying breath, before he managed to ask, "And how much have you discovered of the truth about Duncan MacLeod?" Beyond the fact that he had risen bodily from the grave, Gavin did not add.

Havel ruminated briefly. "You have my assurances that I am very close to discovering the full truth, but before I go further, perhaps it would be better to ask whether you accept Miss Ames' stories about the creature she called Magician?"

"I am not in the mood for fairytales, Mr. Havel," Gavin said, more sharply than was strictly necessary.

"Oh, the Magician was quite real," Havel assured him. "The fanciful soubriquet was just one of the many little games those in military counterintelligence are so fond of. Although the Magician might have commanded the forces of illusion rather than spirits, his ability to transform the real into the false, the truth into lies was nothing short of magical. At the peak of his powers, he and he alone decided what the world saw and did not see."

"In short, it is a spymaster of which you speak," Gavin forced himself to say with a shrug. "It is no secret there were many such men spinning lies designed to urge countless others to offer themselves up for empire, honor, duty, glory."

"I speak not of a spymaster, but rather *the* spymaster. No lesser a figure than the man who succeeded in bringing America into the war when everyone else had failed." Havel paused only briefly before he asked, "Are you aware of how America was finally persuaded to declare war?"

"The Zimmerman telegram, of course. Everyone knows the tale."

"And what a tale it is. Indeed, one might argue that the Zimmerman telegram was one of those fairy tales you so wish to avoid," Havel mused. "For it was one of the most improbable documents ever written. A smoking gun, with Germany's plans to incite war between the U.S. and Mexico neatly laid out—intercepted by British Intelligence by means they conveniently declined to explain."

"Which was why there were so many in America who called it just that, a fairytale," Gavin pointed out with a nod. "Or to use a more vulgar term, a hoax." The Zimmerman Telegram had been the smoking gun the British needed to goad America into the war, but there was no way to reveal it without also revealing that the British had decoded the German's ciphers. The solution had been for British intelligence agencies to publicly claim their agents had stolen the telegram's deciphered text in Mexico. That plan had backfired as most Americans simply disbelieved the claim.

"Hoax. Fraud. Fairytale. The nomenclature doesn't matter. It was an illusion destined to be dismissed like all the others, especially after Hearst featured the conspiracy theory on the front pages of his publishing empire." Havel paused. "And then a miracle occurred. Or if you prefer ... magic."

A miracle too-long prayed for and too-late arrived. For America declaring war had been a faint hope despaired of for so long that when the news finally came, the battle-weary men on the front lines dismissed it as just another rumor to brace them for yet another futile charge across the barbed wire straight into enemy fire. Gavin took a deep breath and said, "Zimmerman stepped forward."

"'I cannot deny it. It is true.'" Havel repeated Zimmerman's words from the press conference that had spelled the death knell of Germany's hope for victory. "And America entered the war within a week. But did you ever bother to ask yourself why? Why would a loyal German civil servant do the one thing that would irrevocably tip the scales against his beloved homeland?"

Gavin raised an eyebrow. "Another miracle wrought by your Magician?"

"Zimmerman's coming forward was the miracle the Allies so desperately needed. A miracle wrought by perhaps the finest spymaster the world has ever known."

"While that may well be true, you can certainly postulate that Zimmerman betrayed his country for far simpler reasons than he was bewitched," Gavin pointed out with a laugh. "Many a man has cast his lot with his enemy for a few zeroes added to his bank account."

Havel's face darkened. "Scoff all you want, but I must warn you that such was the Magician's fatal flaw. His arrogant faith in his own abilities blinded him to the danger of the forces he was about to unleash until it was far, far too late. For he was foolish enough to place all his faith in science and reason, rather than accept the truth that the Old Magicks still roam this Earth. Just because men have long since forgotten to fear them, does not mean they are no longer dangerous."

Old magicks like a ghost who had held out his hand for Gavin to touch? Or the cries of the Gabriel Hounds, which pad at his heels and huff and whine in his ear? "I have no time to quibble over long-vanished magicks or anything else that cannot be proven," he said in sudden impatience. "The past is the past. My concern is the present. What has any of this to do with your burgling Stanton's room? And please do not insult my intelligence by ascribing any magical powers to those pictures or that wretched Book of Shadows. Or by claiming you ventured into his room for any other purpose but to claim them."

Havel dismissed the truth of the accusation with a wave of his hand. "The matter of the camera is a triviality. A side issue, if even that. Ned Adams is a credulous fool, and, were it not directly inimical to my own interests, I would heartily applaud Hollis Stanton's handling of the matter instead of trying to steal from him."

"And yet you chose to steal instead," Gavin said. "Why? What are these interests to which Stanton is so inimical? What do you seek in Woodstock, if not to gain a hold over the Adams' family and their business associates?"

Havel studied Gavin with a condescending smile, as if he found cause for some private amusement. "Very well. I will be completely honest with you," he decided with a shrug. "Call me a madman if you will, but I have come to America to lay claim to the source of the Magician's power. And I will have it by dawn."

The utter confidence in Havel's voice made Gavin waver—albeit only briefly. "And what reason have you to believe such a thing? What reason could any sane man have?"

Havel's smile deepened, as if he had penetrated to the very bowels of Gavin's soul. "Because I was on the H.M.S. *Hampshire* when it sank. And I came face to face with those powers the Magician was too foolish to believe in."

"And what powers are those? Is your Magician to be guilty of every last disaster of the Great War?" Gavin asked. "Would you truly have me believe he murdered Lord Kitchener with sorcery?"

"It would not be the most far-fetched rumor that swirled around Lord Kitchener—or his creature. St. George, they called Kitchener. King Arthur, returned to his people in their time of direst need. And the rumors that began to swirl about his last mission were even madder. That he was the modern Arthur returning to Avalon to raise the slumbering Knights of the Round Table and rally them to his banner once more. That he sailed north not to meet the Russians, but instead to journey to the farthest shores of Ultima Thule to entreat the mystic order of Grail Knights to descend as did the Angels of Mons. And that he had discovered a Book of Shadows that would allow him to summon and then compel the Fair Folk to his cause." Havel broke off, his eyes meeting Gavin's. "Legends, of course. Pretty poetry, nothing more. But every Arthur must have his Merlin."

Once more, Gavin felt the warmth of MacLeod's flesh as he reached out to touch it. "Merlin practiced true magic," he said. "Your Magician, if he existed at all, traded only in rumors. Propaganda, if you wish to use an uglier world. A desperate attempt by the war office to give a battered country cause for hope."

"Rumors," Havel agreed—then added, "But what if Kitchener actually reached the shore of Ultima Thule? And unleashed something terrible there—something so powerful that the H.M.S. *Hampshire* was only the first victim it claimed?"

And what if the Wild Hunt really had charged across the battlefields of the Great War? And what if Gavin really had seen a man die and come back to life? What if the Gabriel Hounds baying constantly at the edge of his hearing were not the product of his own disturbed imagination, but were in fact following his scent?

"Simpler by far to assume that a German spy betrayed the location of the *Hampshire*," Gavin pointed out with a calm he most assuredly did not feel. "Or if you must have your conspiracies, it's possible the ship's position was betrayed by a consortium of American industrialists in retaliation for the U.K. leaking their shipping routes to the Germans in an earlier ill-fated attempt to draw America into the war. Remember, they believed Kitchener bore the blame for that."

"When it was, in fact, a disastrously ill-fated attempt by British intelligence," Havel agreed. "Yet another of the many mistakes caused by the Magician's arrogance." He met Gavin's eyes squarely. "And that alone would be a terrible burden to bear…"

"Enough!" Gavin cut him off. "Let us have done with this farrago of innuendo and speak clearly for once and for all. What does any of this have to do with what happened to those girls? Or Hollis Stanton? Would you have me believe that American industrialists are now working hand in glove with a new enemy? Perhaps they are colluding with the Russian communists in order to rule the world by magical means?"

Havel raised an eyebrow. "Be they Reds or Whites, the Russian temperament has been a slave to magic long before Rasputin's rise to power," he allowed. "But the Americans have no gift for magic. And that is at once their salvation and their downfall. For they alone will not—*cannot*—see Duncan MacLeod for what he truly is."

Which had arguably been the salvation of the civilized world in this most recent conflict, Gavin forbore to point out. "Surely it would be simpler to accept that MacLeod was not the only man who found it convenient to fake his own death in the chaos of battle."

"'The loveliest trick of the Devil is to persuade you that he does not exist,'" Havel said.

Gain snorted. "If you believe in these Old Magicks and believe MacLeod is … not of this world, how do propose to deal with him? Why should you expect to succeed where another, more talented man failed?"

Another small smile from Havel. "Because I do not suffer from the Magician's tragic flaw, Mr. Fellowes. I do believe in magic, when the Magician did not. And that is why, when in his arrogance the Magician cried havoc, he did not let slip the dogs of war, but rather raised the hounds of hell. And tomorrow at dawn, I will complete the working and bring that pack to heel."

Chapter 17

A HOUND GROWLED, its sour breath damp against Gavin's neck. Havel gave no sign of having heard anything, but Gavin stumbled to his feet. "No one could fault me for leaving you to the consequences of your own folly," he snapped, struggling to hide the tremor in his voice. "But common decency bids me warn you one last time. You have no idea of the forces you propose to challenge. And I speak not of any Fairy Rade or magician. I speak of the Americans, who know only one magic, that of Mammon. And believe me when I tell you that they have no scruples about making blood sacrifices in his name."

With that, Gavin threw himself indoors and up the stairs to his room, only one step ahead of the hounds that stalked soft and deadly behind him.

Havel was a fool who little understood the extent of his own folly, let alone guessed that his smug confidence in the power of his own belief would be his undoing. For in his arrogance, he missed one crucial fact: Men driven to desperation become true believers. Just look at the soldiers who had fought at Mons who swore they had seen the angels descend in the form of Henry V's legendary bowmen, even after Arthur Machen himself had stepped forward and gone on the record that he had woven his patriotic fiction out of the whole cloth of his imagination and anyone who claimed otherwise was perpetuating a hoax.

And that had been at the beginning of the war, when desperation had yet to clench first an entire army, and then an entire nation. How much more desperate were those who had managed to survive—live was too strong a word for it—through the trench foot, the fear, the blood, the hopelessness, the grinding futility, and above all the endless mud that sucked down ideals like honor, duty, glory and buried them deep beneath their filth? Many succumbed to the slough of despair, and there was more than one trip over the barbed wire to seek the merciful end they would not deny a suffering beast. But those, like Gavin, who struggled to keep their heads above the tide had clutched at one last spar to keep themselves going. They could not remain content simply to believe in miracles. Instead, like a child trying to make themselves invisible by closing their eyes or a lovesick dairy maid buying a charm from a wise woman, they sought to *will* the miracles into existence.

With that, the choking sludge of memory closed over Gavin, and he slid down against the shuttered door of his room and back into the horror of Belleau Wood, face to face with the Jonah the men had long muttered had doomed them.

The men were only half-right. It was not any fleshly Jonah that had doomed them, but simply a debt. How different that term had sounded when it was but another fairytale scratched out by Gavin's pen moving across paper beneath the flickering light of a kerosene lamp. No, not a tale. Give it its true name: a lie. A pact signed in imaginary blood and paid in fairy gold. Except that the blood was not imaginary now, and the falling mortars proclaimed with every burst that the debt had come due. A pact. A debt. How different the terms seemed when you had faces and names to put to the currency demanded—including your own. How very different the terms seemed when you were the one responsible for dooming sixteen desperate men all for a web of lies. Men who for whatever godforsaken reason believed in your lies and trusted in you.

Gavin looked back at the men crouched in the foxhole. "So how do I tell them?" he asked. "How do I tell them that the rest of the Armies will scramble to safety, while we remain here, heroically dying to save their lives. Shall I bring up Thermopylae? The heroic fall of the 300? Do you propose I set myself up as a second Leonides?"

"Or," MacLeod mused, "you could tell them the truth."

Gavin's jaw set. "And what truth is that?"

"That this is no heroic rearguard action. This is murder, pure and simple. The Americans have demanded the Magician's network of spies and informers as part of their price for entering the war. And as they seek to turn a profit from his labor, they will simply destroy those they cannot bend to their purposes—just as they did Kitchener."

"Along with 736 other innocent souls," Gavin snorted. "So why should I complain about sixteen more who already crouch half-dead and doomed?"

MacLeod studied Gavin for a moment, and then looked down at the map. "The Magician is feared by those who seek to command his magic for he is the only one who can keep them from perverting it and bending it to their own uses. And so they seek to eliminate him by the same means David eliminated Uriah."

"At least, King David had the grace to warn the other soldiers to step out of the line of fire."

MacLeod conceded the point with a shrug. "So what will you do, now that you know the truth? Will you tell them or will you allow them to hope?"

"What choice do I have?"

MacLeod's teeth flashed in the thickening smoke. "Well, I suppose you could always pray for a miracle."

And then the heavens exploded in mockery before Gavin could so much as utter a word. A shell landed with a hollow *whoomph*, and MacLeod was borne aloft on its fireball. Gavin fell to his knees, rapt beneath the skyborne vision that hung illuminated like a saint ascending, before MacLeod was cast carelessly back to the earth, his broken embrace shielding Gavin from the shrapnel that rained everywhere.

So, in death MacLeod had saved Gavin when in life he could not. But what use was the scant extra minutes MacLeod's body gifted to him? What could they possibly matter? Still, life is stubborn and matter they did. Gavin clung to those last seconds with the force of a drowning man clinging to a spar—coming face to face with the truth that he did not want to die—at least not like this. No, not *for* this. Not for a cause he no longer understood. No longer believed in.

Covered in MacLeod's dying blood, Gavin faced the simple question: What debt was so great that it required this much blood money? What had Gavin sacrificed himself for? This strip of mud? The British Empire? A web of treaties signed long ago by men long dead? Why should he—*why should any man*—die for such a thing? For no death could be worth this futile battle over a scant hundred feet of soil—not his, and not the scores of other men whose lives he had willingly sacrificed in the name of the greater good.

But Death was upon him, inexorable and bitter. A dark horde poured forth from the mists of mustard gas that shrouded the battlefield, and Gavin's only, pitiful shelter was a blood-soaked corpse—as futile against the shells that bombarded them from the German emplacement as from the impossible vision that MacLeod's fall released. The Gabriel Hounds were in full cry, and the Tylwyth Teg, the fabled Wild Hunt, pounded in their wake, white chargers with red ears, their hooves striking sparks that shattered into precious stones as pale riders reached snake-like fingers to snatch up souls and bear them off to an unspeakable fate. Neither eternal rest, nor eternal punishment awaited, but eternal chasing after whatever banner might beckon—an endless futile search for purpose in a world that had long given up any claim to such a concept.

Gavin shut his eyes. This was the price of his hubris, and he had no right to protest. A debt was owed. A debt must be paid. So why did he cringe like the basest of raw recruits? He had been the one to set the price in the first place, congratulating himself on how easily his lies masqueraded as the truth. Why was he not willing to bear it now? Was there any truer justice than the eternal fate that beckoned him? He had sent men—no, troops … *necessary losses*—to their deaths, all over nothing more than a stupid fairytale he knew to be a lie. What more fitting sacrifice to the creatures that rained from the sky to feast on men's blood—swooping down from their galloping horses to lap it from the mud, dabbling their fingers to smear it on their faces, then noisily sucking their nails clean of it.

Blood whose coppery warmth was still all too real to him, even though what was left of his reason consoled him that none of this was happening—could ever possibly happen, and he had only to endure a few more moments of this fever dream before he, too, would sink beneath the blessed oblivion promised by the mud.

Yet still, he groveled and sobbed, pleading for one last chance from the creature that loomed over him, his face black and featureless as if he had been wearing a shroud—save for two burning blue eyes. Gwyn ap Nudd, chief of the Wild Ride, King of the Otherworld, Lord of the Tylwyth Teg, his crown a pair of ebony antlers, stretched out his hand for Gavin, as the baying of the Gabriel Hounds softened and drew so close that he could feel their chill breath as they converged to bear him off to Hell.

"A debt is owed," Gavin choked his own epitaph. "A debt will be paid."

The growls softened to a purr, and the muzzles of the Hounds nudged MacLeod's corpse aside, searching for the vulnerable flesh of Gavin's throat …only to draw back with a whimper and a shriek. Growling, they circled him in bewilderment, as if just the touch of MacLeod's flesh had blinded their senses. Stymied, they beat their retreat, their howling growing louder with every step until it swelled into a shout that echoed from trench to trench, from barbed wire to barbed wire. And swelled into a laugh. A great, contemptuous laugh at the folly of Gavin's plea. At the folly of everything that was happening on this wretched battlefield—especially at the folly of the unseen Frenchmen who urged the prudent course…

"RETREAT? HELL, WE JUST GOT HERE!"

The words boomed through the mortar fire, and the Wild Rade swept back, borne inexorably on its receding tide. The creature that loomed over Gavin was equally improbable—and not just because of the gas mask that had distended his face. Even slicked by mud and blood so that it was more a pelt than cloth, Gavin recognized the soldier's olive drab uniform well before the stars and stripes emerged from the fog. The lashed gaiters, tan knapsack with ammo pouches both front and back, a tin helmet strapped beneath his chin, and most of all the lethal looking black rifle could only ride beneath one banner. And as the unseen Frenchmen huddled behind the same rampart of words like honor, duty, and necessary losses that Gavin himself might have used, the American turned to the other Marines converging out of the fog behind them and let sing their battle cry.

"COME ON YOU SONS OF BITCHES! DO YOU WANT TO LIVE FOREVER?"

The cry swelled into a howl, as the Marines crouched, their jaws slavering, their eyes red with fire, the blood-slicked pelt of their uniforms straining to contain the coiled muscles, not of men, but of the *Teufelshunden* the Germans had already begun to call them. Hell-hounds. But the damnation they heralded was not to be Gavin's. He forced himself back to his hands and knees as they sprang past him, too numb to begin the long, slow crawl back to the safety of the foxhole. The *Teufelshunden* surged. The Germans screamed. And Gavin Fellowes lived, if not forever, at least to fight another day.

Chapter 18

THE MAVERICK WAS AS CLOSE to a battlefield as Gavin had seen since the War. Midsummer bonfires smoldered, thickening the gloaming with oily smoke. Forgotten pennons fluttered forlornly. Women in peasant skirts and brightly colored headscarves coaxed porridge to thicken on makeshift cookstoves. Men lay scattered on the ground, numbed by wine and stronger intoxicants. Now and then, an untended child touched one of their faces seeking to decide whether they still lived, just as the stretcher bearers had gleaned the mud for signs of life in the aftermath of the shelling.

Gavin could not have told you what he thought to accomplish here, any more than he could have told you how he had gotten here. All he knew was that the debt that he had thought to settle in the mud of Belleau Wood was about to be paid in full. And that the paws of the Gabriel Hounds padded behind him, cutting off all hope of retreat.

Out of nowhere, a makeshift band rattled out a serenade on pots and pans and tin whistles, and Gavin fell to the ground, certain that the mortars were whistling overhead once more. And when he managed to press himself back to his knees, he was no longer in Woodstock, but back behind the lines beyond Belleau Wood, in the relative safety of a disused chapel that had been converted to a field headquarters, one of a knot of worried intelligence officers who had gathered around the map that had betrayed them to the Americans.

"They want the Magician's networks. They are demanding it all. Names. Codes. Maps. Whatever else you can think of."

"Monstrous!"

"Impossible!"

"Perhaps. But what choice do we have? We cannot afford to alienate the Americans now."

"Do we forgive them everything, then? Do we forgive them even Kitchener?"

"The H.M.S. *Hampshire* was a tragedy, but we will have to leave it to God to call those responsible to account, not the Allies."

"Necessary losses."

"Kitchener himself would agree."

"What man would not consider it an honor to give his life for the greater good?"

Necessary losses. The greater good. Of course, they were right. The 737 souls lost on the H.M.S. *Hampshire* were a cheap ransom for the millions who had already died or were destined to die. But this … this was something more than necessary losses; these souls were Gavin's responsibility. And guilt choked him just as the sea must have choked the drowning men when they lost the will to keep their heads above the water.

With a hasty excuse, he stepped out into the ruined courtyard, where a canopy of stars twinkled in place of a roof. The chapel had been dedicated to a saint whose name had long since been erased from both the altar and the annals of history, but the chapel bell that had once summoned the monks to their prayers now tolled with the accusations of 737 souls who were past rescue now.

The ragged concert ended on a fierce clang of a cowbell, the mists of memory cleared, and Gavin was face to face with Duncan MacLeod once again—a continent and a lifetime away. Gavin's head whirled with questions, denials and accusations, but his lips could only frame four numb syllables.

"I saw you die."

"You know as well as I do that men see what they need to see." MacLeod reached out a hand and helped Gavin to his feet. He offered a slight bow, inviting Gavin to walk with him.

"I didn't just see. I ... felt ... I *tasted*...."

"Men see what they need to see," MacLeod repeated with a shrug. "And when they do not, I sometimes assist them."

"And who assists you? The talented Miss Ames?"

MacLeod raised an eyebrow, arguably as surprised by the abruptness of the question as Gavin himself. "I would suggest that is something you should ask Miss Ames."

"I have tried, but she seems disinclined to pursue the issue."

"Then perhaps you should follow her lead," MacLeod suggested with a faint smile. "Why look for a complex explanation when a simple one will do? They needed a dead body. I gave them one. All the rest is just ... dazzlepaint."

After a moment's hesitation, Gavin conceded the point. "Well I suppose it's more of an answer than *Reach hither thy finger, and behold my hands; and reach hither thy hand, and thrust it into my side?"*

"I make no claim to be a Savior," MacLeod said. "I make no claim to be anything other than what I am."

"Which is?"

MacLeod scrutinized Gavin with those uncanny blue eyes, before he said gently, "I think you know. Alas, knowing is not the same thing as believing, as I would suggest you have already discovered for yourself."

Or so Havel would have it. But Gavin was still not ready to concede the truth of that claim to any creature, regardless of whether he believed in him or not. "But *how?*" he repeated with all the stubbornness of a punch-drunk fighter.

"You, of all people, so bemused by this?" MacLeod asked with a laugh. "Fairy magic or mechanical marvels, what does it matter how the illusion was created?"

"The Magician was no illusion. You know that as well as I do."

"The Magician is at rest," MacLeod assured him. "And so he shall stay."

If only that were true. "It is already too late," Gavin said, with a shake of his head. "Word has gone around about his ... peculiar talents and now everyone seeks him—beginning with Havel."

MacLeod's face darkened. "Havel overreaches and will pay dearly for his temerity."

"Alas, that is, at best, faint reassurance. I care no more about Havel than any other man deluded by his own beliefs," Gavin said. "What I fear is what will happen if the Americans gain control of the Magician and all his tricks."

MacLeod raised an eyebrow. "Then why come to America?"

"The Americans may have once striven to murder the Magician, but they will be equally content to pay him—just as long as he is ready to do business with them."

"And why should he not do business with them?" MacLeod asked, pinning Gavin with his penetrating gaze. "Indeed, it could be argued that the Americans behaved more honorably than the Allies when it came to their entry into the war."

"They brought an end to the war, yes, and saved countless English lives," Gavin acknowledged the point. "But look at how they bargain with their own. Look at the deal they struck with the 146 seamstresses who burned to death because the owners of the factory locked them in to ensure every drop of productive blood they had paid for. Or the eight writers and newspaper editors hanged after the Haymarket Riots all for encouraging workers to strike for a living wage? Suffragists beaten and sprayed with hoses while chained to overhead pipes?" Gavin paused to draw a steadying breath before he added, "Or consider what unholy bargain the Adams family must have struck with the Fair Folk in order to blind themselves to the inconvenient fact that the fortune that allowed them to build their Brotherhood of Artists and frolic with the fairies was forged on weapons of war used to butcher the best and brightest of a generation? Because the Great War wasn't pointless to them—or to anyone else who profited by encouraging men to murder one another..."

He broke off speaking as he realized MacLeod was studying him. "Go on," MacLeod prompted.

"To what purpose? It is too late to right old wrongs. We are at peace. The war is over. No more men will die. We must take our victories where we find them."

"And you are satisfied that what we won is indeed a victory?" MacLeod asked. "Would you delude yourself that this was the war to end all wars?"

"Would you not?" Gavin asked. For in truth, what point was there to any of the sacrifice—the *necessary losses*—if not that? "What did we fight for, if not peace in our time?"

"And what if that is the biggest illusion of all?" MacLeod asked. "What if, already, the seeds of even greater catastrophes are quickening in the most fertile of soils."

The man's cool certainty gave Gavin pause. "You speak of the Russians?"

MacLeod's face softened. "The Russians are children—idealists, as pixie-led as those poor girls who danced in the moonlight because someone told them they were beautiful." He shook his head. "The best among them do believe the events of 1917 signaled the start of a Golden Age. The worst of them know that such a Brotherhood of Man is nothing but a fantasy, an idyll—and seek to bend that knowledge to their own purposes. If the innocents could only see that the result of their Glorious Revolution will bring about a regime whose brutalities will be crueler than the pogroms and starvation from which they fled."

"How can you propose to know that?" Gavin demanded. "Unless you would have me believe you've added soothsaying to your other … singular skills?"

MacLeod laughed. "For a hardened skeptic, you turn easily to supernatural explanations. It takes no magic, not even dazzlepaint, to see the inevitable outcome. The signs are already there for anyone who looks for them."

It was the reasonable explanation. So why did Gavin feel a superstitious dread that MacLeod's blue eyes could see worlds and times far beyond this one? God in heaven! He was falling for the same simple spiritualists' tricks that fooled credulous shop girls. How did this man manage to rattle him so badly?"

"Do you accuse Havel of working for the Communists, then?" he asked with a sigh. "Is that what I should fear? Is that the truth behind this entire sorry episode? Has Havel corrupted the Bloomer Girls in service of his misguided beliefs?"

"Havel matters not." MacLeod dismissed the idea and the man with a wave of his hand. "It is other men, ones like him, you should fear. Men who truly do believe in magic and seek to command it. Men who have embarked on completing Kitchener's mission to find the frozen stronghold of the Grail Court in Ultima Thule, in order to bend its powers to their own. Already they are gathering in Vienna and Berlin, with no lesser purpose than to use magical means to revenge the wrongs wrought on them by the Great War. And they will succeed—and the resultant war will be by far the greater and more terrifying of the two, because this time, it will be fought by true believers instead of skeptics."

Gavin fought down the dread that surged at the utter certainty in MacLeod's voice. "In short, we are to quake against a rag-tag consortium of those who believe in magic?"

"It is not their magic or even their beliefs that you should quake against," MacLeod said. "For Havel and his kind steadfastly believe in the Fair Folk of Ultima Thule, the Seelie Court, and seek to draw them to their aid, just as

Kitchener did. But there are in fact two Courts of the Fair Folk they should supplicate, and they ignore one at their own risk—for the Unseelie Court possesses equally deep magicks as those of their brethren in Thule. Light needs darkness, just as yin needs yang. But the pride of men like Havel blinds them to the beauty and power of anything not created in their image, and if they see the Unseelie Court at all, it is only to bend it to the will of their betters— to enslave it to their own purposes, just as your American businessmen strive to grind beneath their heels the gypsies, Jews, and communists that oppose them." He frowned and looked off into the distance before dragging his gaze back to Gavin. "I give you my word, that is the gravest mistake they can make. Better by far for all of us if they understood that what you grind beneath your heel becomes dust, and dust is the most powerful source of all. From dust you came, and to dust you will return."

Gavin knew it was an effect of the opium smoke swirling across the open field that played upon his tired shock, but suddenly MacLeod seemed to shimmer, as if he were about to dissolve back into the mists of memory— even as his voice seemed to grow loud enough to echo off the surrounding peaks.

"I will stand for the dust. I will stand champion for the dust of the Unseelie against Havel and his kind. You have my word, the blood oath of the MacLeods, Havel will not have the one he seeks. The girl will be returned to you by morning. But that is as much as I can do. The rest is up to you."

Gavin blinked—suddenly uncertain whether he had suddenly just been invited to join a conspiracy to commit murder. "The rest of what? What matters? What do I need do?"

But already the darkness had closed in and MacLeod was nearly invisible. "You will do the right thing. And you will know how when the moment arises."

"A typical spiritualist's answer," he huffed as a surge of anger ripped through him, unlike any since blind fury had driven him from the safety of false ciphers and code books behind the lines in Brittany straight to the front lines of Belleau Wood to witness the chaos the War Office steadfastly refused to admit the Magician had unleashed on the world. "You offer hints and innuendos, seeming to say everything by saying absolutely nothing at all— all designed to prey on the subject's guilty conscience, nothing more."

"Then perhaps the best defense would be to lay one's guilty conscience to rest."

As if Gavin ever could. Necessary losses—a comforting word. But comfort required the one gift Gavin had squandered in the mud of Belleau Wood: Belief.

"I need facts, not words," he said. "If you would charge me with a task, then do so, but pray be specific. For you well know that you have saved my life, and I am under an obligation to you."

MacLeod's teeth flashed in the gathering gloom, just as they had when he suggested Gavin pray for a miracle. "I will charge you with nothing, for the debt that was owed was paid. But now a new debt must be paid."

"And how do you propose to do that?" Gavin said.

"Once again, they need a dead body. And once again, I will give them one. Havel will trouble you no longer. As for the rest, it is up to you." MacLeod's voice drifted from somewhere distant. "But I will beg from you one parting boon—given not out of obligation but of your own free will. Whether you decide to seek justice for the Magician or allow him to rest in peace, I bid you on your honor watch over the waif that calls herself Gipsy Sarah."

Beyond Ker-Ys

DAWN FILTERED DOWN through the sea, softening its inky depths to pale green, and Essie blinked back into the surf that threw her carelessly against the strand, stinging her scraped skin with saltwater and even saltier tears. But as the rising sun warmed the waves, the tossing grew gentler, as if she were being borne toward the surface on the backs of playful underwater creatures. One final nudge, and she was lofted back across the pulsing shoulders of the fire-breathing horse that skimmed across the waves toward a distant city on a distant shore.

Its hooves pounded.

A bell tolled.

A creature cried out.

A waterspout gushed forth. And once more Essie cowered on the wet sand between the Seelie Prince and the sorcerer.

"The sun is rising," the sorcerer said. "And I have returned to meet your challenge. Are you still so certain you wish to meet mine?"

"If I were not, would I be here?" the Seelie Prince said with a fierce grin that exposed pointed teeth. "And you will be the sorrier for it. You have my word, and well you know the Fair Folk cannot lie."

"Folly! You know as well as I do, it is you who will be destroyed." The sorcerer cast a long look at the city that shimmered faintly in the distance. "Or is this a trap? Are you fool enough to hope that this time a champion will ride forth in the Name of the Fair Folk to defend you. To risk their own souls for the very creature who brought about their doom."

"I hope for no champion," the Seelie Prince said. "I will stand for myself."

"But… *why?* Why must you persist in this folly? I propose no vile slavery but rather comfort and pleasure. The terms of the Protocols are not onerous. I pledge you riches, power, glory—all this world has to offer—if only you will serve me. And I will spare the girl's life as guaranty that this is no empty promise."

"The girl's life is not yours to spare, but rather mine to ransom," the Seelie Prince said. "I failed the one girl. I will not fail her friend. I freely accept the alternative as a willing sacrifice."

"Sacrifice for whom? A fallen girl no one cares about?"

"Not fallen," the Seelie Prince said. "Unfallen. Neither of heaven or hell, but of the Middle Kingdom, this earth. As is my kind. Like for like. The exchange is allowed. I claim my right to stand in her place."

The sorcerer stared at him another incredulous moment, and then he shook his head. "Very well then. Choke on your own spite and die. But let us go through the motions according to the ancient formula."

"The deal is struck," the Seelie Prince agreed with a curt nod. "The compact has been sealed."

The sorcerer fell to his knees on the sand and raised his hands to the sky. "The Seelie Prince suffers in exile betraying the Fair Folk—all because he suffered himself to be named. Is there not one champion who will step forward and defend his True Name—and with it the Good Name of all the Fair Folk—in a trial by combat in front of the eyes of heaven, hell, and the worlds in between?"

His words rang off into a silence, interrupted only by the wash of the surf. And the sorcerer laughed.

"No miraculous champion rises to save you. Will you give up this madness now?"

"The compact specifies three cries," the Seelie Prince said.

The sorcerer flung his hands to the sky in exasperation. "Very well, then! I issue the challenge for the second time. Will no one ride forth to save this creature from his folly?"

Once again, the only answer was only the pounding sea.

"This is the third and final cry!" the sorcerer warned. "Will no champion step forth to defend the honor of the Fair Folk? Will no one ride to the aid of their fallen Prince?"

Tap. Tap. Tap.

The answer rang through air, silencing even the wash of the waves.

Tap. Tap. Tap.

The sound took form: One of the buskers from the Maverick, dressed as a gypsy, one eye covered with a patch, her arms akimbo as she contemplated the sorcerer.

"What is this? Some last desperate trick?" he demanded of the Seelie Prince. "You seek to spin a champion out of thin air as you spin fairy food out of acorns? You will not succeed. You *cannot* succeed."

But from the look on the Seelie Prince's face, he was as stunned as the sorcerer. "This is no trick of mine."

"Then what does this mean? Would you have me believe the Seelie Court has at last relented and the Faerie Rade rides to ransom back their lost prince?"

"Look not to the Seelie Court for a champion." The busker laughed, as she swaggered forward, her bootheels ringing impossibly against the sand. "Look not for rescue from those long since scattered by your folly across the Northern Sea. No. Look to me!"

Tap. Tap. Tap. The other foot joined in. The rhythm grew more complicated, and the busker threw her hands skyward as she stopped walking and began to spin, boots and bangles rattling. The sand began to whirl around her, consuming her, until she was nothing but a voice. "Look to the earth and beneath it the molten lava of her core. Look to that which you deem worthless and grind beneath your feet. For I am no creature of the water. I am a creature of salt and dust and heat. I am the sandstorm of the desert. I am the whirlwind that swept up Elijah. I am the fate of Gomorrah!"

Sound and sand swelled into a maelstrom that towered above them, no longer a gypsy, no longer a girl—its only features a ram's horn, a spear, and two iron eyes, one cold and dark, one molten with fire, that shone out from beneath the spinning sand.

"And I accept your challenge," the whirlwind roared. "I will champion the Seelie Prince."

"Who are you?" the sorcerer demanded. "By whose authority do you dare this challenge?"

"By my own authority and none other. And as for my names, I have many. The Egyptians lost in exile call me Black Sarah. The learned of Prague call me Dybbuk and Ibbur. The wanderers of the desert call me Sedeem, Shehireem, Mazikeen. Many call me Djinn. And those who dare, call me by my True Name. For behold, I am Azazel."

The sorcerer paled and a grim smile seemed to fleet across what passed for the sandstorm's face.

"Ah, yes, you recognize that name," the whirlwind snarled. "You have summoned the most powerful of the Sons of Gods. It was I who gifted men with the art of warfare, of making swords, knives, shields, and coats of mail. And it was I who taught women the art of illusion, the magic of ornamenting the body, dyeing the hair, and painting the face and eyebrows—the only way to elude the blind faith heaven demands. And what did I ask of the faithful in return for this gift of their freedom? Not love. Not reverence. Not obedience. Simply the offering of a single goat each year as a mark of their respect." The sandstorm whirled and whistled into a fury. "Respect! How long has it been since you have paid your sacrifice to me for the arts you dare claim? The faithful do not neglect the scapegoat for Azazel."

The sorcerer shrank back. "I meant no disrespect. You will have your sacrifice!"

"I will have my sacrifice, and I claim it now," the whirlwind roared. "I claim the Seelie Prince as my own."

The sandstorm's voice echoed along the strand. And when it finally died away, the Seelie Prince finally found the voice to break his amazed silence. "You are of the Unseelie Court," he said wonderingly. "A knight of Ker-Ys, the stronghold I betrayed in my pride, and yet you rise to my aid when my fellows would not?"

"Are not the Unseelie as jealous of the honor of the Fair Folk as their Seelie brethren?" the whirlwind demanded. "Cannot an Unseelie search for the way to restore our lost honor? Cannot an Unseelie find Ker-Ys—and all the other cities that were lost?"

A smile formed on the Seelie Prince's lips as he gazed upon those two eyes, one burning bright, one cold as winter. "Cannot the Unseelie give an eye for a single glimpse into fairy land?" he asked softly.

"The Seelie Court would send no champion to fight for your honor, for there is no honor left to them as they wander in exile on the Northern Sea. But the Unseelie Court stands ready to defend the honor of the Fair Folk. A fairy prince was captured. A fairy prince will be reclaimed. I stand champion for his ransom. And if I win, I claim that ransom in the name of the Fair Folk. Will you have me as your champion?"

"You promised to stand with me, and I was a fool to not see the truth. I was a fool to doubt you." The Seelie Prince knelt and bowed his head. "Valiant and true fairy knight, I accept with gratitude your gift. And in return the Seelie Court will bend the knee. A debt is owed. A debt will be repaid. For the honor of the Fair Folk."

"A debt will be repaid. The Seelie Court will bend the knee," the storm cried before it turned its sole burning eye back on the terrified sorcerer.

"So, come now!" the storm cried. "Stand and battle with that which your arrogance has summoned and win the Seelie Prince's soul—if you can!"

The storm drove its spear into the earth and flame shot from its tip. Then it raised its ram's horn to its lips and the world exploded into sound. The sea waters raced backwards to the horizon—fleeing the golden sand that shimmered in every direction. The glittering desert heaved, and from its depths the spires of Ker-Ys rose, its bronze walls and golden domes no longer watery and coral-encrusted, but flaming with the heat of the sun.

"The Unseelie Court champions the cause of the Fair Folk!" the whirlwind cried. "Look to Ker-Ys. Look to the citadel of the shivering sands. Look to the lost city that has now been found!" Another strike of the staff, another jut of flame. "Look to the cities buried beneath the shifting sands. Look to Timbuktu, the City of 333 Saints, whose real gold was not that which its greedy conquerors sought, but rather the learning contained in its manuscripts, shrines, and the sacred mosque whose door Men dare not throw open until the End of Days." Another strike. "Look to the libraries of Alexandria and Avicenna, of Banu Ammar, of Antioch and the Serapeum, burned to ash by the brightness of the truths they contained.

"Look to Petra and Palmyra, the Bride of the Desert. Look to the Temple of Solomon with its copper pillars, Boaz and Jachin. Look to the mighty ziggurats of Ur. Look to stern Nineveh with its lion gates. Look to Troy. Look to the Ishtar Gate, the eighth gate that guarded the heart of Babylon.

"Look to Meroe, the ancient capital of the Kingdom of Kush. Look to Saba, the sacred city of Bilqis, the Queen of Sheba, who conquered Solomon with a single smile. Look to Gonur Tepe in the Kara Kum, a sacred labyrinth the size of a city. Look to the Lost City of the Kalahari, built by ancients long before the flood of which an abandoned boat drifting on the sands is the only sign that remains.

"Above all, look to the Gobi, first desert, first sea, whose wondrous island was the stronghold of the last remnant of the race that preceded ours. For does not the *Book of Dzyan* tell us that long before the Biblical Adam and Eve, the Gobi was a huge land inhabited by the Sons of God, who gave up everything for the daughters of man? And if sometimes the sands of the desert shift to reveal marvels that men have only dreamed of, not a native dare touch them for they know to respect the might of the spells woven by Azazel to protect those he loves."

As the whirlwind named them, the fabled cities rose glittering from the sand, and on the walls of each, heralds appeared, lifting ram's horns and conch shells and ivory tusks and golden trumpets to blow upon them, echoing from wall to wall the honor of Azazel, First Champion and Savior of the Fae. And as the bronze gates were thrown open, one after another, the Unseelie Host spilled forth.

Chapter 19

DAY BROKE IN A WILD FLASH, followed by a massive thunderclap that shattered the sky in a shower of midsummer hail. And then, once the torrent of rain and hail subsided, the ground beneath Ker-Ys bathing pool rumbled as if in answer to the storm that had raged from above.

Kate cast a quick glance at Essie's inert form before pulling on the abandoned pair of mud boots, and hurrying out to join the maids, farmhands, and artists assembling to contemplate the storm's aftermath. The lawn sparkled with melting hailstones as if diamonds had rained down from the skies while branches lay scattered about like leafy cudgels from a pitched battle between invisible combatants. The most obvious casualty, however, was the bathing pool which had suffered another rockfall.

Melisandre and Ned swept down from the Great House to survey the damage, but when she caught sight of Kate, she paled and moaned, "Oh, Kate. How could you?"

How could she *what?* Surely even Melisandre would not propose to accuse Kate of causing this? But before Kate could protest, she became aware of soft footsteps trailing her across the grass. She turned to find Essie standing barefoot behind her, blinking against the daylight as if she had just been roused from a peaceful night's slumber.

"Essie?" Kate gasped. "Are you awake? Can you hear me? Can you see me?" She waved her hand in front of Essie's wide-eyed face.

"But *why* Kate?" Melisandre cut her off accusingly. "Why didn't you summon me the moment she awakened?"

Well, for one because Kate had not been aware Essie was awake, and two, because Kate felt herself under no obligation to Melisandre, especially given the hissed conversation they were both pretending she had never heard. But before the angry retorts reached Kate's lips, Essie's eyes lit on Melisandre, and her face set with fear and fury. She pointed in accusation. "You said it was all pretend!" she cried. "You said it was make-believe! That he could do us no harm and that all he wanted was someone to dance with. You never said it was *real!*"

Reactions ricocheted among those gathered. A boy was sent to fetch Miss Smith. Another sent to take the news up the hill to Mrs. Adams. Kate asked the nearest girl to fetch a blanket as she did what she could to cover Essie's flimsy nightdress with her own wrap, and all the while Melisandre continued her tirade in a furious obligato over the concerned shouts and tramping boots.

"Now, see what you've done, Kitty! The girl may have recovered her senses, but she has clearly lost her wits. This is all your fault. I blame you and no one else. Well, you have made your bed and so must lie in it." She threw her hands in the air dramatically. "I wash my hands of the entire affair and leave to you to clean up the mess you've created. Come, Ned! We have no part to play here."

But Essie was having none of it and hurried forward to block Melisandre's retreat. "There is nothing wrong with my wits," she said with a bold glare. "It was just supposed to be dancing, that's what you said. You said he were just a harmless old man what liked to play with the fairies, and what harm could there be in pretending. You didn't say nothing about no sea strands trapped beneath the pool, nor fairy princes riding fire-breathing horses, nor no sorcerer ready to do battle with dust storms wielding spears of fire and battle horns—"

"The girl is completely delusional!" Melisandre scoffed. "Just listen to her. A fairy prince? A fire-breathing horse? Spears and battle horns?"

"No delusion that!" Ned overrode her, his face alight. "But rather a vouchsafed vision of no one less than the genius loci—the very guardian spirit that called me to build my brotherhood of artists on this hallowed ground." He stepped toward Essie as if to envelop her in his arms. "Oh, my dear child, you must tell us exactly what you saw!"

Essie's jaw set, and she crossed her arms across her chest. "I saw a lot of things. And most of them I don't want to see again."

Ned dropped his arms to hang limp at his sides. "But you must. He has chosen you."

"Then, whoever he is, he can darned well unchoose me," Essie snapped. "I'm not staying here another minute!"

"I think you're quite wise," Kate agreed. "The doctor will advise you on recuperation, but I'm certain he would agree that it cannot be healthy for you to remain out here without shoes or socks. We must get you back to your friends at the Overlook Hotel as soon as possible. Perhaps we should gather your things while we wait for a carriage—"

"Impossible!" Ned countermanded Kate with a stubborn shake of his head. "The child has danced upon the waves. She must tell us exactly what she saw while the vision is fresh."

Essie pointed an accusing finger at Ned. "I'm not telling no one nothing—excepting that I'm not going back to that place. Not with you nor no one else. And you can't make me."

Ned's face set with equal obstinacy, but before he could say anything, Melisandre forestalled him. "Of course, no one is going to force you to do anything you don't wish to do, least of all repeating what can only have been a shocking, dreadful experience," she assured Essie. "Our only concern now is to return you to the safety of your friends…"

"*Safety!*" Essie spat. "What do you know about safety? Weren't you the one what told me Gipsy Sarah was mistaken? That what happened to Judith was just an accident so it couldn't happen to me?"

"And it didn't, now did it?" Melisandre purred. "Here you are safe and sound."

"No thanks to you," Essie favored Melisandre with the full force of her accusing, tear-stained gaze. "I went to you direct. I told you I'd have no more of it. I tried to give you back your money. You were the one what refused it. But *why?* I didn't want no part in your charade, and I would never have told!"

Just as the clap of thunder had broken the walls of the bathing pool, so did Ned Adams' world crumble around him. The rapture in his face gave way to childlike disbelief, as if he were watching a magnificent sandcastle being swept away by a rogue wave.

"Told what?" he asked Essie, his voice suddenly high and tight. "What did they give you money for? What did *she* give you money for?"

Essie focused her wrath on Ned. "Gipsy Sarah warned me. And Gipsy Sarah was right. She told me what happened to Judith was no accident." Essie flung her arm out toward Melisandre. "But *she* told me to keep the money, even when I tried to give it back. *She* said it was only pretend. She said it was art. Just like she promised all the others. She said that one day, we'd all be as famous as Lisa Gherardini, the one what posed for the Mona Lisa. She rolled the Italian off her tongue easy as pie and told us we'd be just like her, just like *La Gioconda*. The Smiling One, she said. As if it was our smiles she cared about," she spat.

An angry flush burned on Ned's cheeks as he turned to Melisandre. "What money? Why did you give her money?"

"I'm sure I don't know!" Melisandre gasped.

Essie shook her head in disgust, and Kate shut her eyes as the last vestige of hope that she had misconstrued the conversation between Melisandre and Stanton vanished. But while she could believe Hollis Stanton capable of anything, was she ready to accept that Melisandre had gone so far as to kill a girl?

"The girl is obviously disturbed!" Melisandre cried out. "She should be attended to by a doctor, not made a spectacle of in the middle of the lawn."

But her defense came far too late. Ned's childish rage was no more controllable that his enthusiasms. He clutched Melisandre's arm. "I asked you what money, and I will have an answer! Did you pay this girl to dance with the fairies?"

"How dare you question me!" Melisandre yanked her arm away in a desperate last defense, but defeat already underlay her anger. "How dare you speak to me like that? Was I not the first Fairy Bride? Was it not I who summoned the genius loci from his retreat beneath the water in the beginning?"

Ned shook his head in confusion. "No! It was never you." He whirled on Kate. "It was *you!*" Or were you just pretending, too? Is that why you're here? Is she paying you? Paying you for your scribbling and trances! Paying you to lie—"

Kate straightened her shoulders. "I can assure you—"

"I believed in you. I never believed in *her*, but I always believed in you." Ned's face was a mask of disappointment. "And now am I to believe you're no different than all the others. All the others I had to send away."

Send away? Kate froze in horror as an even more appalling possibility reared its ugly head. Could it be possible that Kate was mistaken in blaming Judith's death on Melisandre and Stanton? Was it not far more likely that their schemes had distracted her from another, darker truth? For when you thought about it rationally, which was more difficult to believe? That Melisandre and Stanton had been driven to violence when a powerless Bloomer Girl threatened their machinations? Or that they were only doing what they could to cover up the grim truth of how Ned Adams "sent a girl away" when she was no longer of use to him?

Enough. No matter which way Kate's imagination raced, there was little she could do—other than to see Essie back to the relative safety of her friends. "I cannot speak for Melisandre, but I assure you that Essie and I have no desire to trouble you any further," she told Ned with a calm she did not feel. "So, I suggest we gather our belongings immediately..."

"No! It is too late for that!" With the swiftness of a thwarted toddler, Ned stooped and snatched a mattock from one of the farm hands who'd thought it might be useful for clearing storm debris. "There is only one answer left now…"

Kate froze in real fear. This could not be happening. Ned Adams was nothing but a petulant, overgrown child—wasn't he? But what might this man-child be capable of when he tossed aside a toy that no longer pleased him?

No, surely not in front of a dozen witnesses.

"Mr. Adams, please, there is no need for violence."

Ned ran toward the pool and down stumbled down it's crumbling sides, sending broken masonry scattering in every direction, as he launched his fury on the stones.

"The gates must be smashed open!" he cried. "The floodwaters must be loosened, and Ker-Ys must sink beneath the waves once more."

He threw himself against what remained of the carved face, smashing the mattock against it rhythmically, blindly, as the knot of appalled on-lookers watched.

"Should we try to stop him?" a workman asked.

"He might do himself a harm," a gardner agreed.

But no one in the shuffling knot of people moved.

"Better do himself a harm than do it to someone else," someone else said.

"Might be some kind of fit," a woman chimed in. "Shouldn't disturb him then. Like a sleepwalker."

Their uncertain congress was broken by the rumble of an automobile, and the group scattered to greet it in obvious relief.

"Mrs. Adams!"

"Mrs. Adams will manage this!"

"Mrs. Adams will know what to do."

The knot of onlookers converged gratefully on Mrs. Adams, handing her down from the automobile like a queen, and bearing her off to manage her husband's mania. But Melisandre hung back, waiting for Hollis Stanton, and Kate slowed her pace to stay within earshot—this time eavesdropping quite deliberately.

"What are you still doing here?" Stanton snapped. "I would have hoped you had the common sense to seize the opportunity to remove yourself from Ker-Ys without troubling us any further."

"In other words, you seek to send me packing like a maid who failed to please?" Melisandre asked with a toss of her head. "I think I'd prefer to let Ned be the judge of that…"

"I think you should prefer to accept the family's generosity in not pressing charges," Stanton snapped.

"I think there are many others who would prefer charges not be pressed besides you."

Stanton's face hardened, and his voice softened with menace. "Be that as it may, you should be very, very careful before you threaten such people. You may well have succeeded in fascinating my uncle, but the playacting is over, and it would be dangerous indeed to attempt to exert your paltry powers over men who would crush you beneath their boot heels without a second thought."

It made no difference how sternly Kate reminded herself that Melisandre was merely reaping what she had sown, she was still consumed by weary pity for her. For Mellie fancied herself ruthless and clever, when in fact her only asset beyond her startling beauty was a feral cunning. And neither beauty nor cunning would be enough to challenge the likes of the Adamses when they were determined to protect their own. That had been a lesson Kate had absorbed instinctively years ago, as she quietly answered the clerics' and teachers' questions about her unseemly drawings. But Mellie was still as childish as Ned Adams in her own way, a faux-naif who reveled in her serene confidence that no one could be crueler than she—completely failing to understand that the surgical precision with which Jean Storrs Adams would eliminate any threat to those she loved would be far deadlier than either Ned Adams' rage or even his nephew's bluster.

Before washing her hands of the whole affair, Kate made one last attempt to intervene. In her best imitation of his aunt's cool command, she stepped toward Mr. Stanton. "Excuse me, but I believe the most discreet way to bring a quiet end to this unpleasantness is for you drive Essie back to her friends. Now." And before he could protest, she turned to Mellie. "And Melisandre, I suggest you consider a brief absence from a situation that causes you so much … psychic perturbation."

Melisandre's beautiful features twisted with ugly indecision, and Kate savored an all-too-brief hope that Melisandre might be persuaded to see reason at last. But a shriek of stone upon stone rent the air, and the moment was lost. Ned had succeeded in his mad quest; the bathing pool was destroyed. By the time they reached it, breathless and panting, there was nothing left beyond a sullen slide of rubble and a foaming rush of muddy water that spilled unchecked through the broken dam.

His mania dissipated; Ned tossed his mattock into the remains of the pool in a wordless epitaph. But instead of being carried off by the rushing water, it landed with a sickening squish on an obstacle that lay just beneath the muddy surface. All watched in horror as the waters receded and a bloated leviathan rose from the mud, its gaudily striped trousers still recognizable as belonging to Josep Havel.

"Oh, Ned," Jean Adams moaned softly. "What have you done?"

"Enough. I will handle matters from here!" Stanton's voice rose above the hubbub that erupted. "We will summon the appropriate authorities, of course, but I will not have my family subjected to vulgar curiosity. Aunt Jean, you and Uncle Ned must return to Meads' Mountain House at once. I will see that Miss Ames and her charge follow as quickly as they can."

He turned back to Melisandre, with a triumphant smile. "And as for you, I would strongly suggest that you would be gone before the authorities arrive, unless you want to find yourself answering some very uncomfortable questions about what misguided conspiracy between you and the unfortunate Mr. Havel might have led to his tragic demise."

Chapter 20

GAVIN CROSSED THE MAVERICK with the same numb disbelief that he and his fellow survivors had lurched among the remains of their American saviors at Belleau Wood, incapable of comprehending the simple fact that they were alive while so many others were dead. At last he found himself outside a shack, half dug into the earth, that reminded him achingly of the trenches. But when he slipped inside, instead of the endless, sucking mud that washed both flesh and spirit into a dull grey, he found a vivid girl with a scarlet patch over one eye, her gaily patterned pants tucked into riding boots, a scarf embroidered with spangles and mirrors tied around her head.

"You're Gipsy Sarah," he said. It was not a question.

"I am many things," she said with a toss of her head. "Most of which are beyond your imagination. But Gipsy Sarah will do for our present purposes."

"Which are?"

"I think you know."

It was no more of a response than the cards dealt out by the mechanical fortune-tellers in glass booths you could find on Coney Island, so it was disconcerting for Gavin's stomach to clench with a foreboding and sickening dread. "I am here to fulfill my obligation to MacLeod," he said steadily. "His last wish was for me to take care of you."

She threw back her head and laughed, a gold tooth glinting between painted red lips. "More like he's the one that needed taking care of."

"Needed? Does that mean he is gone—for good this time?"

"His work here is finished. He has done what he needed to do. The rest is his legacy to you." Silver bangles jingled as she threw an arm toward the only one of MacLeod's creations that remained, a magic lantern that gleamed dully on the plain wooden workbench, flanked by a rack of hand-painted slides. "As is this."

"What sort of legacy is that?" Gavin asked. "I am no child who plays with toys."

"That remains to be seen," she said with another laugh. She pulled three slides out of the rack and laid them side by side in the simplest tarot spread: past, present, future. "Perhaps the answer lies in here."

"Do you propose to tell my fortune then?"

"Men tell their own fortunes," Gipsy Sarah said. "If only they have the courage to turn out the cards."

If only he had the courage. But what if he had no more courage left? What if his greatest desire was to do exactly what Jean Storrs Adams did, and cocoon himself in his own ignorance in a place like Mead's Mountain House, a refuge that was "not exclusive, but endeavoring to guard against uncongenial introductions"? Had he not suffered enough *uncongenial introductions* already to justify such a retreat? The silent answer gleamed from Gipsy Sarah's gimlet eye.

And Gavin selected the first plate from the spread and slid it into the projector.

The image that emerged was familiar from every newsreel scrolled out in every theatre across America. A stout man in military uniform, an equally stout woman in a broad-brimmed hat, both entering an open top car. A crazed assassin shooting at point blank range. The man collapsing from a shot to the jugular, shouting to the woman, "Sophie, Sophie! Live for our children!"

It was not to be. They died together, the stout man muttering the most fitting epitaph for all the Magician's machinations, "It is nothing."

Nothing it was. And nothing it should be. What was past was past, and so it should remain nothing but a grim chronicle that Gavin would prefer to forget. Gambit against gambit, move versus counter move on the chessboard that was America's entry in the Great War. False hopes engendered by the Angels of Mons and the martial music of George M. Cohan. A score of provocations, the sinking of the Lusitania only first among them. The atrocities in Belgium. The threat of unrestricted submarine warfare— long before the Zimmerman telegram…

The ugly pictures raced across Gavin's memory as surely as if they were cranked out by the jerky hurdy gurdy of MacLeod's machine. An implacable tale of hidden puppet masters who had pulled the strings while the good and the bad, the golden and the ordinary, the English and Huns, had died—all for one fell purpose: To enrich the coffers of the men whose entire profit lay in prolonging the carnage— the dealers in arms, steel, oil, and transport.

"No more!" Gavin snapped, pushing himself away from the machine.

Gipsy Sarah's only response was to push the second slide toward him. Gavin had known the truth of this tale as well, of course, and the knowing had shocked and horrified him, but seeing the plan on paper, a matter of map coordinates and shipping lanes was nothing compared to witnessing the terror unfold through the rapid succession of slides. A ship slipping across the fog-shrouded North Sea, risking all on desperate mission to Russia to bring an end to the war that had already cost England so dearly. Or, as other, more desperate rumors had it, a vessel bearing none other than Arthur himself returned in the form of Lord Kitchener, on a mission to return to the reaches of Ultima Thule and sound the trumpet that would raise the slumbering Grail Knights to his cause.

But beneath the waves, a U-Boat slid in its wake, a silent predator. A lantern signal broke briefly through the darkness. And the Russian envoy—who was in fact no envoy at all, but Josep Havel, bundled in an astrakhan coat—climbed out of the lifeboat he had stolen to the safety of a waiting launch.

Then came the hell—the more fearful for the silence of its approach. Indeed, the sea seemed to settle, the fog seemed to clear, and a brilliant shaft of moonlight casts its peace upon the waters...

A spray. A sudden rise, as if the ship were reaching for the heavens, imploring their mercy.

Next followed the desperate discipline of seamen of every nation. The bow was righted. All hands swarmed on deck. The lifeboats deployed—and lowered into the churning waters.

The keel cracked. The mast fell.

And then the screams of drowning men.

"The Magician's secrets." Sickened, Gavin looked up at Gipsy Sarah. "Why did MacLeod not take them with him?"

"They were not his to take."

Gavin's jaw set. "Then they should be destroyed."

"And so they will be. You have only to give the word," she said. "But that is your decision to make and no one else's."

Once more, Gavin hesitated, once more envying Jean Storrs Adams' capacity not to see what she simply cared not to see.

"Why me?" Gavin asked, knowing the question to be rhetorical at best, meaningless, in truth.

"MacLeod did not share his reasons," Gipsy Sarah said. "Only his purpose. And his purpose was for you to bear witness to the truth that lies beneath those slides."

"How can I bear witness to something I have never seen?"

"Something you have never seen?" she asked. "Or something you still do not wish to see?"

She pushed the last plate toward him, and shamed, Gavin turned back to the magic lantern and slid it into place, already knowing the impossibilities he was about to witness. But knowing did nothing to abate his terror as he found himself back in the cold, dark sea, the cries of drowning men growing fainter and hopeless with every wash of the waves, until even the crash of the surf on the distant shore died away into a forgotten echo. And even now, here in the safety of another land altogether, beneath Gipsy Sarah's mocking gaze, there was much of Gavin that wished to simply sink beneath the waves and allow himself to be subsumed into the blessed peace of oblivion.

But even as he sought to yield, a faint glow appeared on the horizon. And the crash of the surf turned into the pounding hooves of a black horse that skimmed the waves, breathing fire from its nostrils.

Of course, the light was naught but *ignis fatuus*, St. Elmo's fire. But as it crackled across the waves, strange and terrible shapes emerged. Barges with black sails, each one a floating bier for a knight in sea-stained armor, who lay amidships his skeletal fingers folded over his salt-stained sword. One by one, they hove into view, drifting toward the maelstrom beneath which the H.M.S. *Hampshire* had vanished—where they too were drawn beneath waves…

Only to erupt into light and noise—as silent waves swelled first into sea foam, and then into white horses with red ears and red eyes, who bore their ghostly riders skyward, their hooves scattering precious stones wherever they struck the clouds.

Gavin spun away from the magic lantern in dismay. "It is a lie!" he said hoarsely. "Kitchener never tried to raise the Grail Knights. Kitchener never believed in the power of the *Protocols* any more than I … *anyone* did. The book was a forgery, a hoax—nothing but another meaningless fairytale like the Angels of Mons, meant to bolster Russia's flagging spirits and strike fear in the hearts of the Americans. It was the Germans that destroyed Lord Kitchener, not some Faerie Rade."

Gipsy Sarah eyed him narrowly. "The Germans?" she asked. "Or the Magician, who in his hubris as a master of lies, released a force far too powerful to control, a real and ancient magick that the world has fled for the safety of their dying God, or for the even more elusive refuge of science and reason?"

"I do not believe in fairies!"

"I think the more important question is whether they believe in you," Gipsy Sarah said with a laugh. "But peace. I was not speaking of them. Yes, the Sons of Heaven gifted the Daughters of Man with the ancient arts of illusion, just as they gifted their brothers with the art of weapons and war. But such gifts go far beyond rouging and kohl. Much more dangerous are illusions like patriotism, or pride, or honor, which unleash in their wake the true force of the Wild Ride. For what more terrifying weapon can there be than those who cling to no banner, and yet gather to any banner that dares lay claim to ride at their head? The rule of the Mob. Chaos unleashed. Profit unlimited. And what man more powerful than the one who commands it?"

"Even if it is true that such a power in fact exists, how would you suggest it is commanded?" Gavin countered. "Surely not by painting illusion upon illusion—whether you name them magic or science or religion or art or even civilization?"

Gipsy Sarah met Gavin's gaze with the full force of her single eye. "I think you know the answer to that question."

"Then I'd say you significantly overestimate me," Gavin snorted. He turned for the door. "I came here to fulfill an obligation to Duncan MacLeod. Not to listen to his fairytales, no matter how cunning his illusions."

He made to go, but she planted herself in the way, arms akimbo. "Duncan MacLeod did not underestimate you, when he placed you under that obligation," she said. "Instead, he trusted you, and sacrificed himself so that the truth could at last come out."

"Whose truth?" Gavin shook his head. "The Magician's? It strikes me he is beyond justice now."

"Will you never tire of playing with words?" she asked, shaking her head in an impatient jangling of beads and bells. "How has such sophistry served you so far? Can you not see that what you must do now is speak the truth? For it is only by calling things by their True Name that illusion can be stripped away so we can see things as they are."

"If soldiers in the trenches had named things truly, we would have had two armies of deserters. Which many of us who witnessed the destruction in the trenches might have been the best thing for all concerned," he retorted.

"But instead, the Magician fed them illusion after illusion to believe in," Gipsy Sarah said implacably. "And in doing so, unleashed a force he was powerless to control."

Gavin shook his head. "Words," he said. "Just words."

"And what can be more powerful?" Gipsy Sarah countered. "What are words but truth and lies. And the time is come to have done with lying. Now MacLeod calls you to give things their True Name. It is time for you to speak the Truth about Judith. The Truth about Essie. The Truth about Rachel and Miriam. The Truth about Lord Kitchener and 736 other doomed souls. Even the Truth about Josep Havel, whose sole crime was to venture a peek into fairy land. But most of all you need to speak the Truth that will finally set *you* free."

Chapter 21

Gavin arrived back at the Mountain House so exhausted that its staunch respectability, which normally oppressed him, now beckoned as a welcome refuge. A few hours spent in the east dining room trading trivial comments about the excellence of Mrs. Mead's vegetable garden amongst guests with impeccable references while sipping on nothing stronger than a glass of the late Mr. Mead's ingeniously cooled spring water, suddenly seemed as close to heaven as the information travel booklet had promised. But still, as he stood and limped toward the front door, the Gabriel Hounds padded close at his heels.

He froze, fighting down the impulse to call for his horse and ride straight to the West Hurley railway station, where he would send for his baggage to follow. But what was the use? He had fled the hounds across a continent and then an ocean. There was nowhere left to run.

He reached for the door, only to have it swing open to admit a worried maid who informed him that the Adamses begged him to join them immediately in one of the rustic tents on the edge of the fields—another one of the late

Mr. Mead's innovations, designed to attract guests who wanted a taste of camping without giving up any of the amenities offered by the Mountain House. But he guessed the Adamses' motivations in choosing such a location had nothing to do with fresh air and everything to do with a privacy that even the stout oak doors of the rooms the Meads had designated for private evening entertainments such as charades or card games could not provide. Which could only mean that the situation was dire indeed.

The assembly that awaited confirmed his opinion. The rugs, cushions, and bedding that were so proudly promised in the information booklet had been pushed rudely aside to make room for a ring of chairs that could only be described as a court of judgment. Ned Adams shivered in a ladder-backed chair that served as the defendant's seat. His wife waited to pass judgement in a rocking chair, while Hollis Stanton served as an impromptu bailiff, standing guard by the open tent flap. Kate Ames and Essie were squeezed together on a wooden bench commandeered from beneath a neighboring tree, apparently having been granted temporary status as witnesses.

Concern flashed across Kate's face as soon as she saw Gavin, but she hid it immediately, as she helped Essie to her feet. "Perhaps we two should squeeze over onto the cot," she suggested. "Miss Smith has warned that you might be subject to further dizzy spells, so it might be best to sit where you could easily lie down."

It was nothing but a graceful excuse to cede Gavin the bench, where he might stretch out his leg more comfortably, but he accepted the kindness gratefully. He had a feeling he would want to be seated to hear the news they were about to impart.

"Has something happened?" he addressed himself to Miss Ames. "Beyond, of course, the glad news that the young lady has apparently recovered her senses, that is?"

"Miss Smith predicts a complete recovery from what can only be described as a singularly nasty shock," Kate told him. "Unfortunately, the same cannot be said for Mr. Havel."

So, it was just as Duncan MacLeod had foretold: Josep Havel, Impresario, would no longer trouble Gavin Fellowes or anyone else. "Then he is…?"

"Dead," Stanton informed him. "Drowned in that infernal pool. Damned thing should have been torn down long ago. I've already given orders to have it razed. At least what's left of it after my uncle got through with it," he finished with an ugly look at Ned.

And thereby hung a tale—and not a pretty one, Gavin was certain. But he refused to let himself be distracted from the matter at hand. "What happened?" he asked.

"Who knows?" Stanton replied with a shrug. "It seems most likely that he was foolish enough to venture forth during this morning's storm. When those hailstones were at their height, the sharpest-eyed man could not have seen to place one foot in front of the other. He must have stumbled in and hit his head on a rock."

"No, he didn't!" Essie erupted in furious protest. "That's not what happened at all, for I saw it for myself! Havel was the sorcerer what challenged the fairy prince, the shining stranger that rode his horse across the waves and caught me up out of the water. They bargained for my life, and then the champion Azazel arose from the dust in a whirlwind, and fought back the water, and everywhere the lost cities began to rise, and the horns began to blow…"

Her voice began to ratchet upward, and Kate laid a soothing hand on her arm. "There are drugs that can make you see things like that, things that were never real. I'm sure the people who paid you to dance with the fairies gave you some such thing, in order to make the pictures more convincing. And that was something they never, ever should have done. You have every right to be very angry with them, but you would be wiser if you simply tried to put them out of your mind forever, and with them, that vision. For neither can hurt you any longer. What you saw was nothing worse than a nightmare, a bad dream."

Her voice betrayed nothing but calm reason, yet it was clear to Gavin that she was at least as troubled by Essie's tale as the girl herself was. In fact, he might have even gone so far as to say that Kate was struggling to convince herself as much as she was struggling to convince Essie. Even worse was his rapidly evolving certainty that she might have a far harder time convincing him, especially after his conversation with Gypsy Sarah.

"Or maybe even he was struck by lightning or a falling branch," Mrs. Adams seconded her nephew's version of events. "Who knows what kind of misadventure awaits anyone foolish enough to venture out in such weather? The mountains are beautiful, yes, but the traveler does well not to underestimate their dangers, as our hosts have so often cautioned us."

"And does the coroner concur?" Gavin asked, his voice carefully neutral.

"The coroner will of course exercise due consideration in making his decision, for he is a man of conscience," Mrs. Adams allowed. "Woodstock is but a village, and things work differently here. What benefit could there be to any more scandalous verdict? The stain on Mead's Mountain House would be irreparable."

Even more irreparable would be the stain on Ker-Ys, as well as the entire Adams' family, but Gavin forbore pointing that out, conceding her point with no more than a polite nod.

"Besides, what does it truly matter whether the man drowned himself by accident or deliberately?" Jean Adams warmed to her theme. "Whatever it was, it was by his own hand. It is no shame to put the needs of the living first, and the coroner is a man who understand as much."

In other words, the coroner was a man whose conscience would guide him into delivering a satisfying verdict, a tidy little package that would allow them all to return to the ordinary living of their lives with no permanent scars from risen dead men and impossible visions whether nightmare or no. "So, the only question is whether it was an accident or self-harm?" Gavin pressed. "There can be no question of murder? No question of the fatal blow being struck by another man?"

"It wasn't another man! They weren't men, either of them," Essie cut in hotly. "They were creatures like nothing you've ever seen. And they killed Mr. Havel, just like they killed poor Judith! Dragged her off beneath the sea—just as they tried to do to me…"

"Silence, girl! You're in enough trouble as it is," Stanton snapped.

"What trouble?" Essie retorted. "I told her I didn't want to! I told her I was scared! I tried to give back the money—"

"Money you were paid to help blackmail my uncle! The very fact of which could see you in prison if you don't keep your mouth shut."

Kate and Essie both erupted in furious protest, but Stanton ignored them. Instead, he turned his attention back to Gavin. "Even if another man struck the blow, it was Havel's own hand that felled him as surely as if he had raised a gun to his own temple. The man was a blackmailer. Being killed by a victim he himself had driven to desperation is nothing more than the inevitable consequence of his own actions."

"Many people might take that as a confession," Gavin pointed out, his voice schooled in calm deception. "Unless, of course, you are shielding another man?"

Ned Adams scrambled to his feet. "I never touched him!" he protested. "I never touched any of them. I only look. I never touch."

"Of course, you didn't, my dear," Jean Adams said. "And Mr. Fellowes was implying nothing of the kind. Now do sit back down…"

"If I propose to shield my uncle, it is only from the likes of *her.*" Stanton spun on Essie. "Tell them the truth of what you did to my uncle! Tell the truth now if you do not want to sleep in a jail cell tonight! Tell them what that she-devil made you and all those other poor girls do!"

"I was only to dance with him." Essie's lip trembled. "I swear on my mother's grave I was only to dance."

"Blackmail!" Stanton roared, as he stabbed an accusing finger at Ned. "Blackmail of a helpless, confused old man— and a blatant attempt to ruin our entire family. Do you know what such pictures of my uncle's fairy dancing would do to the share prices of our holdings if they were ever leaked to the press?"

Gavin raised an eyebrow. "And so it is your duty to your family that justifies your taking measures to ensure that would never happen?"

"Of course, I took measures!" Stanton said. "I have made no secret of the fact. For this is not the first time someone attempted to use my uncle's ... predilections against him. But you have my word that I am determined it will be the last. The fate of Josep Havel is nothing but the final nail in the coffin. The case for removing my uncle from his position in the company is compelling enough in its own right that I did not need to dirty my hands by killing that odious man. Although I will say freely that I don't mind that Nature was kind enough to save us the trouble of bringing the monster to justice."

Justice? What justice? Surely, Josep Havel was not the most dangerous monster that stalked among them. But what protest was there left for Gavin to make? Stanton's threat was clear. If anyone dared question the verdict of death by misadventure, Stanton would strive to throw the blame on an innocent girl and a bewildered and besotted old man, all to protect the family holdings.

"And what of Judith?" Essie demanded. "You'd have us believe she drowned herself, too?"

"Judith was less fortunate than you," Stanton warned. "A wise girl would be very careful to keep it that way."

"Please, Mr. Stanton! What point is there in threatening Essie, unless you propose to cause a relapse?" Kate said. "She is understandably quite confused about what actually happened to her, but surely it is clear that you are dealing with a girl who has been through a terrible experience at someone's hands—be they fairy or human. She is owed your consideration."

"Fairy or human? How ridiculous. And I owe her nothing. We all know at exactly whose hands she has suffered; the same hands that used her to blackmail my uncle," Stanton said. "The girl should be grateful for her narrow escape. And the woman who used her as a cat's-paw should count herself fortunate that I am content to send her packing, rather than prosecute her."

"I assume you speak of Melisandre?" Kate asked incredulously. "Surely, you cannot be accusing her of murder now? Judith maybe, at least if she had the element of surprise. But how could she possibly have overpowered a man of Havel's stature?" She almost blurted out that she had overheard Stanton and Melisandre conspiring, but what had she actually heard?

"Melisandre was never anything but a tool," Stanton snorted. "There were other, stronger hands at work."

He made to turn away, but Kate was having none of it. "Perhaps you would care to share with everyone exactly to whom those hands belonged?" Her voice edged with a dangerous undercurrent Gavin found himself unwilling to interpret.

"Josep Havel is hardly the only one to put his wartime experiences to profitable use in peacetime," Stanton answered her, his voice as tinged with meaning as hers. "Automatic writing. Seances. Blackmail. Tricks of the trade, learned in the service of our country. But who controls them when they seek to turn their service to a different master?"

Gavin sprang to his feet, ignoring the pain that surged through his bad leg. "Essie, Melisandre, and now you would accuse Miss Ames? How many others will follow? Use your head, if you have one! Miss Ames was not even in Woodstock when the girl was killed!"

"I do not accuse Miss Ames. I accuse her masters. Men like the Magician. Men like Duncan MacLeod. Spymasters."

Kate's eyes narrowed. "I have good cause to believe it was not Duncan MacLeod for whom Melisandre was working."

"And I have good cause to suggest that you be very, very certain that you can prove your accusations," Stanton retorted. "There are laws against slander in this country."

Kate's voice was sharp as a blade. "There are laws against murder as well."

But Gavin interrupted, impelled by the truth of MacLeod's last words as they came rushing back to him: Havel would trouble him no longer. The rest was up to Gavin. "Do you accuse Duncan MacLeod of being the Magician then?"

"What do I care what name you give him? Names are just another spymaster's games. Let us be adults enough to call them what they truly are: Thieves, traitors, and liars all. We are well to have done with the lot of them."

"I would remind you that Miss Ames is under your aunt's particular protection," Gavin pointed out.

Stanton smiled at Gavin all too knowingly. "And I would say she has another protector as well. But what do I care?" he said with a shrug. "Melisandre has already admitted her guilt by fleeing, and by all accounts Duncan MacLeod has vanished as well. As far as I'm concerned, they've done us a great favor. I'm sure we can all agree that the more quickly we put this painful episode behind us, the better it will be for all concerned."

He glared at Ned. "Especially for you, Uncle. I think the less our investors know about how nearly you led us all into disaster, the better for all concerned. But surely you can see that you are in no position to do more than serve as a figurehead any longer. I will speak with the companies' lawyers immediately."

Briefly, Ned bristled with the feral desperation of a cornered animal. "I did nothing wrong! I only looked. I never *touched.*"

Jean Adams laid a hand on his arm. "Of course, you didn't. You and I well know that you are incapable of doing otherwise. You seek them only in service of your Art. But there are other people, people not blessed with your unsullied soul, that might find cause to doubt your purity."

Gavin turned away before Jean Adams could see the pity that twisted his face. Was this how she managed to cope? Was this the pretty story she recited like a bedtime prayer so she could sleep at night?

As abruptly as it swelled, Ned's defiance collapsed, and he turned to his wife, eyes brimming with tears. "But I have still been a fool," he said brokenly.

Gently, Jean Adams held out her hands to her husband. He knelt as he took them and collapsed sobbing into her skirts.

Chapter 22

THE RULES ABOUT GAMES in Mead's Mountain House were straightforward. Guests were encouraged to participate in such evening entertainments but asked to confine their conviviality to the parlors set aside for such use, so as not to disturb either the Office or those guests who preferred to relax on the piazza. Gambling was obviously strictly forbidden, but, according to the travel booklet, other card games were encouraged as were classic parlor games such as Fictionary, Squeak Piggy Squeak, The Minister's Cat, The Sculptor, Change Seats!, Are You There, Moriarty?, Fruit Bowl, Pass the Slipper, Consequences, The Laughing Game, Wink Murder, Lookabout, Forfeits, and Elephant's Foot Umbrella Stand. Back when Mr. Mead had been alive, he had been famous for leading boisterous rounds of charades.

Of course, such frivolity was out of the question in the aftermath of the sudden and shocking demise of one of their guests. By unspoken accord, the Adamses were afforded their privacy in one of the twin dining rooms, while the rest of the guests kept their table conversation decorously quiet over the homemade chicken and dumplings. Unwilling to join either group, Gavin wandered out onto the piazza, taking a book at random from one of the shelves in the parlor to discourage anyone who might think to engage him in casual conversation. It was a silly piece, written by a not usually silly man. According to the bookseller's notice tipped behind the last page, its author, one Dexter A. Hawkins, was better known for such sober-sided tomes as *Relation of Education to Wealth and Morality, and to Pauperism and Crime* and *The Anglo-Saxon Race: Its History, Character, and Destiny*. But the mountain air had impelled him to deliver a series of mock lectures for the entertainment of the other guests at the Overlook Mountain House, which were now collected in the leather-bound volume entitled *The Traditions of the Overlook Mountain* that Gavin now held in his hand. This copy was affectionately inscribed to the Meads, the proprietors of "The Oldest House in the Southern Catskills."

No sooner had Gavin opened the volume than he wanted to cast it aside, for the book was a bit of legend piracy at least as egregious as that of the enterprising Mrs. A.E.P. Searing, resituating such tales and legends as were collected by scores of lady folklorists in Gavin's own English countryside, to the wild natives who dwelt on the summit of the mountain that loomed above him. Dartmoor's druid libation bowls and processional ways had been replaced by the terrible Altar Rock, where the primitive tribes performed their sacrifices and war dances. The crystal caverns of bards and wizards were transformed into a fissure that was called the Cave of the Sybil. There was even an Arthur's Seat to guard it, in the form of a yellow birch, where first the Sybil's jealous father and then an enamored scion of the British Royal Family, held watch over the lovely shaman.

In a second cave, called the Lovers' Cave, lived an Indian with such an impossible wife that the estranged couple lived in separate caverns, until the exasperated husband finally received instruction from the witches who occupied the nearby Witches' Glen to "Lash her, lash her"—which was said to explain the origin of one of the most prominent family names in Woodstock.

Those same witches were called on to intervene when a man brought home a wife from a neighboring tribe, only to have his mother dismiss her as "too fat" and "holding her head too high." The witches proposed the following test: If the woman could squeeze through the crevasse at the entrance to the glen, and then squeeze beneath the overhang beyond, she was not too fat, nor did she hold her head too high. The husband, who genuinely loved his wife, agreed to the test. And when a kindly witch pulled aside the hazel bush that blocked nearly half of the crevasse, the woman was able to pass through both challenges easily.

Gavin closed the book and tossed it away. Once upon a time, when he had been a callow youth at Balliol College, he had been an eager antiquarian himself, and had spent his summers tramping the countryside to collect such legends with as much enthusiasm as Mrs. Searing or Dexter Hawkins. But the War had left him with nothing but contempt for people like the good guests of Mead's Mountain House, so securely fortified by their temperance and respectability that they could enjoy such tales as an evening's entertainment. How likely would they be to enjoy such stories if they had ever heard the howls of the Gabriel Hounds as they drew ever closer, had tasted the cold stink of death in Gwyn ap Nudd's breath, had seen the Wild Ride converging on the dark hulk of a ship sinking in the North Sea, their long fingers stretching greedily for the souls of the doomed men? If only, like Miss Ames, he had found a way a tame such bitter memories by recapturing them and transforming them back into charming fantasies for children. But, alas, the stains upon his soul were too great.

As if summoned by the mere thought of her, a pale figure emerged from a copse on the far end of the lawn, like one of the white ladies that haunted the Hudson Valley as surely as they did England: jilted brides shimmering on cliffs where they had thrown themselves to their dooms; runaway countesses spooking horses and riders at the crossroads where the highwaymen they loved had been hanged; mad wives pining away in locked family towers. Slowly, she stretched out a hand and beckoned to him. And Gavin obeyed, crossing the lawn to her with the uncertain tread of a man who knows he follows the will-o'-the-wisp, yet remains helpless to resist his doom.

But the lady that awaited him was no pixie; rather, she was very much a creature of this world. Alas, it was not the creature of this world he had hoped it be, for it was not Miss Ames. Instead it was Melisandre who awaited him, her flowing sleeves exchanged for a neat traveling costume; her red-gold curls tucked up tidily beneath a hat.

She smiled bitterly at his obvious disappointment. "Have no fear. I am not here to beg you to plead on my behalf. I am branded the disgraced villainess, and I will vanish as such. A good actress knows how to time her exits."

"And yet you came to find me. Why?"

She tossed her head, and a rebellious curl escaped. "I will not stay and fight to defend my good name. But I will not suffer for another. I would have all the guilty named."

Foreboding clenched Gavin's chest. Was she about to name Kate Ames as a co-conspirator? "Do you speak of Duncan MacLeod?" he asked evenly. "Or someone else?"

"Duncan MacLeod?" She laughed, her teeth flashing in the darkness. "Why on earth would Duncan MacLeod want to disgrace Ned Adams?"

Gavin nodded slowly. It was the question he had been asking himself all along—the piece of the puzzle that refused to align with the others no matter to which angle he turned it. And it had only grown more perplexing now that he had seen the magic of MacLeod's mechanical marvels for himself. Now, not only did the prospect of MacLeod stooping to blackmail for profit fly in the face of everything Gavin had known of a man who had given his life's blood to save him, but it was impossible to believe that such a master craftsman would ever be content to create such cheap effects as Ned Adams' vulgar fairy photographs.

But if MacLeod were not the one to place the Magician's arts in the service of embarrassing Ned Adams, what other suspects remained—other than Kate Ames, that is? And that was a possibility that Gavin increasingly could not accept.

"Blackmailers don't want to disgrace their victims," Gavin pointed out as evenly as he could. "Blackmailers want their victims to pay so they are not disgraced."

"Perhaps," she conceded. "But you are, by all accounts, a learned, logical man, Mr. Fellowes. A true skeptic, it has been said. So, I bid you ask the logical question: Who truly benefits from Ned Adams' disgrace? Or as your courts of law would have it, *cui bono*?"

It was the question any logical man would ask himself, and it admitted of only one answer. "Hollis Stanton."

"He has longed to prise the family holdings from his uncle and aunt for years," she agreed. "And many would argue it is the right thing to do."

"And is that why you assisted him?" Gavin asked. "Because he convinced you of the righteousness of his cause?"

She stiffened. "Do not presume to judge me, Mr. Fellowes. I helped Hollis Stanton save his family from ruin—nothing more."

"Saved them how?" Gavin asked. "By humiliating his aunt and making his uncle a laughingstock?"

"All I did was make an old man happy for a little while. And help him escape the clutches of that witch of a wife—if only temporarily."

And while the final tableau of Ned Adams sobbing into his wife's skirts like a chastened child roused in Gavin more than a little sympathy, he was obliged to point out, "Some would argue that kidnapping and drugging young women is an unduly *forcible* way of ensuring a man's happiness."

"There was no question of kidnapping!" Melisandre protested. "The girls came to Ker-Ys willingly. And if we offered them a few stimulants to make their dancing more convincing, well they accepted them of their own volition."

"And were they murdered of their own volition as well?"

Her face lit with undisguised fury. "Not a single one of those girls was harmed," she said. "They were paid for their efforts and then were paid to disappear—quite handsomely, I might add. Mr. Stanton does not stint when it comes to such things, I can assure you. They are all safely back in the city, and comfortably the better off for their efforts."

"With one rather obvious exception."

Her face darkened. "Judith was different. Judith was an unfortunate mistake."

"Particularly unfortunate for he."

"Judith was Josep Havel's creature, not ours," Melisandre snapped. "He was the one who persuaded her to spy and steal, and there would be more than one who would agree the responsibility for her death lies at his door and no one else's."

"A convenient stance to take when the man is dead," Gavin retorted. "But since he is not here to speak for himself, perhaps it is time for you to tell me what you know. Who is this Josep Havel? Why did he have to die? What part does he play in this entire sorry episode? Or was he simply another mistake as well?"

"Havel was a calculating villain. I don't think he believed any of the nonsensical stories about magical spies and faerie armies and the H.M.S. *Hampshire*'s last voyage to Ultima Thule with which he filled Judith's head—and which ultimately led to both their deaths. Such tales were naught but a way to turn her to his own purposes, and nothing more."

Melisandre might see matters that way, but Gavin was less certain. Still, he pressed her, "What were these purposes exactly?"

"What do you think?" she demanded with an eloquent shrug. "What answer is there ever? Leave the fairies aside, and once more ask yourself *cui bono*? Who had an interest in hiding the truth behind that last clandestine meeting aboard the H.M.S. *Hampshire*? Who here in America most benefited from keeping a sodden, hopeless war on a far, foreign shore alive?"

"Stanton?" Gavin asked, strictly suppressing the sudden surge of hope he felt at the prospect, for he knew only too well that his natural dislike of the man and his concern for Kate Ames were clouding his judgment.

"There was plenty of profit to be made in staying out of the war, so we could sell arms to both sides," Melisandre said with a shrug. "If you don't believe me, you might want to confirm what I've said by inspecting the Adams' family profit and loss statements for the past five years."

"And so Havel came to Woodstock to blackmail Stanton?" Gavin pressed. It made sense, and. more importantly, it completely removed Kate Ames from any question of blame. "All the rest was just talk meant to mislead and distract? Pixie dust scattered to blind everyone to his simple and sordid purpose here: blackmail?"

"Surely, you can't believe that the Allies were desperate enough to turn to witchcraft to win the Great War." Melisandre's voice was casual enough, but her eyes were as appraising as a riverboat gambler's as she gauged his reaction.

Gavin's jaw set. "What I believe is not important. The question is what Havel believed. Did he come here to blackmail Stanton, or did he truly believe that one of those girls possessed the secret of commanding the Fair Folk?"

Melisandre raised a shoulder. "I told you what I think, but perhaps Kate is in a better position to answer that question than I."

Gavin stiffened, and Melisandre smiled at the clear evidence her shot had struck home. "And I see with that I have finally brought you to my cause. Very well then, Mr. Fellowes. I make no apologies for who I am or what I have done. Nor do I ask anything more from you than that you see to it that *all* those who have done the same or worse answer for their deeds as I have. And with that the time is come for me to go."

She moved to slide back into the shadows to disappear forever—before she could satisfy him as to one last, burning question.

"Wait! *Please*," he forced himself to add more moderately.

She raised an eyebrow. "Yes."

"What of Miss Ames? You have opened an issue without closing it."

He strove to phrase the question as nothing but a bid for completeness. A dispassionate query. But he failed abjectly to disguise the emotion that choked his voice, and Melisandre shook her head in mock despair. "Ah, Kitty. Ever since we were first called, it has always been Kitty. I suppose I shouldn't be jealous. If only she offered even the faintest hint of being aware of her power over men."

His chest unclenched. "So you would suggest she is … completely unaware …. You can assure me she paid no willing part in this—"

Melisandre studied him with a malicious smile. "If you care so very much to know the answer," she suggested, "the simplest approach would be to ask her yourself."

Chapter 23

GAVIN HESITATED AS HE SAW Kate emerging from the Office of Mead's Mountain House, having finalized her conveyance to the West Hurley railway station and down to New York City for the following morning. Might it not be simpler to let her do just that? Why press for the truth? Why even press for a farewell? What business was it of his? Why not simply turn and run once more—away from the Catskills, just as he had run away from England, staying one step ahead of those damnable hounds.

But, he realized, even if he could evade the Gabriel Hounds, he could no longer run away from himself. "If this is to be farewell, Miss Ames," he said, intercepting her in the lobby at the foot of the narrow stairs and offering her his arm, "then would you at least allow me the pleasure of a parting stroll down to Mead's meadow."

She hesitated only briefly, before accepting his arm and stepping out into the summer evening. They walked down the broad road in silence. Only when they had settled on a shady bench with one of Overlook's fabled views of Indian Head Mountain, did Gavin venture to speak.

"I suppose you can see a profile there, if you try," he began conventionally enough. "Only a cynic would point out that every mountain range seems to have its recumbent giant, from Albion in England to the Nephilim trapped beneath the Caucasus."

"What did people desperate enough to flee across an ocean have to bring with them other than their legends?" she asked.

"Neither Ned Adams nor his wife could be described as such people," he said. "And yet they chose to bring the tale of Ker-Ys to Woodstock. I trust you know the legend?"

"I think none of us who have summered with the Adamses could possibly forget it," she answered with laugh. "It was rather pounded into us every evening. Gradlon, the Seelie Prince, betraying his own kind all for the love of a woman, the Sorceress of the North. Gradlon, turned fugitive from both the Fair Folk and Christianity seeking refuge with the only court that would have him— only to betray his hosts' kindness by seeking to transform Ker-Ys into a Christian citadel and fortifying it from the ancient magicks of the sea with a series of mighty walls and canals. But his efforts failed and left him and the holy saint Winwaloe, the only survivors of the terrible flood that overwhelmed the city, galloping across the waves on the back of Morvarc'h, his magical black horse that breathed fire through his nostrils."

Gaving nodded. "Or so the traditional story goes. But in truth there were not two, but rather three who survived the drowning of Ker-Ys. Gradlon and Winwaloe, yes, of course. But what of Gradlon's daughter, whom Morvarc'h bore on his back as well?" Gavin met her eyes. "At least until the saint commanded him to throw her down into the waves, so that he himself might survive."

"Ah yes, his sinful daughter. A sorceress like her mother, and a wanton like her father, seduced into betraying Ker-Ys by the devil who called himself the Red Knight."

"A devil? Or one with the power to command devils? A sorcerer. A Magician." Tired of prevarication, Gavin pulled the maps out of his pocket, willing his fingers not to betray him by trembling. "But enough talk about fairytales. Let us speak frankly, instead of in metaphors. I have here two maps, one true, one false. Two maps that Josep Havel came to America to seek. Two maps, one of which I am certain cost Josep Havel his life. The question is, for which one was he killed?"

Once more, he pulled out a map to confront her. This one was an ordinary nautical chart. "On the face of it, it must have been this one—which, I am certain, was one of the papers Havel was seeking in Stanton's room—rather than Ned Adams' pathetic fairy pictures. For would you not agree that this is the map of the American shipping lanes given to the Germans in a misguided effort to draw the Americans into the war? And if the other papers Havel succeeded in stealing were equally incriminating, they could even now see the perpetrators hanged for treason. Surely, the murder of one man, especially a blackmailer, would seem a simple price to pay to protect oneself from the rope."

She raised an eyebrow. "Are you accusing me, Mr. Fellowes?"

"You drew this map. You drew it as part of Mr. Thayer's secret disinformation project at the behest of the Magician. And if Josep Havel came to America to discover evidence of that plot, any and all who worked for the Magician and could be exposed for treason would have ample cause to kill him. So, I beg you to tell me why I shouldn't go to the authorities with evidence that would hang you for murder. Or treason."

A moment's pause. Then she raised a shoulder with that self-containment that both irritated and captivated him, as she pushed the map back toward him. "Blackmail is blackmail, Mr. Fellowes, no matter how justified you believe the cause."

"I am not a blackmailer, and my cause is far more than a simple matter of what I believe justified!" he snapped. "This map alone is evidence enough that Josep Havel came to these shores to discover evidence of American clandestine meddling in the Great War, only to find himself murdered for his pains. And while I do not weep for Josep Havel any more than I would any other blackmailer, the enormity of the plot he threatened to uncover is such that I cannot allow it to pass."

"Then why do you not take what you know to the authorities?"

"Firstly," he said, "I don't believe you capable of such a foul plot. And secondly, even if you were involved, the thought of you hanging would break my heart."

The words spilled out before he could stop them, and the two of them stared in appalled silence, as if the words had been splashed all over the grass beneath their feet. Then her face broke into the most genuine smile he had ever seen. "A memorable declaration, if not precisely a pretty one," she said. "How can I not tell you what you wish to hear after that?"

He did his best to hide his furious flush and rush of emotions and pressed the map toward her once more.

"Then, if you would be so kind, what I wish to hear is everything you know about this map and how it might be connected to the sinking of the H.M.S. *Hampshire* and the assassination of Lord Kitchener."

Her flush arguably equal to his own, she took a moment to compose her thoughts—or, Gavin could only hope, her own emotions, before she said, "In truth, I've already told you most of what I know. I've already explained that I was engaged, as part of Mr. Thayer's studio, in a private arrangement with British intelligence to create illusion and disinformation. Dazzlepaint. One part of that arrangement involved disguising maps of the Atlantic to protect American shipping lanes against the looming threat of unrestricted submarine warfare by the Central Powers. Then word came that someone had betrayed our codes to the Central Powers and all of American shipping was at risk."

She smiled bitterly. "We soon learned that was not true. Just one more bit of the Magician's own dazzlepaint. One of scores of attempts that failed to bring America into the war before the Zimmerman telegram finally succeeded. But when the plot was exposed as another of the Magician's illusions, Washington reacted more violently than if it had been true. For, as a born and bred English gentleman, the Magician did not fully appreciate one important fact about Americans. You can threaten an American's honor. You can threaten an American's life. But whatever you do, do not threaten an American's business interests. And that's what threatening the shipping lanes did."

Gavin nodded slowly. "What exactly did Washington do?" he asked, although he was certain he already knew the answer.

"New orders came to Mr. Thayer from Washington. Henceforth, his work would be only in service of his own country. No more work for the Magician. And our first assignment was to trick the Magician into revealing his identity so the Americans could bring him to justice and eliminate him and his tricks once and for all. They claimed he'd gone mad, obsessed by the idea that he'd created a Book of Shadows that gave men the power to command the forces of the Fair Folk, who now roamed the battlefields of the Great War, leaving chaos in their wake." She raised a shoulder. "More fairytales, of course. The men who wished to seize his networks for themselves sought to silence the Magician because they knew he and he alone was powerful enough to oppose them and undermine their own plans. And so, the men in Washington struck a dreadful bargain with both Allied and Central Powers. The goal was to hunt down the Magician and divide his secrets between the Germans and the Americans." She shook her head and looked out across the lawn.

"A despicable bargain, and you may ask why the English were party to such a deal."

"And do you have an answer to that?"

"The answer is that they were willing to sacrifice one of their own as the price paid for America's entry into the war."

In other words, the Magician himself was just another necessary loss. There would be many who would argue there was justice in that. Gavin pulled out the second map, the one that was stained with Duncan MacLeod's blood. "And they asked you to assist in the pursuit by drawing once more?"

A small nod. "The first attempt on the Magician's network was meant to be a tale so patently obvious that it could be tracked easily through his contacts. Mr. Thayer was asked to encode false information revealing Lord Kitchener's secret mission to Ultima Thule to wake the sleeping Grail Knights and raise them to England's cause." She shook her head. "Unfortunately, the Americans' false information was all-too-fatally true. The coded message included the exact coordinates that the German U-Boats needed to target the H.M.S. *Hampshire* and sink it. Despicable as it might have been, it was precisely the catastrophe the men in Washington sought, for with it came a triple coup—in a single blow, they managed to map the Magician's networks beyond a doubt, rid themselves of one of the few leaders able to inspire a victory that might bring the war to a premature close, and turn a tidy profit by speculation in stock market shares that would be affected by the news of Kitchener's death."

Which was a tale Gavin had heard too often to believe it was anything but the truth. "Did no one try to stop them?" he asked, knowing the answer before she spoke it. "Did not *you* try to stop them?"

"I did what I could. And Duncan MacLeod did even more. He sent urgent cables in the name of the Magician to the war offices of both the Allies and the Americans, warning them that under no circumstances should Lord Kitchener set sail."

"And yet the H.M.S. *Hampshire* did set sail," Gavin said. "The question is, why."

"The explanation we received in the aftermath of the disaster was that the Magician had cried wolf once too often. Why should Washington have any reason to think the Magician's claims were anything other than more dazzlepaint, another not-too-subtle attempt to draw

America into the war." Another small smile. "At least, that would have been the official verdict—if in fact any official details of the case had been allowed to escape. As for the unofficial verdict, well, rumors of conspiracy had been swirling for long before that. Indeed, poor Kaiser Wilhelm was closer to the truth than he knew when he protested the entire war was nothing but a Masonic plot."

"Whereas you propose to blame … who? The Rosicrucians? The Jesuits? Perhaps the Knights Templar?"

She laughed. "Which villains would you prefer? The Elders of Zion in Biarritz? Churchill conspiring to lie about the Battle of Jutland with his Jewish friends so they all could make a killing in the stock market? The Communists assassinating Lord Kitchener to keep him from completing a top-secret mission to Russia to replace the Boshevized Jews with loyal men of impeccable English breeding and so prevent the Russian Revolution?" She shook her head and let out a long sigh. "Communists and Jews today. Suffragists and Gypsies tomorrow. Or the Irish and the Haymarket anarchists. But tell me, do such conspiracy theories seem any the less likely if you substitute the words 'Titans of American Industry' for any of those other names?"

She pushed the map back toward him a second time. "Surely there's no need to spell out matters for a man like you. If you wish to discover the truth behind Lord Kitchener's assassination, all you need do is ask yourself the obvious question. Who are the only people who profit from a war?"

"*Cui bono*?" Gavin seconded her with a nod, feeling a rush of relief as his theories were confirmed. "Who profits from a war other than the industrialists? The steel magnates. The oil barons. The arms manufacturers. The munitions suppliers. Krupps or Carnegie, theirs was the true alliance: German and American, brothers beneath the skin, hand in glove with no greater gods than gold and silver. Or dollars or marks or francs or even pounds, whatever the case may be."

"And William Morris be hanged, those are the fortunes without which artistic idylls such as Ker-Ys could not exist. And as far as I'm concerned *should* not." Once more, she met him with those peculiarly penetrating eyes. "Men such as Abbott Thayer have assumed that a weakness of determination and a natural female modesty are what keep me from seeking artistic greatness as a painter. Nothing could be further from the truth. Art for art's sake is a will o' the wisp. A phantom. The worst kind of illusion wrought for the worst possible purpose: an artist's tribute to his own genius. For what worse chimera could there be? Art was never for art's sake. Take the Acropolis. The great medieval cathedrals. The illuminated breviaries. The gilded coffins of Egypt. The ceiling of the Sistine Chapel. All of them were art in service to *something*—created by artists that submitted themselves to a far greater force than themselves—a sacrifice to which today's brand of egoists have proved themselves sadly inadequate."

She drew a steadying breath. "You ask me whether I believe in the truth of automated writing. And the truth is, I do not know—any more than I know whether the Magician's efforts succeeded in raising the Fair Folk to the Allies' cause. But I do believe that the purpose of art is to create magic, just as I believe that the only way to do that is to submit oneself completely to a power that exceeds oneself. For art whose only purpose is to display the genius of its creator is nothing but excess. A vulgar decoration just like the stuffed birds and bell jars and ceramic mantel ornaments with which the Victorians sought to clutter their houses. No, I am proud of being an illustrator, for books are art that create magic. Stevenson compared them to frigates; I think of them rather as portals, but whatever the metaphor you choose, books weave new worlds for people who have been told they have no place in this one. And that is the cause to whose service I take pride in placing my art, rather than simply in service of some meaningless notion of glory or profit. I may never see my bust in the Pantheon, but I will have the dignity of knowing that my illustrations in their own small way created magic—even if that humble magic was nothing more than allowing a child to forget their unspeakable circumstances for at least a moment ..."

Recollecting herself, she paused to grope for words, then concluded, "Whatever needs forgetting."

She spoke with a passion he had not known her capable of—her eyes sparkling, flush rising to her cheeks, her lips parted. And Gavin found himself consumed with wondering whether she might ever react with similar ardor to ...

He forced away the ungentlemanly image and deliberately returned to the matter at hand. "You said you did what you could," he said, looking down at the bloodstained map. "Did such efforts include this?"

"Of course." She wasted no time studying it. "When the men from Washington first came to us in search of the Magician, I did what I could to prevaricate. I pleaded my weak woman's brain. I told them that Andrew Piper's sad fate had caused me to doubt—no, to *fear*—my own powers. But the men from Washington were adamant, even going so far as to charge me with conspiring with Duncan MacLeod to turn the Magician's networks to our own private gain. So, I drew them a map, Mr. Fellowes. I drew them a map of fairy land." Her fingers traced the bloodstained figures fondly. "I made it as detailed and elegant as any of Mr. Thayer's angel paintings. And as illusory. Or so I thought."

"Or so you thought?" He raised an eyebrow. "Surely, you would not suggest you mapped for the Americans the true way to fairy land?"

"I drew them a picture instead of the truth," she said. "The same sort of picture I draw now. I drew them a map of fairy land—a fanciful, pretty thing, fit only for children. A lie, Duncan MacLeod would have called it. A tall tale, others would say. How was I to know that while the picture concealed the truth about the Magician's network of spies, it betrayed the fatal truth of what the Magician had inadvertently released?"

"Which was?"

"Chaos," she said. "The chaos that erupted when the Magician's web of lies was exposed for all to see—and to seize for themselves if they dared. For that is the essential difference between our world and the Realm of Faerie. Truth commands loyalty, while illusion's only loyalty is to whoever can best command it. Call it by whatever name you will, Faerie Rade or disinformation, the fact remains that there is only one name to describe an army that rallies to any banner with equal passion."

"Chaos," Gavin agreed, as the flood of memory unleashed by MacLeod's magic lantern threatened once more to overwhelm him. "And what man might not risk all to command such power?"

"A wise one, many would say." Again, the faint smile. "One who had learned from the Magician's mistakes. But there are very few of them, it would seem."

Including one Gavin Fellowes himself. But he shook off the memory. "What happens now?" he asked. "For we both know that Havel was neither the first, nor will he be the last. Who is going to raise the banner to command the forces of chaos the Magician raised?"

She met his gaze with those singular green eyes. "At the risk of impertinence, Mr. Fellowes, I would suggest you might know more of that than I. For you did serve with Duncan MacLeod at Belleau Wood, did you not?"

Chapter 24

GAVIN RETURNED TO MEAD'S Mountain House and a world transformed. The croquet pitch now traced the map of fairy land. The quoits two gentlemen were engaged in tossing landed on the lawn with the force of elf-bolts. A roiling sea serpent threatened to rise from beneath Mr. Mead's ingenious system of galvanized steel coils. Was this what love felt like? Was Gavin suddenly seeing the world through Kate Ames' eyes instead of his own?

Or was he simply regaining faith in his own vision? Gavin paused to take another look at those coils. It was not their resemblance to a sea serpent that had drawn his eye toward them. Rather...

Yes! That was it. That was what his own eyes bade him see. Not the coils, but rather where they led: to the Meads' spring house, an entirely more businesslike affair than the one at Ker-Ys—and a very convenient place to hide the stolen papers he sought. His step quickened, his limp all but forgotten. The spring house was a wooden structure set deep into the mountain's slope just like the one at Ker-Ys, but the inside was order itself, with milk, cheese and meats stored on shelves to take advantage of the natural cooling of the running water. It cost Gavin only a moment's searching to find the sole spot of disorder, an oilskin-wrapped packet tucked into the rafters with housewifely prudence.

He waited until he was back in the warmth of the sunshine to tear it open—and was glad he did. Even muddied and sullied as it was, Piper's forgery exuded the power of a masterpiece. But what a terrible power it was. Pure evil pulsed from the embossed swastika and title on its cover: *The Most Sacred Protocols of the Germanenorden Walvater of the Holy Grail.* The Magician's last spell—and the unholy magic that had sealed Havel's doom.

"As for the rest, it is up to you," MacLeod's voice floated across the distant breeze.

But *why*? If this madness was destined to be brought to America, how could one Englishman hope to fight it without losing his own reason in the process? For Gavin had seen no shortage of such Books of Shadows or the societies that created them in the course of his work before and during the war. The Teutonic Order. The *Reichshammersbund.* The Thule Society, they called themselves now. All of them dedicated to the same purpose: To restore the lost strength of their Fatherland by returning to the ancient pagan rituals and the Aryan Truth discovered in the *Eddas* and sagas. Many of their initiates had openly welcomed the outbreak of the Great War as a testing ground to forge anew the knightly steel of the Germanic soul and save its people from the softness wrought by the scheming of the Jews and the weakling doctrine of the dying Lamb of God. Not that the Germans were alone in the proliferation of such secret societies. The English had their Order of the Golden Dawn and Knights Templar. The Americans had their Freemasons. The world had Madame Blavatsky and the Theosophists.

But even if Gavin knew this evidence was incontrovertible proof of the truth behind the murders of Josep Havel and Lord Kitchener, not to mention 736 other souls, it would hardly stand up in the court of reason, let alone a court of law.

"What would you have me *do*?" he sighed.

"Well, I suppose you could always pray for a miracle," MacLeod said with a laugh.

As if a miracle could provide any innocent explanation why the title and text of this German spellbook was in English. There was only one possible explanation for that, and it lay in the three words stamped beneath the swastika, "New World Lodge." Three words that pronounced the death sentences of first Lord Kitchener and then Josep Havel and the girl Judith. How many more were destined to die now that the damn thing had been brought to America?

Too many. Gavin's path suddenly clear to him. This was no time for praying and this was no time for miracles. This was time for true magic, illusion and fairy dust, the stuff dreams were made of. He had no smoking gun with which to confront Stanton directly. But confrontation would not win this battle. No, this assault had to trace the coward's path of circumlocution, feints, and treachery—a web of half-truths and insinuations that Gavin Fellowes had once spun more fluently than the Fair Folk themselves.

"Abracadabra," Duncan MacLeod whispered, his voice as low and close as the soft snuffling of hounds.

Gavin announced himself with no more than a perfunctory tap on the door, before accosting Stanton where he worked on his papers in one of the Mountain house's private rooms. "I apologize for interrupting you, but I have heard some disturbing rumors that force me not to stand on ceremony. Whispers are circulating that your uncle was not Havel's only chosen victim here in Woodstock. Indeed, many are saying that the entire unfortunate episode involving those pictures was nothing but a diversion to draw away suspicion, while he set his hooks into far more powerful, more dangerous men. Not that I believe the whispers, of course, but I felt it only gentlemanly to make you aware of them so that you can silence them as firmly as possible."

Gavin observed Stanton's reaction with calm dispassion. An innocent man would have sprung to his feet in outrage. Instead, Stanton's face slid into the appraising mask of the champion fencer Gavin had once been.

"Indeed," Stanton said. "And may I ask what the rumors suggest his true purpose here was?"

Once Gavin allowed the old talents to emerge, they unfurled rapidly, and the truths, half-truths, and lies began to weave themselves as fluently as Kate Ames had sketched the details of her drawings. Gavin needed no pen or magic lantern to create the scene as his power had always lay in his command of words, be they true, false, or somewhere in between. "Havel not only claimed to have survived the sinking of H.M.S. *Hampshire*, he claimed to have been the one who gave the signal to the U-Boat."

Stanton's jaw tightened. "So he was a German spy. That makes his death doubly fortunate."

"Not a spy," Gavin said. "A traitor operating at the behest of a secret conspiracy to murder Lord Kitchener—and send 736 other souls to watery deaths."

His directness was deliberate, although he had held no real hope of shocking Stanton into a confession so easily. As he anticipated, Stanton merely shrugged. "There is no shortage of such theories about the sinking of H.M.S. *Hampshire*, any more than a score of other events during that unfortunate war."

"But Havel was in possession of much more than a theory. Havel knew. Havel knew the True Name of the puppet masters who had directed him to assassinate Lord Kitchener: The New World Lodge of the *Germanenorden Walvater of the Holy Grail*. This was the knowledge that Havel came to America to profit from. And this was the knowledge that led, not only to his death, but to the death of the girl he sought to make his cat's-paw."

Gavin pulled out the Book of Shadows and laid it on the desk. "This was the prize for which Josep Havel risked his life—without ever understanding the nature of its true power. Your uncle's stolen copy of *The Most Sacred Protocols of the Germanenorden Walvater of the Holy Grail*—written in English and belonging to the New World Lodge. Just the knowledge of its existence provided the *carte de visite* with which Mr. Havel gained entrée to the first circles of American society. For this book is nothing less than the proof of a terrible conspiracy that could have changed the course of the Great War. And proof of why Lord Kitchener was murdered."

"As I said, there is no limit to the number of theories surrounding Kitchener's death," Stanton said with a shrug. "One of them may even be true. Now if you will excuse me…"

"There was no question that Lord Kitchener was sailing to Russia at the personal invitation of the Tsar to bolster both their resources and their commitment to the fighting on the Eastern Front, where the situation was rapidly deteriorating—as was the political situation at home. The question was which Russians?" Gavin pressed his case implacably. "The wilder accusations were that Lord Kitchener sought to install a network of Englishmen to replace the Bolsheviks and Jews and so bolster the Tsar's position. But what if Lord Kitchener's mission was to unite the Russian aristocracy and the Bolsheviks against a common enemy?"

A muscle twitched in Stanton's cheek. "And what enemy is that?"

"A secret network of industrialists and financiers who had been meddling in almost every aspect of the war. A secret network of *American* industrialists, who were sending arms to Germany despite the blockade and the embargo. A secret network of industrialists that was conspiring with their counterparts in Germany to divide Europe between them and split the entire continent into two separate empires—not military or political empires, but two *business* empires. For the business of America is business," Gavin's mouth twisted with contempt. "Profit at any price. Even if that price is prolonging a war that cost civilization nearly a million souls."

"Those are serious accusations," Stanton said, but he could not disguise how the tic in his jaw grew more pronounced. "A man would be risking at least a libel suit if he flung them around without proof—if not more severe retaliation."

"The same retaliation that Havel suffered?" Gavin retorted. "Not that I have any sympathy for a blackmailer.

But justice belongs in the courts of law, not the hands of a few powerful men."

Stanton stared at him for a moment, then shrugged again and laughed. "You are as fatally naïve as he was. You think you understand, but you have no idea. So, fine. I will tell you the truth—in the faint hope of saving you from your own folly. Havel was no blackmailer, but rather he was as credulous a fool as my uncle. He came to America not to extort money or even information, but solely in search of the powers that ritual proposed to raise. He believed in runes and grails and the ancient Aryan magic that he proposed to harness through such nonsense, as if the secrets of true power had ever been contained in reading the Eddas and the German mystics."

Gavin conceded the point with a shrug. It made no difference. Even if Melisandre was wrong about Havel's credulity and even if his motivations had been as mad as Andrew Piper, they did nothing to change the grim reality of the motives of the men who had murdered him. "And in his mad pursuit of an alchemical fairytale, he inadvertently posed a very real threat to a secret society that sought to bend true power, not make-believe power."

"A network where like-minded gentlemen could discuss matters without the interference of the rabble or the nation." Stanton smiled unpleasantly. "Not all that very different from the network our founding fathers used to break free of English chains, really."

"Freemasonry?" Gavin snorted.

"Give it any name you will. Havel came to America with no other purpose than to resurrect and wield the Magician's magic quite literally. And doing so, he gravely jeopardized those who sought to bend the book's power to far different purposes."

"And what threat did Havel offer to such men? Losing their fortunes?"

"Of losing any last vestiges of civilization that remain here in the United States, after we saved the rest of the world!" Stanton said, his voice tinged with fervor. He threw a hand in the direction of the road to the Overlook Hotel. "For the love of God, think, man! Do you know what the Jews and communists would do if they got wind of such a story? Because mark my words, those are the ones who threaten us today. Jews. Communists. Union agitators. Suffragists. All of them radicals intent on overthrowing every freedom this country enjoys. And I for one have no intention of letting them do it."

"By resorting to murder?"

Stanton's face hardened. "By joining forces with those who command far more effective means of commanding the rabble."

"Those such as the *Germanenorden Walvater of the Holy Grail*? Or whatever they happen to call themselves now?"

"They call themselves the Thule Society now, and they have already shown their worth by quashing the Bavarian Revolution last spring. The Bavarian Soviet Republic lasted barely a month when the *Freikorps* marched beneath the banner of the Thule Society. And we in America are not willing to give those agitators even that month. We will strike them first, before they can organize. And believe me when I tell you, this village will be among the first targets they strike."

Woodstock. This village of madmen and Bohemians and Bloomer Girls practicing their folk-dancing in the midst of canny innkeepers with ingenious systems of coiled galvanized steel pipes? What would be the next threat to civilization? The fledgling film industry that had migrated from the cliffs of the Palisades to sunny Hollywood? Writers, illustrators, and publishers? Magic in all its forms ground beneath the heel of the industrialists' profits? Gavin struggled to keep the contempt out of his voice as he said, "Be that as it may, you must admit, that does give you a powerful motive for killing Havel."

"I didn't kill Havel." Stanton dismissed the accusation with a casual wave. "I paid him. I freely admit it. Paid him to take action to preserve the safety and stability of our nation. Although I will warn you in no uncertain terms that if such accusations were ever to be made public, I have friends in Washington who understand that I acted from the highest principles. And would take the strongest measures to make sure another blackmailer did not arise to take his place," he added meaningfully.

Gavin met his gaze, ignoring the clear implication beneath his words. "And will such strong measures involve bringing Havel's killer to justice?"

"What justice?" Stanton asked with a shrug. "Melisandre is gone, fled with her accomplice, MacLeod. Good riddance to them both. What point is there in pursing the matter any further?"

"MacLeod!" Gavin said sharply. "I thought you accused Havel of being her co-conspirator."

"And why could there not be three? Indeed, what could be more likely? What clearer explanation of Havel's murder—if in fact murder it was—than a falling-out among thieves?" He waved a hand as if swatting a fly. "It happens all the time."

"Indeed," Gavin allowed. "So you would now have it that Duncan MacLeod is responsible for Josep Havel's death?"

"I would have it that whoever is responsible is only an instrument of justice." Another pointed glance from Stanton. "Indeed, one might argue that, whatever the killer's motives, he was acting for the greater good of his country."

Or at least the greater good of Hollis Stanton and his friends' balance sheets. "So there will be no pursuit of MacLeod as a murderer?"

"Why should there be? He served the greater good by doing things most men cannot. For it is not every man who has the strength to kill another when it is needed. My friends in Washington would believe the only decent thing to do is leave such a creature to whatever scant peace he can find."

Or consign him to a lifetime's running—not unlike the hell that Gavin currently inhabited. "Or perhaps they fear what he might reveal if he were found?"

"And you, Mr. Fellowes, do you fear what MacLeod might reveal if he were found? Would your secrets stand scrutiny in the broad light of day?" Stanton's gaze was sharp, knowing. Taking Gavin's silence for the answer it was, he turned back to his papers with a satisfied smile. "There's no reason for us to be at odds, Mr. Fellowes. And over what? What does it matter whether that wanton conspired with Havel or MacLeod or both to disgrace my uncle? There can be no doubt that either one of the two of them killed Havel. Their fleeing proclaims the guilt. So let us lay the matter to rest and move forward. We avoid scandal and justice is served in its own imperfect way. I will leave it to MacLeod's personal furies to see to justice on any higher plane."

Chapter 25

TWENTY-FOUR COPIES, Andrew Piper had said, his bandaged hands testament to his fear. One book for each of the twenty-four protocols. A game, at best. At worst, sheer madness. But now Gavin must face the fact that the madman had not been mad at all. The madness lay out here in the real world, not inside a disturbed mind—and the danger those twenty-four books represented went far beyond raising some unholy spirits. For the darkness of the occult could always be defeated by the light of science and reason, but the conspiracy he had unearthed—no, face facts, the conspiracy he had launched—was beyond the capacity of either scientist or magician to comprehend.

It made no difference to protest that he hadn't known. Who could possibly have known what he was unleashing? Even if he had known at the time, why would he have paid any more attention to the Protocols than a score of other illusions—the angels of Mons, the leaked maps of the shipping routes, the faked code book that was the key to the Zimmerman telegram. Just one more game, exactly as Piper had described it. But now the stakes had been laid on the table for all too see. Twenty-four copies for twenty-four men. And every one of them Gavin's responsibility.

His shoulders slumped as he searched the jagged silhouette of the Devil's Path for help that was destined to never come. And why should it? Gavin didn't believe in the Devil, any more than he believed in magic. But he did believe in evil. And he was now face-to-face with the fact that he had unleashed pure evil on the world.

Twenty-four books. Twenty-four Protocols. And twenty-four men. Rich, powerful men seeking even greater riches. Even greater power. What could one man hope to do against that?

"You could always pray for a miracle," MacLeod's voice drifted across the summer breeze.

But there was no miracle awaiting Gavin when he paid his final visit to Ker-Ys. Jean Adams and Miss Smith were briskly supervising the shuttering of the colony for the season, sensible cotton aprons tied over their dresses. "For the few artists who have not already left are all quite in agreement that it would be impossible to continue working in this atmosphere," Jean said. "Miss Smith has graciously offered to find them accommodations in one of the many other boarding houses in town."

The past, too, was to be equally neatly shuttered away, according to the farewell tea Miss Smith had laid out for them on the verandah. Miss Smith herself did not join them, but instead diplomatically excused herself to finalize the arrangements to remove the beehives to a nearby farm. The bees must be told, she explained, and their permission sought, just as any apiary must be solemnly informed of events in their keepers' lives, such as births, marriages, or departures and returns in the household. If the bees were not put into mourning by solemnly decorating the hives with scraps of black cloth before they were removed, then their new keeper ran the risk of their producing no more honey or leaving the hive forever.

"And so we must all learn to bow to wisdoms and forces greater than ours," Jean Adams supplied the moral to Miss Smith's homily. She was restored to her rightful place in the center of the group, a chastened Ned kneeling adoringly beside her. Hollis Stanton smoked against a pillar, keeping a careful eye out for pilferage as the farmhands packed the wagons with the family's belongings. Essie had been quietly removed as befitted an uncomfortable dependent, but Kate Ames had been allowed to remain and lend a hand with the packing up.

"As the Reverend Parker instructed us all in his famous abolitionist address, 'I do not pretend to understand the moral universe, the arc is a long one, my eye reaches but little ways. I cannot calculate the curve and complete the figure by the experience of sight; I can divine it by conscience. But from what I see I am sure it bends towards justice,'" Jean Adams continued. "We must be content that we have seen justice served in the cases of Josep Havel and Melisandre and teach ourselves that pursuing any further redress would simply be revenge. For as Christians, we must always hold ourselves above motivations that can only sully us."

In other words, sweeping the callous murder of a young girl under the rug was the only moral thing to do. "So, we are to consider the case closed?" Gavin asked with a neutrality he did not feel. "No effort will be made to bring the murderer to justice?"

"There can be no question of murder," Stanton protested. "Both the girl and Havel met their death by mischance. A tragic coincidence, nothing more."

"Quite possibly," Gavin allowed. "But would it not be best to quash the rumors that inevitably attach themselves to such unfortunate coincidences with a thorough investigation?"

"To what possible end?" Jean asked with a sigh. "Justice for that poor, dead girl? Better we devote our efforts to justice for the rest of her kind and leave her to plead her case in a higher court. We must have faith that the guilty, if there are in fact such men, will answer for their actions in this world or the next."

"And such men ought to be grateful that the family is willing to leave it at that." Hollis met Gavin's eyes. "Mr. MacLeod was lucky to make his escape this time. If he has any friends, they would do him a service by convincing him of that fact."

"So you do, in fact, accuse him now?"

"Would you suggest another culprit?" Stanton asked. Not waiting for Gavin's response, he crushed out his cigar. "I have it on good authority that the man has vanished. What clearer admission of guilt might there be?"

So this was how it was to be played. "And if Duncan MacLeod is not your man?"

"Oh, he is. Unless, of course, you are suggesting we investigate the remainder of his associates," Stanton said with a pointed glance at Kate Ames.

In other words, if Gavin did anything to pursue the issue, Stanton would not hesitate to destroy not just him but anything and anyone he cared about—beginning with Kate Ames. Gavin's throat clenched. "If you have an accusation to make…"

"You go too far, Hollis," Jean intervened. "The girls are more sinned against than sinning, and it behooves us to treat them as gently as we can."

"You are as ever an innocent, aunt! These girls are no better than they ought, and you would treat them as if they were queens!"

The breeze quickened, sending a rogue current that curled around Gavin's ear and swelled into an expressive snort. "What does he mean, 'as if'! I'm a queen already, I'll thank ye to know. Queen of the Gypsies. Ruler of the Joint Courts of the Seelie and Unseelie. Captain of the Wild Ride. And High Chieftain of the Fair Folk, who needs no kindness from the likes of her. The Fair Folk will claim the bread and butter left on the hearth by any housewife as an honest debt honestly incurred, but we spit upon any morsel thrown from the table by the charity of those such as her."

"Mr. Fellowes, are you quite all right?" Mrs. Adams asked.

"Of course, you're not all right!" Gipsy Sarah snorted. "And you'll not be all right until you do what you must to make things right! So, I have said, and so shall it be!"

"I was simply attempting to consider what direct efforts might bring justice, if not for Judith, for the rest of her kind, as you suggested," Gavin said, keeping his voice even with no little effort.

"First and foremost, we must rid ourselves of that pernicious influence at the Overlook Hotel," Stanton said.

"Indeed, there is little we can do to protect those poor girls from those who would take advantage of them as long as such institutions continue to preach their false gospels," his aunt agreed. "These sad events have clearly demonstrated that the likes of these trade unionists cannot ever be tolerated among the good people of Woodstock again."

"And what of Essie? Will an exception be made to tolerate her?" It was Gavin's lips that formed the last, even if it was Gipsy Sarah who spoke them.

"Essie will be tended to, of course," Mrs. Adams assured him. "And every effort will be made to help her recover her wits, although I gravely fear it may prove a hopeless task. But if she does, there will be a place for her in the settlement schools. And if she does not, which I believe is far more likely the case, she will be treated gently, for her delusions are punishment enough for her misdeeds."

"*Her* misdeeds?" Gipsy Sarah said with a laugh. "How does a girl's trying to look out for herself compare to the betrayal of nations in the name of profit?"

Gavin had no answer to that, so he did what he could to ignore her insistent voice—or as his rational mind put it, an obvious and unlovely auditory hallucination.

"And as for Judith?" Gipsy Sarah pressed. As did her unwilling ventriloquist.

Jean Adams answered him. "Ah, Mr. Fellowes, we must not judge her too harshly. She was only a product of her environment, as with all of her kind. As was her unfortunate fate."

"And what of *her* fate and *her* kind," Gipsy Sarah scoffed. "I think not much of her chances when she is called to stand before the Twin Courts of the Fair Folk."

"But you have my assurance, she will not be forgotten," Jean went on. "We shall name a scholarship for her— and her sad example can only encourage its recipients to eschew her failings and choose a wiser path."

"And if a girl would not choose your path?" Gipsy Sarah demanded. "If she would prefer to throw your self-serving goodness back in your smug, smiling faces? What of that girl? What of Miriam? What of Rachel? What of MacLeod? What of *us*?"

The angry cry rang out across the mountains, echoing from the crags of the Devil's Path to the cliffs of the Escarpment, then rebounded in a deeper timbre: "What of me?" it boomed. "Horatio Herbert Kitchener, Field Marshal."

"Robert David Macpherson," another voice floated down from the peaks to join him. "2nd Lieutenant."

"Leonard Charles Rix, clerk," a thin, reedy voice offered.

"Matthew Mcloughlin, Detective Sergeant, Protection Officer."

"James Walter Gurney, valet."

"William Shields, valet."

"Henry Surguy, valet."

"Francis Peter West, valet," the voices continued to toll.

"John Albert Aburrow, Officer's Cook, First Class. H.M.S. *Hampshire*."

"John Downes, Third Writer, H.M.S. *Hampshire*."

"George Nicholas Donnelly, Able Seaman."

"Albert Edward Austin, Leading Seaman."

"John Donald MacGregor, Ordinary Seaman."

"John Briscoe," a higher, youthful voice piped up. "Signal Boy, H.M.S. *Hampshire*."

"Alfred George Charles Brockway, Boy Telegraphist, H.M.S. *Hampshire*."

"Alfred Burrows, Boy First Class. H.M.S. *Hampshire*."

"Philip George Alexander, Chaplain," a deeper voice added a final benediction, before another gust of wind brought another set of voices.

"John Coull, Skipper. H.M. Drifter *Laurel Crown*. Lost in the minesweeping operation pursuant to the sinking of the H.M.S. *Hampshire.*"

"George Petrie. Deck Hand. H.M. Drifter *Laurel Crown.*"

"Thomas James Baker, Engineman…"

Closer and closer, the voices crowded, not just 736 names, but millions. Soldiers and civilians. Women and men. Turncoats and patriots. Truth-tellers and spies. Germans, Russians, Americans, French and British. All their voices echoing from peak to peak, then dying away into the scratching of a quill across a scroll that stretched into the distance as far as the eye could see, inscribing each of the lost into the infernal Domesday book of which Gavin was the author.

"Twenty-four books. Twenty-four men," Gavin protested to the madman who had embroiled him in this hopeless task. "What can one man hope to do against so much?"

But when the scribe looked up from his work and turned, it was not Andrew Piper, but rather Duncan MacLeod who said, "With the right man and the right book, one will prove more than enough."

Chapter 26

ONCE MORE, GAVIN MOVED through the Maverick like one of Dante's wraiths, the dead following him in silent procession, urging him toward the little cabin rooted into the hillside and its magic lantern that spun the fates of lost cities and lost souls. But after a long futile search, Gavin sank against a rocky outcropping, defeated. MacLeod's cabin was nowhere to be found—nor was there any man or woman who could remember such a place, or even recall a waif who called herself Gipsy Sarah.

With the right man and the right book, one will prove more than enough. MacLeod's voice echoed in Gavin's head as he snorted at the volume he held in his hands. "Well, if you are the right book, I am by all appearances the wrong man."

The wretched text stared back mutely. And the grudging nugget of faith that had buoyed Gavin's spirits began to dissipate. What did it matter that twenty-four men in America believed in this book's power? He of all people knew it for the cheat it was. Naught but a copy-book collection of legends and fairy stories culled from the imagination of a Balliol-educated fool who had been too smug to see he was awakening forces darker than those wielded by the Prince of Lies himself. Jaded as he was now, how was he supposed to find the imagination to pretend that it contained spells powerful enough to counteract the dark magic Stanton and his friends would unleash first on America—and then on the world?

A murmur of discontent rippled amongst the dead as they pressed around him, reminding him that despair was the coward's choice—and one that would bind him to them for the rest of his life. He sighed and tried to ignore them, even though he knew well that those who lacked even the dignity of a grave could still feast on flesh weaker than their own.

Closing his ears to the insistent hum, Gavin picked up the cracked volume and opened it to the first Protocol.

"The Summoning of the First Guardian of the Seelie Court," he read. "And with him the drowned Guardian of Ker-Ys…"

He heard a soft footfall behind him, and for a moment, he almost believed. But it was no Seelie Prince that approached, nor even one of the shades that threatened to haunt him for the rest of his life. This tread was familiar. And human.

"Not that way," Kate Ames told him.

"Go away," he said without turning. "This is my own fault and none of yours."

"Blame does not matter. The only question you must consider now is, how can you summon them?"

"How do *you* propose I should?"

"You must call to them by name," she said. "One at a time, you must call them by their true names. For nothing in this universe, not even men, can resist the power of true naming and true seeing. And while you name them true, I will draw them as I see them, and they will have no choice but to assemble—and then to ride."

And just as she had managed to arouse other, more carnal feelings he had thought he was no longer capable of, he felt the sullen nugget of hope rekindle and burst into a brilliance that rivaled the evening star winking into view above him. Maybe, *just maybe*, this *was* the right book, and, unlikelier by far, maybe he *was* the right man. If Kate Ames was with him, he could at least try to believe it was true.

Kate arranged herself beside him on the rock and reached into her bag. Gavin watched as she drew out a charcoal and sketch book. She opened to a clean page, situated it on her lap, and gave him a nod. He drew in a deep breath and, keeping his eyes fixed on that lone star in the sky, he spread his hands in supplication for those who no longer had flesh or bones to plead for themselves.

"I seek the Seelie Court," he said. "I seek the *Aos Sí*, the *sídhe* that still bless Ireland. I seek with equal respect the Unseelie Court—the bogies, bogles, boggarts, abbey lubbers and buttery spirits."

He began uncertainly, but his voice slipped into an incantatory rhythm of its own accord.

"And I seek their brother courts, the Tylwyth Teg and the Bendith y Mamau. The shining Ellyllon and the Bwbachod of the hearth, the *Coblynau* of the mines, the *Gwragedd Annwn* of the lakes maidens, and the hags of the mountain, the *Gwyllion*—I humbly seek their aid.

"I seek the Piksies of Cornwall. I seek the great Cailleach of Scotland. I seek the Mooinjer Veggey, the little people who bless the Isle of Man. I seek the Korrigan and Nains of Broceliande in Brittany. I seek the Santa Compana, the Nubeiro, and the meigas of Galicia.

"I seek the merry satyrs and shy nymphs of the Grecian woods to leave off their endless chase and race to my aid instead.

"I seek the will-o'-the-wisps, the *Feufollet*, the Ignisfatus, the Jack o'Lantern, the Jenny Burnt-Tale, the Kitty Candlestick.

"I seek the kindly Zana of Romania, and her sister, the Asturian Xana, who guide and guard children and other good people who enter the woods.

"I seek the duende and the Nahuatl *ohuican chaneque*, the dwellers in dangerous places.

"I seek the Encantado, risen from the Portuguese waters as snakes and dolphins.

"I seek the Peris who wander Persia in penance in hopes of finally being granted entry to Paradise…

He continued his solemn invocation deep into the night, as the darkness fell and bonfires flared to life on every side. As he spoke, Kate sketched, covering page upon page, until he at last sealed the solemn litany with the words, "I seek you all to rally to my aid behind the greatest of the Sons of Heaven, chief of the earthly angels, neither fallen nor saved, first among the Unfallen, Azazel."

The bonfires flared, then died.

Silence fell, and so did darkness, leaving Gavin prone on an unknown seashore, surrounded by shadows. When his eyes adjusted and he could at last discern the shapes that crowded in from every side, he scrambled back in fear. The companies massed in silence—twenty-four of them, he knew without counting. The Teufelshunden padded softly behind the dog-headed saint, Christopher. The dark sails of the barges of Avalon bobbed at an anchor in the harbor, surrounded by selkies and merfolk and the white steeds of

Neptune and Manannan mac Lir that rode in the vanguard
of the Faerie Armada. The Frost Giants, the Sleeping Giant
Albion, the Great Earth Spirit Manitou, and the Giant of
Mont Saint Michel needed no mounts, nor did the Great
Boar Twrch Trwyth. The Hag Ceridwen was an army in
herself, shifting shape from greyhound to otter to hawk to
hen, at the head of all the poets she had fed from her great
cauldron of inspiration. The Lambton Worm slid upon its
belly at the head of the Company of Dragons. The rising
sun glinted against the fantastic armor forged by the elves
of Nibelheim.

Then Gavin saw MacLeod astride a fearsome black
charger, at the head of a band assembled beneath the fabled
Fairy Banner that bore his family's name. Their eyes met,
and MacLeod's pointed teeth flashed. "So, at last comes
your miracle," he said. "And mine as well."

He said no more—nor did any of the others. The
assembled companies were waiting—but for what? What
name had Gavin forgotten? What last command must he
give?

"Peace," MacLeod assured him. "You have done your
duty and played your part. It is up to another to command
us now."

Silence fell once more, and this time it lasted until the
rising sun became visible in the east. Only then did the
assembled host begin to ripple with excitement, as did the
sea. Two figures crested the waves, then glided across the
surface onto the beach. The first was a Bloomer Girl with
the face of a lioness, her white cotton blouse soaked not
with saltwater, but with the blood that dripped from the
sword she carried. She was accompanied by a one-eyed
crone, who lumbered beneath the weight of a basket.

When the lioness stopped at the edge of the sand, the crone laid the basket in front of her, then backed away with a reverent curtsy.

The lioness' lips drew back to expose her fangs, as she plunged the sword into the basket, spearing its grisly contents and thrusting a grim trophy aloft: A man's head so soaked with blood it was unidentifiable. And when the rising sun drew level with the head, bathing air, land, and sea in a molten glow, the lioness threw back her head and loosed a full-throated roar.

That was the signal the massed companies had awaited, and with an answering cry, they rode, taking to the sky in a mass of pounding hooves that sent sparks flying down from the clouds to ignite the St. Nicholas fire that raced across the sea.

Gavin listened to their hoofbeats fade—and then return, this time in the form of a terrified boy astride one of the Mead House's cobs who burst though the morning silence of the Maverick, crying, "Come quick, come quick! Mrs. Adams sent me to find you as there's been a horrid accident at the quarries."

A knowing glanced passed between them, and Gavin and Kate rose to their feet as one.

"An entire wall let go and slid down right on the loading platforms," the boy continued. "They're saying it's a mercy no quarryman was hurt. But as for the gentleman what ordered the load of stone ... Well, what they're saying about poor Hollis Stanton is too terrible to believe." The boy paused and gulped. "They're saying a sheet of rock sliced his head right off and carried it clean away. They've searched all over the quarry, but no one's been able to find a trace."

Chapter 27

THE EXPLOSION OF THE MUNITIONS stored in the castle on Bannerman's Island, following hard on the heels of the death of the arms magnate who had built it, was only the harbinger of a series of disasters that spread like wildfire down the Hudson Valley and out across the nation. An air ship filled with visiting German dignitaries burst into flame upon docking. Oil well upon oil well across Texas went bust. The Chicago stockyards were paralyzed by a mass stampede when the railroad tracks buckled beneath a heat wave that gripped the Midwest. The loading docks in San Francisco harbor collapsed into the bay. Construction on the great skyscrapers rising up along the Manhattan skyline ground to a halt, as ironworkers refused to climb scaffolding so given to collapse that even the Mohawk skywalkers from Canada, who balanced fearlessly on girders a thousand feet in the air, returned to their native lands with tales of dark curses. It was as if the forces of Chaos had chosen to ride across America. A curse, some said, while the more religious-minded warned of Armageddon and the Four Horsemen rising from the ashes of the Great War.

The aftermath of the quarry disaster at Mead's Mountain was considerably more sober—as befitted a wake. Gavin found Kate Ames contemplating the unseasonably hot fire burning in the massive bluestone fireplace of Mead's reception room. He paused for a moment, watching as she paged through her sketchbook, tearing out each sketch she had created the previous night.

She looked up as he pulled up one of the stiff, ladder-backed chairs to sit beside her. "It seems a shame to burn them, for you've captured their likenesses exactly. Seelie and Unseelie both," he allowed. "But you are correct. It must be done."

"Such things are not for human hands," she agreed. "Icarus. Dedalus. Faust. Friar Bacon. Canute. And now Havel. There will always be those who seeks to command powers they are too puny to control—and in doing so, destroy others along with themselves. We must do what we can to return the secrets of the Fair Folk to beneath the Hollow Hills."

It was all that passed between them in the way of excuse or acknowledgement of what they had shared as the bonfires of the Maverick flickered in the darkness around them. It was too soon to say more. Instead, they concentrated on this Viking funeral, crumpling page after page and tossing them into the fire, where they flamed, curled, and writhed, then vanished back to the invisible world.

When the last page dissipated into smoke, Gavin laid the stained volume that had caused all this trouble on the embers. It would be burned whole, as was necessary with such terrible power. They fell silent as the flames licked, then rose, and salty steam began to rise from the cracked leather cover.

In that silence, Gavin wrestled with himself. It was indeed too soon to speak of what had happened at the Maverick; in fact, there might never come a time to give words to an experience so beyond human understanding. But there were other things to speak of, other matters that lay unsettled between them. And if he walked away without settling those matters openly, if he took the coward's path of escorting her down to the railway with no more said than a courteous farewell, it would be forever. If he did not speak now, he would never be strong enough to share such awful intimacy with another again. But was he strong enough? Could he bear to give voice to a truth that horrified him and laid him bare? And what of Kate Ames? Would she welcome being shouldered with such a burden, or would she flee in justifiable repugnance?

"I have no more understanding of the power of that book any more than I can explain the events of last night, but I must tell you what little truth I do know." He drew a deep breath, then forced out his confession in measured syllables. "I did not pursue Duncan MacLeod to Belleau Wood to warn him that the *Germanenorden Walvater of the Holy Grail* sought to murder him and seize the secrets of both his networks and the *Protocols*. Duncan MacLeod came to Belleau Wood to warn me. For I am the Magician, not he. I am the man who spun the webs of illusions that fueled the Great War, from the Angels of Mons to the Zimmerman telegram. And I am the one who created the *Protocols* as yet another trick to bolster the resolve of the Russians and convince the Americans that the Germans were intent on infiltrating the highest echelons of their society if they did not declare war. I never so much as saw the finished book." He looked at it now, pages curling.

"It was nothing to me but words conjured from my own imagination. And yet those words loosed the scourge of chaos upon this world."

"I know." She spoke the two syllables simply.

He drew a sharp breath and sat back in his chair. He had been braced against many responses, but not that one. "For how long?" he asked, when he was finally able to match her serene dispassion.

"From the first time I saw you at the West Hurley railway station," she admitted with a sly smile.

Once again, she had not failed to surprise him, and he sensed—no, *hoped*—that would never change. "More of your vaunted true seeing?" he asked with a laugh.

"It takes no true seeing to know the Magician for what he was: A trickster. A clever cheat. An accomplished liar. Criminal talents when the world is at peace. But deadly necessary when the world is at war."

Which was seeing truer than Gavin particularly liked. But he persisted, "And yet you still got in the carriage with me. Were you not afraid to be carried off by a demon?"

"You are no more demon than you are criminal," she said with a quirk of her lips. "As I have already told you, here in the Middle Kingdom, only men can lie. And you, Mr. Gavin Fellowes, are a man. Nothing more, nothing less."

Gavin could not bring himself to smile at that—not yet. Once more, silence fell, and the two of them watched the dying fire, as the last bits of the *Protocols* twisted like drakes and salamanders, then vanished into the aether.

"I understand it is no defense to claim I had no idea of the book's true power," he finally said. "Indeed, many would argue that it is a far worse crime for a man to raise such unholy powers solely through ignorance and unbelief."

"The greatest trick the Devil played was convincing the world he didn't exist," she concurred.

Another moment's silence, before Gavin burst out, "Dammit, Duncan MacLeod died for me. Be it truth or illusion, Duncan MacLeod gave his life to save mine. The Gabriel Hounds were baying for me. MacLeod came to save me. He died covering my body with his own."

"An illusion, as you yourself have said. Your enemies in America needed the body of the Magician. They needed to know he could never rise to oppose them before they dared wield the powers that were rightfully his to command." She reached for a poker and stirred the embers. Then she turned and looked squarely at Gavin. "Duncan MacLeod gave them their corpse. It was a gift freely given—and a gift I would suggest you freely accept." She shrugged. "For it is said it is not wise to reject gifts from his kind."

Gavin huffed out a breath. "In other words, I'm to play the coward and let another man's name be besmirched for my misdeeds?"

She shook her head and replaced the poker. "Mr. Fellowes, you did not kill Havel or Judith. Stanton did. And Stanton has paid. If MacLeod prefers his name be signed to that meaningless IOU we call justice, I can only say it is ill-luck to refuse him. Besides," she added, "I'm not at all sure that 'man' is the correct term for whoever or whatever called himself Duncan MacLeod."

Gavin's jaw set. "Pretty as such an explanation might be, I am not one to be bought off by fairytales."

"Nor am I one to spin them—at least if I am not being paid handsomely for the effort," she added with a quick smile. She was quiet for a moment, then said, "Perhaps the only reassurance I might offer is that regardless of who or what Duncan MacLeod is, and regardless of what real or imagined missions he might choose to embark upon, the only true fact we know is that he chose you."

Which was answer enough—and yet no answer at all. "But ... *why?*"

"It is not the way of the Fair Folk to explain themselves," she said. "They follow their caprices when it comes to humankind—whether for good or for ill."

"And which is this? Good or ill?"

"We won the war," she said. "Beyond that, I suppose it is your choice."

He drew a deep breath as he watched the glowing embers. "I don't suppose you have any sage advice on how I am expected to make such a choice."

She pondered that, and finally offered the only answer she could. "Maybe you should try believing in magic."

"As you do?"

She cocked her head and studied him with the same amused consideration she had when he'd declared himself so vehemently on the piazza. "Perhaps we should try to learn together," she finally offered.

He froze for a moment that seemed as endless as the lists they had invoked under the stars the previous evening. It was Kate Ames' green eyes watching him, but it was Duncan MacLeod's voice that whispered in his ear, *'Tis a lucky man to be granted more than one miracle.* Gavin swallowed hard and finally found his voice. "I would be privileged to submit myself to your tutelage."

Rising to his feet, he offered her his arm with old-fashioned courtesy, and they went out to call for the carriage that would take them down to the railway station—together.

Epilogue

AS BEFITS EVERY ANCIENT SEA, the Mediterranean brims with Old Magicks. Many of them are monstrous and dangerous, but a few are kind. First among the kindly are the dolphins, sacred to Aphrodite, herself born of the sea foam. For how could those that serve the goddess whose radiant beauty was born of the basest act of violence and betrayal be anything but kind? Kindness even tamed the trickster god, Dionysus, Lord of Chaos and Misrule, who punished the brigands that dared capture him by transforming their oars into sea snakes and causing them to leap into the sea in panic. But the god quickly repented of his cruelty and transformed them into dolphins rather than leaving them to drown. Gentle St. Nicholas of Myra also succors storm-tossed seafarers, sending stones floating across the waves to save those who have fallen overboard. And St. Elmo sends his fire to light the masts of ships caught in thunderstorms to reassure fearful sailors their patron still watches over them.

No less miraculous than these stories were the tales of those who saw the Lost Company of Ker-Ys sail through the pillars of Hercules from beyond the western sea to bend the knee before far older magics than their own. Those who claimed to bear first-hand witness have long since been carried by the dolphins to the Islands of the Blessed, but to this very day, desperate desert dwellers clinging to life and makeshift rafts amidst the pounding waves, whisper stories of strange magic beneath the waves. Some tell of a barge with billowing sails embroidered with golden apples and bearing three sad-eyed queens whose task it is to carry away the storm-tossed to the Blessed Isles. Still others describe the red ears and white coats of the Gabriel Hounds, their angry howls softening to a growl that presages death. But then there are the few—the very fortunate few—whom the Fair Folk have chosen to bless for reasons only they know. And those are the ones who will swear to their tale of three mighty shouts shattering their hour of darkness. Three shouts that herald a fire-breathing, coal-black horse pounding to their rescue across the waves, and like the kindly dolphins, delivering drowning men to the safety of shores far beyond the Pillars of Hercules and across the western sea.

Acknowledgments

Thanks to the Historical Society of Woodstock, Woodstock Town Historian Richard Heppner, and archivist JoAnn Margolis, for guiding me through the Historical Society's invaluable archives. Thanks to Fern Malkine-Falvey for a meticulous fact-check. Thanks also to the Woodstock Byrdcliffe Guild which lovingly maintains the Byrdcliffe Art Colony, where I am privileged to live. All errors and flights of fancy are purely my own.

Thanks to eagle-eyed beta reader Tina Debellegarde.

Finally, I am grateful to return to the talented team at Amphorae and the capable editorial hands of Kristina Blank Makansi.

About the Author

Erica Obey graduated from Yale University, and her interest in folklore and story led her to an MA in Creative Writing from City College of New York and a PhD in Comparative Literature. She began publishing articles and then wrote a book about female folklorists of the nineteenth century before she decided she'd rather be writing the stories herself. There are three places you can find Erica when she's not writing: on a hiking trail, in her garden, or at the back of the pack in her local road race. Her favorite kind of vacation is backpacking across Dartmoor or among the hills of Wales in order to find new and exciting legends to inspire her own writing. *Dazzlepaint* is her fourth novel and the second in a series of historical suspense romances inspired by the stately homes of the Hudson Valley.